MURDER ACROSS THE LINES

A totally gripping crime thriller full of twists

JANICE FROST

Warwick & Bell Book 2

Joffe Books, London
www.joffebooks.com

First published in Great Britain in 2021

Cover art by Dee Dee Book Covers

ISBN: 978-1-80405-054-5

CHAPTER ONE

Jane
21 May 2019

The droning of a motorcycle turned heads in the small group of pedestrians waiting at the crossing on Burton Road, its thrum intensifying as the bike veered into view and began overtaking the queue of traffic building up as the lights switched from green to amber. It showed no signs of slowing.

At the last moment, its driver swerved sharply to the right, skidding to a halt in front of a startled girl standing at the kerbside.

A heavy-set man in leathers jumped off the passenger seat and headed purposefully towards her. Sunlight flashed briefly off the visor of his helmet as he pulled her briefly into a tight embrace, only to cast her aside again. He remounted the bike, which roared off, running the lights, smoke belching from its exhaust and tainting the air of the spring morning.

The girl made an unsuccessful grab for the pole of the traffic lights, then pitched forwards on to the road to the accompaniment of gasps from startled onlookers.

A panicked voice screamed, "She's been stabbed!"

Jane Bell, an off-duty special police constable, rushed forward and dropped to her knees beside the girl. Concerned bystanders pressed around her. "Stay back! I'm a police officer. Is anyone here a medic? Has anyone called 999? We need police and an ambulance. Now!"

People began jabbing at their phones. No one questioned Jane's authority. Not so long ago, she'd have felt helpless in a situation like this. Now, just over a year in the job, she knew exactly what to do.

Except, she wasn't a medic. She'd received only a rudimentary training in first aid. The denim jacket she'd removed and rolled up to press against the wound on the girl's chest was soaked through already. The girl's skin was cold to the touch, her pulse weak, lips and fingernails shadowed blue — all signs that she was rapidly going into shock. Her wide, frightened eyes fixed on Jane's. She struggled to speak.

"Help her," a woman cried, her voice urgent, desperate. *Accusing.* Again, Jane's training helped her to stay calm.

A man handed her a blanket retrieved from the boot of his car, and she placed it over the girl. She was a scrap of a thing, just into her teens perhaps, and looking frail and undernourished. If she had been stabbed in the heart, as Jane suspected, her chances of making it to the hospital were not good.

Jane held her hand and whispered, "It's all right. Help is coming." Behind her, a woman began to sob. Jane wished she would move out of earshot.

She stroked the girl's hair and held her hand. She was little more than a child. A gurgling sound came from her throat. *The death rattle? Please, no.* Jane held her breath.

The girl was still trying to speak. Jane leaned in until her ear was almost brushing the girl's lips, and she was able to catch a single, breathless word: "Nate".

"Nate." Jane repeated the name aloud, so that the girl would know she had heard.

Someone was giving a running commentary on the ambulance's progress. By the time the wail of approaching sirens was heard, the girl was already unconscious.

The crowd of stunned bystanders now included drivers who'd abandoned their cars to see what was going on. A few people were weeping. One woman crossed herself, clearly believing the girl to be dead. There was so much blood.

The paramedics arrived and rushed to the child's side. An Initial Response Vehicle pulled up, reminding Jane of her duty as a police officer. "Did anyone see what happened? Get a number plate?"

Several people spoke at once.

"It was all so fast—"

"Two men on a bike—"

"The one on the back got off—"

"Didn't even see the knife—"

"He took something from her—"

"Couldn't see their faces—"

Jane sifted through the cacophony of voices. One stood out. "Who said that he took something?"

A woman in a floral dress stepped forward and raised her hand. Jane was an ex-teacher. When she asked a question, people tended to respond like that. "What did he take? Did you see?"

"A bag. One of those little backpack ones?" She seemed uncertain.

"She's right. I saw that too." A man, his voice shaky.

"Me too . . . I think it was khaki."

Jane looked across the road at a café with a green awning — *Veganbites* painted in red across its window. The café was owned by some friends of hers, Frieda and Karun. Maybe there'd be other witnesses inside.

One of the PCs from the IRV asked the bystanders to remain so that statements could be taken. The other approached Jane.

"Nice work, Jane." It was Tim Sterne, a PC Jane had worked with a lot, particularly in her first few months on the job.

"Geez, Tim. She must be all of thirteen years old."

"I know, lass. It's always worse when they're kids. As it seems to be, more and more these days." He touched her shoulder. "Knife attack, I take it?"

"Yes. I was standing practically next to her when it happened, but I didn't see the knife. I don't think anyone did. There was no time to process what was happening, and the sun was in my eyes. All I registered was the bike screeching to a stop. He was off and on again in a flash. Now I know why witnesses often sound vague and unsure of themselves. You don't register what you're seeing when it happens like that. You can't take it in. Sorry if I'm repeating myself, Tim."

Tim shook his head. "No, no, you're fine, lass. It's the shock."

"You know what, Tim? I don't think it was a random attack. It was like they were targeting her."

They were interrupted by a grave-faced paramedic signalling that the ambulance was about to leave. Was it Jane's imagination that he shook his head ever so slightly?

Tim's corresponding sigh seemed to confirm it. "Well, much as I hate to say it, this is potentially a murder scene now. I'll update the control room, start securing the area and request CID and Forensics."

A little half-heartedly, Jane asked, "Want me to stick around and help out for a bit?"

Tim pointed at another response car drawing up nearby. "No need. Cavalry's here, but you'll be required to provide a statement as soon as possible."

Jane stuck around long enough to give Tim a quick account of what she'd seen, then left them to it. She crossed the street and headed for Veganbites. Frieda was standing by the door.

"What's going on, Jane? A customer told me there's been an accident on the other side of the road. She saw a motorcycle go right up on the pavement. Then we saw the ambulance and two police cars—"

"Is she still here? What else did she see?" Jane scanned the room.

"No. She was on her way out. That was all she saw. I looked across and thought that was you I saw on the pavement. You were standing next to the police car when the crowd dispersed a bit."

Jane sighed. "A young girl, a child, was stabbed."

Frieda gasped. "Is she—?"

"I don't know. I think it was her heart. There was an awful lot of blood."

"Oh my God, Jane. Did you see it happen?"

"Yes."

Frieda gave her a hug and led her to a table near the counter. "Sit down. What can I get you?"

"Tea's fine."

Frieda returned minutes later with a large teapot and three cups. Her husband Karun joined them, bringing cake.

"Sugar. For the shock." He cut three slices. Jane pushed hers away. She told them what she knew.

"I thought we'd left that sort of thing behind in London. We moved to Lincoln, thinking it was a quiet place," Frieda commented. "But why? Why would someone just randomly attack an innocent child?"

"Was it random? Were they after her phone?" Karun looked at Jane.

"I don't know. They snatched her bag."

Karun gave her a knowing look. "Well, if it wasn't her phone they wanted, I bet I know what they were after — drugs."

Jane nodded. "That would be my guess. Drugs, or cash collected from clients — drug users."

"Do you think this was something to do with county lines? It's been in the news a lot lately," he said.

"Sadly, yes. It could be, but it's best not to jump to conclusions. It might simply have been a robbery." *Yeah, right.* Karun, too, looked sceptical.

"County lines. That's when drug dealers in cities send kids to the country to sell their drugs, isn't it?" Frieda said.

There was a bit more to it than that, but Frieda was essentially correct. City drug gangs were going 'up country' — expanding into new markets in county towns and rural areas. They recruited children, some of them shockingly young, as couriers to transport drugs and cash between locations. County lines operations were infamous for their use of extreme violence and intimidation. Jane shuddered, recalling some of the facts about the trade that she'd learned recently.

"Yes, more or less."

"Poor girl." Jane suspected that Frieda was thinking of her young daughter, Neela. Karun too, probably, for he reached out and took his wife's hand.

Jane's main concern at that moment was for the victim, but she couldn't help wondering, *who was Nate?*

CHAPTER TWO

Nate
July 2018

Nate Price had been looking forward to moving up to secondary school. He'd been placed in a form with his two best friends from primary school — that would make things easier than being in a class full of strangers.

Then, at the beginning of the summer holidays, his mum had dropped a bombshell. "We're moving. Start packing. We've got to be out by the end of the week."

"Where are we going?" It wasn't a big deal. They'd moved around a lot in the four years since his dad left them. Never very far.

"To a nice housing association maisonette." She beamed at him as though it was the best news in the world.

"What's a maisonette?" Nate asked.

"It's like a flat with upstairs as well as downstairs. The one we're moving to even has a garden."

Nate's eyes widened. They'd never lived anywhere with a garden before. Then he noticed his mum was looking at him the way she did when she had something to tell him that he might not like to hear.

"It's in Lincoln."

"Lincoln? What about my new school? I can't travel all the way from Lincoln to Gainsborough and back every day. It'd take for ever."

She laughed. "There are schools in Lincoln, silly."

"But all my friends are going to Gainsborough. Charlie and Alfie are going to be in my form."

The whine in his voice tipped her mood. "Don't go spoiling this for me, Nate. This is a great opportunity. A fresh start. Things are going to be different when we move. You'll see. Now go and start packing."

Nate knew better than to argue. He looked at the row of lager cans on the coffee table to see how many she'd had. Three. She'd be starting on the spirits soon. Best be off before then.

He saw her reach for a fag as he headed for the stairs to his bedroom. Who did she think she was kidding saying things would be different this time? He might have believed her if she didn't come out with the same old crap every time they moved. There was some truth in what she said, though. Things were always different when they moved. Only seldom in a good way.

Nate took the stairs two at a time. He made sure to slam his bedroom door extra hard before leaning back against it and casting his eyes around the tiny room. It wouldn't take long to pack. He didn't have much.

Back when he first started school, he'd been invited to other kids' houses for tea. He couldn't believe how much stuff they had in their bedrooms — toys, bookcases filled with books, wardrobes and drawers full of clothes. They had other things that he didn't have too — bedcovers with Spider-Man, racing cars, or football logos on them, pocket money to spend on more stuff.

He remembered the time when Charlie Sullivan came round to his house and asked him where all his toys were. Nate had pointed at the red plastic crate in the corner of his bedroom. It contained an assortment of toys from the charity shop, most of which were broken or he'd outgrown. They'd ended up watching telly downstairs until tea was ready. Spaghetti hoops on toast, not a proper meal like the one Mrs Sullivan had made when he went to Charlie's house.

It wasn't long before the invitations to go to other kids' houses dried up. Nate began to notice the mums in the playground nudging each other and looking at him in a certain way. Only two of them had continued to welcome him round for tea — Charlie Sullivan's and Alfie Colgan's.

Nate had been friends with Charlie and Alfie all through primary school. He'd gone to their homes at least once a week for years, and to Charlie's most Saturdays. Their parents didn't have a great deal of money, but even from a young age, Nate sensed that there were many ways in which his friends were better off than him.

He liked going round to Charlie's and Alfie's, and not just because their mums cooked proper dinners. He got free school lunches, but his own mum never made anything much for their evening meal. In the past couple of years, she'd mostly left him to fix something for himself from whatever was in the fridge, or the cupboard, or she'd give him some money for a takeaway. Nate rarely saw his mum eat. Maybe she didn't need much food because she didn't use up any energy lying around all day. Or, maybe she was just too full up from all that drinking.

Nate knew his mum was an alcoholic. Not when he was little, but when he was about eight or nine, some kids in the playground started taunting him about it. He'd looked the word up in a dictionary and knew immediately that they were right. Before then, he'd thought she was just ill or tired when he came home from school and found her slumped on the sofa. Now he knew it was because she drank too much alcohol, and it was slowly poisoning her.

Another thing Nate knew was that he was, 'known to social services'. He'd heard his teacher whisper it to one of the other teachers once. He didn't know what it meant, so he'd asked Charlie's mum. She'd told him that his mum wasn't very well and that people were keeping an eye on him in case they thought she wasn't able to look after him properly. Nate didn't ask what might happen to him if these people decided his mum couldn't look after him at all.

"Is everything all right at home, Nate?" Whenever an adult asked him this question after what Charlie's mum told him, he was always careful to tell them everything was fine. He made up stories about his mum, saying how great she was and how she took really good care of him. He knew what happened to kids who were taken from their families. He'd seen it on the telly. They were put in homes where people did bad things to them. That wasn't going to happen to him.

CHAPTER THREE

Steph
24 April 2019

Steph made a quick phone call to cancel an afternoon appointment. She was sharp with the receptionist when he asked when she thought she'd be able to reschedule. "Who the hell knows?"

People who worked for therapists must get special training on how to remain polite when dealing with arsey clients. There was the briefest silence before the receptionist replied in a calm voice, "That's perfectly all right, Ms Warwick. You let us know when you think you might have some time and we'll reschedule. You take care now."

DI Warwick. Was it so difficult to get her title right after all these months?

The last thing she'd wanted to do was cancel her appointment. It wasn't that she looked forward to her sessions with Dr Bryce, but they were necessary. That much had become apparent to her a year ago in January when she'd suffered a series of flashbacks that had compromised her ability to do her job and had put her life — and the lives of other people — in danger. She'd been saved by the prompt action of a special constable — a rookie at the time — called Jane Bell.

Steph made her way out to the car park. There, she caught sight of her colleague, DS Elias Harper pacing up and down, gesticulating wildly. Drawing nearer, she heard him proclaim, *"Let me play the lion too. I will roar, that I will do any man's heart good to hear me. I will roar that I will make the Duke say 'Let him roar again. Let him roar again.'"*

He wasn't mad, merely rehearsing. Elias was keen on amateur dramatics. Steph clapped, slowly. Elias's face reddened. "Oh. Er, morning, boss. Didn't realise I had an audience." He hurried to hold the car door open for her. Steph didn't thank him. She'd told him repeatedly that she didn't like him doing that. He wasn't her chauffeur, and she didn't expect it of him. All he was required to do was drive.

"You okay?" he asked.

"I'm fine. Stop asking."

"I hardly ever ask."

"Well, it seems like you always are." Elias fell silent. "So, what is it this time?" Steph asked, trying to make up for her shortness with him. "*Hamlet? Macbeth?*"

"*A Midsummer Night's Dream.*"

"Is that the one with the ass?"

"Yes, Bottom. Me."

Steph snorted. "That I have to see. When do the tickets go on sale?"

"I'll let you know."

After a short drive, they pulled up behind a response car parked outside a barber's shop at the bottom end of the High Street. "This is it."

They'd been called to the scene of a suspicious death, that of a young man in his twenties whose flat was above the shop. Steph looked around. This area of the High Street was characterised by small independent shops and businesses — nail parlours, hairdressers, takeaways, mortgage brokers, electrical repair shops — Steph took in all of these, and more, at a single glance. She didn't often come this far south of the town centre. Maybe she should.

Investigating a case like this would normally fall under the remit of the East Midlands Special Operations Unit — Major Crimes, known as EMSOU-MC, but they were otherwise committed. The local EMSOU DCI had agreed that Steph and her team would investigate.

Similarly, as a DI, Steph should not really be so directly involved in investigations, but the reality was that all hands were needed on deck these days, and this suited her fine — she'd had enough of sitting at a desk when she worked in a bank.

The street entrance to the victim's flat was via a green, wooden door to the left-hand side of the barber's shop. A uniformed PC guarding the entrance greeted them and gave them directions. "Morning, ma'am, Sarge. Up the stairs, turn right."

The communal stairwell was dimly lit and smelled strongly of rotting fish. Steph noticed Elias cover his nose. The source of the smell was a torn plastic bin bag on the landing opposite the victim's flat.

They paused for a moment to suit up before entering, watched by another PC, who brought them up to speed. "Morning, ma'am, Sergeant. Victim's in the kitchen. Name of Nicholas Burke. Went by the name of Cole. Looks like he's been suffocated and there are signs of torture."

Cole Burke was lashed to a kitchen chair. His purple-red face looked like a raw steak wrapped in cling film. Some of his fingers had been hacked off.

The young PC rambled on nervously. "He's ripe. I reckon he's been there a couple of days. His neighbour, Brian Sykes, raised the alarm when he opened the letter box and got a whiff of him. Terrible way to go, suffocation. Takes longer than people think too. Imagine staring into your killer's eyes through that plastic bag and seeing no hint of mercy in them. Chilling."

Steph sensed Elias's eyes on her. She refused to look at him. It was probably killing him not to ask if she was all right.

Just over a year ago, she'd experienced partial suffocation at first hand, only she'd been luckier than Cole Burke.

She realised that her hand was at her throat, and quickly diverted it to rub her nose, as if that had been her intention all along. At least Burke's face — what was left of it — wasn't changing into that of her violent and abusive ex-lover, Cal, before her very eyes. The therapy must be working.

Steph had been having nightmares about Cal for years. He'd killed her best friend, then come after her. At the last moment, he'd changed his mind and cut his own throat right in front of her. She'd watched him bleed out for too long before she'd called the police, a detail that she'd only ever revealed to Dr Bryce.

Bryce assured her that she'd almost certainly been in shock, that her delay in acting had been understandable in the circumstances, but deep down Steph couldn't shake her belief that but for those few seconds' hesitation, Cal might have been saved. That's why he'd come back to haunt her. Even when Dr Bryce pointed out that it wasn't Cal but her own misplaced sense of guilt that was haunting her, Steph clung to her belief. Maybe one day, given time and enough persuasion, she'd let herself believe she was innocent.

Back in January, things had taken a deeply disturbing turn — Cal had begun popping into her daytime thoughts. She'd transposed his features on to that of a murderer, and tried to save his life, almost getting herself killed in the process. She didn't need a shrink to point out the irony of her attempting to save the murderer whom she had temporarily believed to be Cal. So deep was her need to change what she had done — or more accurately, not done — when Cal was dying before her eyes, she'd tried to rescue him this time around.

This was the fate from which SC Bell had rescued her. Steph had made up a lame excuse to explain her behaviour and even gone as far as to attempt to blackmail Bell into not reporting the incident.

The incident was also what had finally propelled her into therapy. She couldn't afford to lose it like that while on duty again, still less, put other lives at risk besides her own. Even so, it hadn't been her decision. Bell and Elias had conspired behind her back, finally agreeing not to report her, on condition that she seek help.

"I recognise him actually," the PC said.

The sound of his voice refocussed Steph's attention. She assumed that he meant he'd come across Cole while on duty. She was right.

"He's been done for dealing in the past. Did some time a few years back."

"You think this is drug-related?" Elias asked.

"Got to be, hasn't it? There'll be some evidence of it when they search the place, I'll bet you."

Steph thought he was probably right. If Cole had been dealing, he could have been targeted by a disgruntled customer, or been involved in some sort of territorial dispute with a rival. It happened every now and then, but this level of violence wasn't standard.

Elias voiced her thoughts. "Bit over the top, isn't it? Why torture the poor bloke?"

The PC had a ready answer. "You don't need me to remind you that drug-related violence is getting nastier." Steph knew what he was going to say next.

"All this county lines business. Gangs from the big cities getting themselves established out here. They need to assert their authority over the local dealers, and they don't do things by halves."

He was probably right. The county lines phenomenon had exploded the myth of rural peace and tranquillity. The kind of extreme violence associated with organised crime was no longer the preserve of the big cities. Gangs were becoming business savvy, extending their markets into county towns and rural retreats and building up big customer bases using untraceable or 'burner' phones to maintain their anonymity.

As well as being associated with sickening violence, the practice was becoming synonymous with child criminal exploitation, sexual exploitation and human trafficking, among other crimes. Kids, some of them as young as eight or nine years old, were groomed and then coerced into working as couriers to transport drugs from the cities to the country. Those at the top were protected by a hierarchy of lower-level operatives.

"People are often tortured as a punishment or to obtain information. What did Cole's killers want from him?" Steph looked around. Cole's flat was in good condition. The kitchen was spotless. Even the four empty takeaway pizza boxes were stacked tidily beside the bin.

The main room was arranged around a huge flat-screen TV linked to a games console. A number of controllers lay on the floor nearby. A set of shelves housed neatly arranged games and comic books. In one of the two bedrooms, they found boxes of trainers of various sizes, and heaps of still-wrapped clothing, with their tags. Designer sportswear mostly — football shirts, hooded tops, and joggers.

Elias held up a clutch of tops. "Think he was grooming kids with this lot?"

"Most likely," Steph said. "Cool older man offering clothes, entertainment, probably ciggies and takeaways, in return for delivering a package or two. Maybe even some cash thrown in." She picked up a black hoodie, sizing it up. "Not exactly man-size, is it? Probably fit a twelve-year-old." She placed it back on the pile, carefully. "Where's his phone?"

They returned to the kitchen and asked the PC if he'd seen it. He shook his head. "No, ma'am."

"Let's hope it turns up in a thorough search when Forensics are done." She turned to Elias. "Let's speak with the neighbour, Sergeant."

They crossed the landing between the flats. A cat had appeared from somewhere and was licking at the remains of a tin of mackerel fillets. Elias shooed it away and tucked the tin deep inside the bag. "She'll cut herself on that."

The man who answered their knock screwed up his nose, as if offended by the stink of his own rubbish. "Police," Steph said, showing her warrant card. "We'd like to ask you some questions about your neighbour."

"Best come in then." He shuffled down the hallway in front of them. The smell inside his flat was no better than the fishy one outside, although it was more complex — a nauseating cocktail of rank drains, body odour and cat's piss. Steph half-expected Elias to tie a handkerchief around his nose and mouth.

At least Sykes wasn't a hoarder, Steph thought, appreciating the sparsely furnished sitting room. In a hoarder's house you never knew what might be lurking under the clutter.

Burke's neighbour invited them to sit down. Steph made a beeline for a hard chair, leaving Elias to perch on the edge of a shiny, dirt-ingrained armchair. She asked the neighbour, "Can you confirm that your name is Brian Sykes, and that it was you who called the police regarding Mr Nicholas Burke?"

"Yes, I'm Brian Sykes all right, and it was me that called the police. I knocked on Cole's door to ask if he could sort out my Wi-Fi. There was no answer, so I looked through the letter box. That was when the smell hit me, and I called you lot. Have a fall, did he?"

"No," Steph said. "I'm afraid he's died, and we're investigating the circumstances."

"Bloody hell. Poor sod. Far too young for that."

"How well did you know him?" Elias asked.

"You mean what was he like? Nice enough bloke. We'd always say 'hello' when we met on the stairs, and he'd take my rubbish down if he saw it outside my door. Young bloke like him isn't likely to have much to say to an old codger like me, but he'd always give me the time of day, I'll say that for him. Had a lot of youngsters visiting him, mind. Cousins of his, but they never made any noise, not that I could hear anyway, so I can't complain."

Steph leaned forward. "Tell us about his cousins."

"They were young lads mostly."

"How young?"

"I was getting to that. Teenagers, I'd say, though a couple of them looked a bit younger, I reckon. Eleven or twelve, maybe?"

Steph asked if he'd heard any names. Brian thought for a moment. "Little'un was called Nate, I think. There was also a man called Wes. Never heard their surnames. Can't think on the others. Sorry."

Steph reassured him. "That's all right. Just knowing a couple of first names is helpful. Did Cole tell you they were his cousins?"

"I asked them what they were doing hanging about on the pavement outside once, and they said they were waiting for Cole. Said they were cousins of his. I didn't let them in, mind. For all I know they could have been up to some mischief. I let a stranger in once, and he mugged me as soon as the door shut behind us. Once bitten and all that. I didn't care that they were just skinny kids. I wasn't going to take any more risks after that."

Steph asked Brian if he could describe Wes and Nate. "One called Wes seemed a bit sullen, like. Bit of an attitude, if you ask me. Youngster was chirpy, though, used to give me a smile. Big gap-toothed grin, he had."

"The small one. Nate? He had missing teeth?" Steph asked.

"No, not missing. Thought he was missing one at first, mind, then I realised there was just a big gap between his two front teeth."

"A diastema," Elias said. Brian and Steph looked at him. "That's what it's called. An extra wide gap between two teeth. Easily correctable."

"So, it's fairly noticeable?" Steph asked Brian.

"Oh yes. Hard to miss, if you can miss something that isn't there in the first place." He laughed at his own joke. "As I come to think on it, he was here a few days ago. Might even have been the day Cole died." As if it had just hit him, he added. "So, he's really dead then, that young fella across the landing? Never would have believed it. Would have thought he'd be around long after I was dead and gone. I never heard a thing. Far as I know he didn't call for help or anything. Then again, my hearing's not what it used to be. Wouldn't be able to catch more than the gist of what you're saying now, but the replacement batteries for my hearing aid arrived yesterday."

Cole wouldn't have made much noise with a bag wrapped around his head. He'd have had no breath to scream. They'd probably gagged him when they took his fingers. Steph winced at the thought. "The sullen man. Can you describe him?"

"He was a right ginger."

"He had ginger hair?"

"He did, though it was shaved close to his head. But he was proper ginger, you know? With the ginger eyelashes and freckles."

"Anything else you can tell us about him?"

"Not that comes to mind. Being ginger was his most distinguishing feature. That's what you call it, isn't it?"

Steph thanked Mr Sykes, reminding him to get in touch if anything else came to mind. Elias offered to take the rubbish bag down to the bin.

"Very kind of you, Officer. Takes me an age to get down there, with my back the way it is. It's downstairs and turn right along the passage to the back door. Don't shut the door behind you, mind, or you won't get back in."

Halfway down the stairs, the flimsy bag burst, strewing rubbish down the remaining steps. The stink made them gag.

"Jesus, Elias. Why do you have to be such a do-gooder?" Steph pulled a spare pair of latex gloves from her inside pocket. "Here. Make a start while I see if he's got another bag."

She returned, moments later, with a dustpan and brush and another flimsy bin bag. Elias was tying a handkerchief around his hand. "Cut my finger on that bloody tin."

Steph began sweeping up the rubbish he'd gathered up. "I'll sort this out. You go upstairs and run some water over that."

She took the bag of rubbish to a wheelie bin in a small yard at the rear of the building.

By the time she returned to Burke's flat, her nostrils were so accustomed to foul smells that she scarcely registered the scent of death, which was just as well. As the SIO, she was likely to be stuck there for some time.

19

CHAPTER FOUR

Jane
21 May 2019

While Jane was drinking tea and eating cake in Veganbites with Frieda and Karun, a young woman, looking not much older than the girl who'd just been stabbed, walked into the café. It was Thea Martin, one of Jane's ex-students. Her face lit up when she caught sight of Jane.

"Hey, Jane. Wasn't expecting to see you here this morning. Any idea what's going on at the traffic lights? There's about three police cars and everything's at a standstill."

These days, everyone seemed to expect Jane to know everything about every piece of activity in the city, criminal or otherwise. It didn't bother her. She just regretted she couldn't be more informative. Still, on this occasion she could enlighten Thea.

Frieda got in first. "A girl was stabbed in front of Jane."

Thea's eyes widened. "Oh my God, Jane. What happened? Is she going to be okay?"

"She was attacked, stabbed by a man who jumped off a motorbike. I don't know if she'll survive." Jane's tone said it all.

"That's terrible! Did you know who she was? Was she local?" Thea gasped. "I might even know her if she went to my school."

"There are a lot of schools in Lincoln, Thea."

"I know, I know. It's unlikely, but it's possible, isn't it?"

Her excitement was slightly unnerving. Jane ignored the question.

"You're a bit early," Karun said to Thea. "Would you like to join us for tea and cake before you start?"

Thea had a part-time job at Veganbites. She worked weekends and occasional evenings, if there was a function going on, and she would be working there full-time in the school holidays. "Mmm. Is that your famous carrot cake, Karun?"

"It most certainly is." He cut her a slice.

Jane had grown fond of Thea in the months when she'd tutored her to help her catch up on her studies after an illness that had kept her out of school for a while. She was no longer tutoring her, but a bond had formed between them.

Thea lived in a large house in a village on the outskirts of Lincoln. She was alone a lot of the time because her parents were sailing around the world with some friends on their yacht. Her older brother checked in on her from time to time, but not often enough, in Jane's opinion.

"How old was she?" Thea asked.

"She didn't look more than twelve or thirteen," Jane said.

Thea seemed less surprised than Jane would have expected. There was a reason for that. "Someone at my school was stabbed a few weeks ago. He was in year eight. He was okay, though. It was drugs-related."

Jane nodded. She'd heard about the incident from PC Tim Sterne, who'd been nearby and hurried to the scene. It hadn't happened on school premises, so she hadn't worried too much about Thea, but she had intended to talk with her about it.

"And people are forever being stabbed on the Cathedral Estate," Thea declared.

21

Jane shook her head. "That's not true." But she acknowledged that Lincoln wasn't exempt from the rise in knife crime occurring in the nation as a whole. The statistics were alarming, but of course could be misleading.

Frieda looked worried. "Thea has got a point. They say attacks involving knives are spiking nationally. There's reports in the *Post* every other week."

Jane offered some words of reassurance. "It's not always what you think. A lot of knife crime occurs in domestic settings and involves people who know each other."

Jane thought it prudent not to mention that more knives and other bladed weapons had been recovered in random stop-and-searches this year than in previous ones. She and her colleagues were also attending more knife-related incidents than ever before.

"We're being proactive, carrying out more stop-and-searches and educating people about the dangers of carrying knives. The problem is getting the government to see that it's not just urban areas that are blighted by knife crime. Rural areas are affected too. We need the resources to deal with it."

"We had some police officers give us a talk about knives at school last week," Thea said. "They mentioned something I'd not thought about before — that carrying a knife can turn a small incident into a serious one. Like they gave a real-life example of an argument over a parking space that ended up in a near-fatal stabbing."

"Yes. I've done some of those talks," Jane said. She thought of a story she'd heard about a young lad who'd turned up at a police station in one of the coastal towns soon after such a talk. He'd handed over an eight-inch zombie knife, a picture of the Grim Reaper on its handle. The owner was twelve years old. "We try to focus not just on the crime itself, but the repercussions for the wider community, including friends and family, of both victim and perpetrator."

Thea began gathering up the mugs and plates. "Time I got to work."

Karun excused himself too. "Those mushroom-and-leek pies won't make themselves." He followed Thea into the kitchen.

Frieda lingered. "I can't get that poor girl out of my head. You were right when you said that becoming a parent makes you see the world as a hostile place full of potential dangers for your child. I can't even bear to watch the cosiest of crime dramas on TV anymore. Anything even slightly violent makes me afraid for Neela's future."

Jane couldn't get the girl out of her head either. Just over a year ago, she'd become involved, tangentially, in a murder investigation that had led, among other things, to her being suspended from her special constable duties. Since then, she'd resisted the urge to become involved beyond her role. It hadn't been difficult. The crimes she dealt with as an SC were mostly minor ones.

This case was different, and not just because it was a murder. It felt almost personal. She couldn't help but feel an emotional pull towards the girl, as well as a responsibility. It wasn't going to be easy just to let it go.

Frieda grabbed Jane's wrist. "Oh my God. Janie, is that who I think it is?"

Jane followed Frieda's gaze to a woman in a car that had just drawn up across the street. She ducked. "Bloody hell! It's DI Up-Herself Warwick."

The case Jane had become involved in the previous year had been led by DI Stephanie Warwick. It was an understatement to say that the DI had taken an immediate dislike to Jane. Her hostility towards her was compounded when she discovered that Jane, a lowly special, was meddling in her case. It had been Warwick who'd had her suspended. Things had become complicated. Jane had saved Warwick's life, but she'd also colluded with Warwick's colleague, DS Elias Harper, in forcing Warwick to seek help for a mental-health issue that had impacted on her role as a senior police officer.

Frieda laughed. "She can't see you, Jane. This table isn't visible from across the road."

"Did I just duck? I couldn't help it. It was a reflex action." Jane sighed. "Looks like she'll probably be the senior investigating officer on this case."

"Is that a problem? I know you don't like her, but she's good at her job, isn't she?"

Was she? Jane had witnessed Warwick being very bad at her job. Was that fair? There had been a reason — Warwick had been mentally unstable at the time. Reluctantly, Jane agreed. "It's not that—"

"I know what it is. I know you, Jane. You're drawn to this girl, aren't you? You want to be involved, and you know DI Warwick will forbid it."

There was no point in denying it. "You're right, I suppose. I just want to know more about her, particularly how she came to this tragic point in her life. She looked undernourished, neglected. Someone should have been looking after her, and someone should care about why this happened to her."

Frieda looked her in the eye. "You missed something out." Jane raised an eyebrow. "Who. You want to know who killed her. You want to find that person and hold them to account."

Frieda did, indeed, know her well. "Yes. I do. I want justice for her. But she's not dead yet, remember." *Is she?*

DI Warwick stepped out of the car. She turned her head slightly and fixed her gaze on Veganbites. Jane resisted the urge to shrink back in her seat. She hoped Frieda was right about their table not being visible from outside, for she could have sworn that Warwick was staring straight at her. It was a relief when Warwick turned away and walked towards the scene of the crime. Jane felt a stab of envy. She wished she could take her place.

Frieda patted her hand. "Have you come across DI Warwick much since the case last year?"

"Not at all, thank goodness."

"I told you she stopped coming into the café after that time when she visited and went on about how she was so grateful to you for saving her life, didn't I?"

"Yes, you did."

Warwick had been much less effusive when thanking Jane in person. She'd sounded grudging. Moreover, she'd tried to blackmail Jane by hinting that she'd do all she could to help her be reinstated as an SC if Jane agreed to keep quiet about the state of her mental health.

"Pity. She really liked our coffee, and I think she liked talking to me. Still, I suppose she didn't want to risk bumping into you here."

"I suppose not."

A couple walked into the café and asked if they could have a table. Frieda got up. "I'll bring you a fresh cup of tea when I've served those two."

Jane didn't decline the offer. She heard the couple asking Frieda if she had seen the 'accident' as they called it, and if she could tell them anything about it. Jane hoped Frieda wouldn't send them her way. She had no desire to discuss the incident with complete strangers.

DS Elias Harper had got out of the car after Warwick. Jane had met Elias on a few occasions in the past year. The first time he'd still had his leg in plaster after being assaulted by the killer they'd all been pursuing. She'd asked him to meet her for a drink at a pub on The Strait, a narrow passage leading from the top end of the High Street to the bottom of Steep Hill, telling him that she needed to speak with him urgently about DI Warwick.

She'd told him the truth about the events at Walter Street. How Warwick had twice mistaken the killer for someone called 'Cal'. How she'd run into his burning embrace as if into the arms of a long-lost lover, trying to save him. Even when she caught alight and was in grave danger, she'd struggled against Jane when she pulled her away. Jane had needed to shake her, and scream at her to wake up and see that the man she was trying to save wasn't Cal, whoever that might be. Elias had had no idea.

"None of that was in your statement," Elias had pointed out immediately.

"She asked me to agree to a slightly different version of what happened." Jane had coloured as she told him this. She wasn't proud of what she'd done. "Instead of saying that I'd had to pull her off him, she asked me to state that he'd grabbed her and tried to pull her into the flames with him when she was attempting to smother the fire with her coat. That explained her injuries and still showed me in a heroic light, which she probably thought was important to me. It wasn't. My only concern at the time was to drag her to safety. You should have seen her, Elias. It was like she was hallucinating."

Elias had listened with a grave look on his face. He seemed genuinely shocked when Jane mentioned that Warwick had tried to blackmail her.

"I think she was quite desperate at that point. I'm not sure why I agreed to alter the facts, even if it was just a slight shift in perspective. I know I shouldn't have done it. It certainly wasn't what she said about getting me reinstated that made me agree. I think it might have been because I felt sorry for her."

Elias nodded. "I know what you mean. There's something about her, a vulnerability that makes you want to get beyond that prickly exterior and find what really makes her tick."

Jane sighed. "I don't particularly like her, but I do think that something really terrible must have happened to her to make her the way she is. She's so hostile and defensive. Maybe this Cal did something to her. And I feel I need to understand her to overcome my dislike of her. I hate that she makes me behave like her." She noticed that Elias was about to protest. "It's true! She makes me see a side of myself I don't like very much."

"Your dark side," Elias said with the faintest of smiles. "DI Warwick certainly has one of those. I admit I'm at a loss to know how we can reach the other side that we both suspect is there."

"What are you going to do?" Jane asked. "I've confided in you because I've noticed how you are with her. She doesn't get under your skin, does she, the way she does with other people? You seem to have infinite patience with her."

"How do you know it's not just that she's my boss? That I have to bite my tongue because of the difference in our ranks?" Elias asked. It was a fair question.

Jane smiled. "I know another softie when I see one. You care about people. You care about her." Elias nodded. "So, what do we do about your boss?"

"We should report her. If she's unstable, she could present a risk to others." He thought for a moment. "I don't want to report her though. I believe in second chances. If you agree, I'll confront her, demand that she seeks help. I'll tell her that if she doesn't agree, we won't hesitate to report her. With any luck, she should appreciate that we're doing her a favour, risking our necks for her, not going after her. That okay with you?"

"Yes. I was so hoping you'd say that. It'll be better coming from you. Mind you, it will give her even more reason to hate me, knowing I dobbed on her to you. But it can't be helped. It's not like I'll be seeing much of her again. She's going to be furious when you broach it with her, you realise that, don't you?"

Elias grimaced. "Hell, yes. I'm not looking forward to it."

Jane met Elias again when he'd had an opportunity to speak with Warwick. She asked him how she had reacted. Predictably, she'd blown a gasket.

"Her initial fury was directed at you, of course," Elias told her. "She ranted on for a good ten minutes about that effing interfering special. When she calmed down, I told her, bluntly, that if she didn't agree to getting some sort of help, I'd report her to the superintendent. She went very quiet after that. It was like she'd blown hot and then she was icy cold, but still smouldering."

"And? Did she agree?"

"She agreed. But I'll be keeping an eye on her, watching for signs of stress. If she shows the slightest hint of mental instability, I'll confront her. She's going to be really pissed off about the amount I'm going to scrutinise her, but I can't allow her to lose it on the job again. This is something that could affect her decision-making and her ability to react in an emergency."

"I'm sorry, Elias. I'm afraid I've put a burden of responsibility on your shoulders."

Elias shook his head. "Not a burden. A responsibility, yes, but not a burden."

Looking through the window of the warm and cheery café at the scene of the recent stabbing, knowing that DI Warwick was likely to be the SIO on the case, Jane was certain of one thing — however much she'd hoped to avoid crossing paths with Warwick again, it was now inevitable. Not least because she was a significant witness, and Warwick would need her to provide a statement very soon.

CHAPTER FIVE

Nate
5 August 2018

The day before his move to Lincoln, Nate went round to Charlie's house for a goodbye tea. Charlie's mum, Mrs Sullivan, had invited Alfie too. She'd made Nate's favourite meal — hunter's chicken with roast potatoes, vegetables and Yorkshire pudding, with loads of lovely thick gravy. Charlie and Alfie groaned when they saw it. They would have chosen pizza and chips. Nate liked that Mrs Sullivan said she loved cooking for him because he appreciated proper food. He didn't tell her that it was because until he started coming to his friends' houses for tea, the only vegetables he'd set eyes on were frozen peas. Mrs Sullivan made his favourite pudding too. Apple crumble and custard. He had seconds.

After tea had come a surprise. Going-away presents! A new school bag from Mrs Sullivan, a pencil case full of pens and other stuff from Charlie, and a calculator from Alfie. There was something from Alfie's mum too, a ruler set, and some dinosaur erasers. There were good luck cards too. Nate choked up a bit when he opened them. Mrs Sullivan tousled his hair, told him she expected him to keep in touch. Even Charlie's dad had signed the card.

Mrs Sullivan and Charlie dropped him home. His mum was in the kitchen, taping up a big cardboard box on which was written 'kitchen drawers'. She wasn't drunk. She'd been teetotal, as she called it, for a couple of days now, which was great, but even sober, her moods were all over the place. She said she was suffering from something called withdrawal, which meant her body was trying to get used to doing without alcohol. Nate always tried to gauge her mood before he opened his mouth.

This evening she was jittery, excited about the move. Nate too was on edge. It was good to see her happy, but he wondered what she'd be like when the novelty wore off. She was acting like this move was going to make everything better. It was hard to be positive when he'd seen her this way before and knew how it would probably end up: his mum — *Angie* — back on the bottle, his hopes that life might get better crushed like one of her fag ends.

He tried to hide the new bag containing his presents, but his mum could be quite sharp when she wasn't drinking. She spotted it straight away. "What's that you've got there, babe? A new bag?"

"It's for school. A going-away present from Charlie's mum." For a moment, he thought she wasn't going to say anything. Then she started.

"I'd have got you one if you'd asked, you know. You don't have to go begging from other people."

"It was a present."

She yanked it off his shoulder, and he heard the contents rattle against each other. "What've you got in there then?" She tugged at the zip, turned the bag upside down. Nate looked on in dismay as the pencil case and the calculator hit the floor. The pencil case was okay. It didn't open, but the back of the calculator came off. He dropped to his knees to retrieve it.

"You've broken it!"

Angie spoke in a mocking tone. "Don't be such a crybaby. It goes back on. Give it here." She swiped it out of his hand.

"Give it back!"

She held it tauntingly out of his reach. Nate lunged forward and managed to knock it out of her hand. This time it made a worse clattering sound when it hit the floor tiles. Tears stung Nate's eyes when he saw the big crack on the display screen. Even if it still worked, it was spoiled. "I hate you. You're a cow and an alcoholic. Everybody says so."

She screamed at him then. Called him a little shit and said he was worse than his dad. Nate drowned out the hateful words by yelling right back at her. Then he grabbed his new bag, scooped his presents inside and went up to his bedroom.

The following morning, Nate woke up in his Gainsborough bedroom for the last time. The removals van was due at half past nine. When he came down for breakfast, he found a small rectangular parcel on the kitchen table, wrapped in red paper. His name was written in his mum's writing on the attached tag.

Inside, was a new calculator. It was rubbish compared to the one Alfie had given him. His mum must have gone out to the supermarket first thing to get it before he woke up. He knew she was trying to put things right, but he couldn't forgive her. It was her fault the other one was broken. It probably hadn't even occurred to her that Alfie's one meant something to him. It was a present from his friend. He'd have liked it even if it had been as crap as the one she'd given him.

Angie tried to sweet talk the removals men into giving them a lift to the new house. "Sorry, love. It's against the rules," the older of them said. So they had to get a bus to the station and take the train to Lincoln.

Nate had only ever been to Lincoln on school trips. He'd been to the castle and the cathedral, and the Museum of Lincolnshire Life. Once they'd gone on a Roman tour with a man dressed up as a centurion. He'd loved all that. History was his favourite subject at school.

When he saw the cathedral from the train, his spirits lifted. His mum sat beside him, reading a magazine about celebrities. She didn't even look up. They'd hardly spoken to each other all morning. Neither of them mentioned the calculator. She must have known he'd opened it because he'd deliberately left the wrapping paper on the table, but she hadn't asked if he liked it, and he hadn't thanked her for it.

Angie looked around after they exited the station. "It's changed a bit since the last time I was here. That bus station wasn't there for starters."

Someone overheard. "It's the new one. Just opened earlier this year." It was a man who'd been in the same train carriage as them. Nate had seen him looking at Angie, but she'd been too absorbed in her magazine to notice.

"Just here for the day, are you?" the man said.

Angie ignored him, so Nate said, "No, we're moving into a new house today."

"Just you and your mum, is it?"

Turned out Angie had been listening. "That's none of your business. Piss off."

"Excuse me—"

Angie grabbed Nate's wrist and pulled him away. "What have I told you about talking to strangers? If I hadn't stopped you, you'd have been telling him our new address and inviting him round for tea."

"I wouldn't. I'm not stupid."

Angie guided him past the bus station. "It's not that far. We can walk."

It was soon obvious that his mum had no idea how to find her way to the new house. She kept stopping to ask people for directions, and it seemed to take them forever to get there. Luckily, the lady from the housing association was still waiting for them when they finally arrived.

"I let the removals people in. They turned up about two hours ago." Thankfully, she didn't seem annoyed about Nate and his mum being late. "I'll just show you around, then you can sign for the keys."

Nate thought it looked quite nice from the outside. His mum had told him it was a maisonette, and that it had stairs

32

inside. They'd only ever lived in flats before, so stairs were exciting. And there was a garden! Something else they'd never had.

The woman's name was Helen Wood. She wore glasses with mosaic-patterned frames in turquoise, red and yellow, which made her look quite weird. She had white hair like an old person, but she didn't look that old.

There was a flat underneath their maisonette. Helen Wood told them they would have to make sure they didn't make too much noise and disturb the elderly tenant who lived there, or he'd probably bang on his ceiling with the end of his walking stick, like he'd done to the previous tenants. Angie assured her that they were very quiet.

They had to wait outside the front door for the removals men to manoeuvre the sofa through. Nate asked if he could see his bedroom. Helen Wood smiled and led them upstairs. There were two bedrooms, one bigger than the other. "I expect this will be yours," Helen Wood said, pointing to the smaller room. "It has a nice view of the garden." She had explained, as they mounted the stairs, that the back garden was theirs. The smaller one at the front belonged to Mr Thom downstairs.

Nate had already looked at both rooms and decided he liked the smaller one better anyway. It was lighter. When he crossed to the window and caught sight of the rectangle of grass surrounded by tall hedges, he forgot all about being mad at his mum for breaking his calculator.

"Look, Mum! A proper garden."

The housing lady smiled. "You've got the best spot at the end of the block, so one side of your garden isn't next to anyone else's. And this block looks out on the playing fields belonging to the primary school." She pointed at a cluster of low buildings on the other side of the field.

One of the removals men shouted up, "Where do you want this, duck?" Nate followed his mum and Helen Wood back downstairs, where there were two rooms — a kitchen big enough for a table, and a sitting room with a door leading to a little balcony with railings painted blue. His mum really liked the balcony.

If it hadn't been for the prospect of starting a new school, Nate would have been okay with the move. Charlie and Alfie had promised to keep in touch. Their mums both said Nate could come for sleepovers at the weekends whenever he liked.

A thought occurred to him. Maybe Charlie and Alfie could come for sleepovers here. He'd been watching his mum as they toured the house. She'd seemed really happy.

Maybe she really was going to stop drinking and this really was going to be a fresh start. Maybe this time it would be different in a good way.

CHAPTER SIX

Steph
25 April 2019

The morning after attending Cole Burke's murder scene, Steph and Elias interviewed Luca Esposito, the owner of the barber's shop below Cole's flat. His Italian grandparents had settled in Lincoln after World War II and set up the business that Luca still ran today. Steph expected him to say that he was far too busy cutting and shaving to notice any comings and goings to Cole's flat but, as luck would have it, he was a smoker.

"I go out every so often for a ciggie and sometimes I used to see kids go in and out of there." He nodded at the street door to Burke's place.

"Ever speak to any of them?" Steph asked.

Luca laughed. "Only the ones cheeky enough to ask me for a smoke. But, sure, I'd nod at them in passing if they looked my way."

"What about your staff?" she asked.

"I employ five people — two of them, Serge and Bruno, are my cousins, and there's a young lad, Noah Shore, who's only been with me for a few months. Don't know what he's doing working here — he's a gifted stylist and I'm lucky to have him. I expect he'll be moving on soon. This is just a stopgap for him. Noah probably knew Burke best. He chatted to him whenever he cut his hair. They were of an age. Serge, Bruno and Noah are all in today. I can give you contact details for my two other members of staff."

"Thanks," Steph said. "Cole Burke's neighbour mentioned a boy and a man who were frequent visitors to Cole's flat. The boy looked about eleven or twelve. He had a wide gap between his two front teeth. The man had red hair. Do you remember either of them?"

Luca turned his head to exhale his cigarette smoke away from them. Pretty pointless given the way the wind was blowing. Steph waved her hand in front of her face. Luca noticed and apologised. "Filthy habit, I know. I'm cutting down. Vaping more than smoking now. Yes, I think I know who he means. It did strike me as a bit odd, the ginger-haired man and Cole hanging out with kids. Would have thought they were paedos, only they didn't seem the type."

He dropped his cigarette stub, extinguished it on the pavement, then kicked it away from his shop doorway towards the gutter. "Tell you what, though. The small kid couldn't have been in school much. He used to turn up at all hours of the day. I don't know about the evenings because we close at half past five. Ginger guy's been coming around for about a year, but he only started bringing the kid with him last October. There were other kids before that."

"How well did you know Burke?"

"Not well. We talked about the usual stuff when he came in. Football, mostly. He used to take the piss out of me for supporting AC Milan." He shrugged in a way that emphasised his Italian ancestry. "I have family in Lombardy. I used to spend the summer holidays with my hordes of cousins there."

"Did you ever ask Burke about the kids who came to his flat?"

"He said they were his cousins. They weren't a nuisance."

"You mentioned that the little kid was absent from school a lot," Steph said.

"None of my business."

Then why mention it? It seemed that Luca's concern for the children's welfare had not extended to alerting the authorities. Not that he was alone there. It was always a safer bet not to get involved, especially where drugs might be involved, and Steph suspected that Luca must have had some idea of what Burke had been up to and had chosen to look the other way.

Serge and Bruno were happy to answer questions. Neither of them knew Cole Burke other than as an occasional customer. The newest member of staff, Noah Shore, agreed he'd been on friendly terms with him. None of them could think of a reason why anyone would want to murder Burke.

Steph squinted across the busy road at the buildings fronting the street on the other side. As on this side of the road, they were mostly Victorian and early-Edwardian two-to-three-storey houses of red brick, almost all of them converted into shops and businesses. Some had flats above. There was some slight hope that a resident looking out of one of the windows around the time of Burke's murder might have seen something of interest. Staff of local businesses and residents in the vicinity would all need to be interviewed — a job for the house-to-house-enquiry team.

While they were standing on the pavement, a man in a black hoodie and faded black jeans approached the street entrance to Burke's flat. After looking somewhat shiftily from side to side, he pressed the buzzer of the entry system. Steph and Elias exchanged a glance. Burke's body had been removed from the premises the day before, but Forensics were still up there gathering evidence.

Steph called out to the man. "Excuse me. Are you looking for Cole Burke?" The man turned to see who was calling out to him. He took one look at them and bolted. Some people just had a radar for identifying police.

Steph swore under her breath. Dodging startled pedestrians, she and Elias took off after him, pursuing him down a side street. It was one of many leading off the High Street to the Sincil Dyke, a canal-like watercourse of pre-medieval or even Roman origin that flowed through the low-lying land east of the High Street.

"He won't get far," Steph called out to Elias. "This ends in a cul-de-sac." Steph hoped she was right in thinking that this was one of the streets off the High Street that didn't lead to a bridge across the dyke to Sincil Bank on the other side. She was right, but where the road curved round, there was a junction leading to a row of three or four modern houses ending in a fence, behind which lay the dyke. She watched the man stop short at the fence and then attempt to scale it. She rolled her eyes. Elias grabbed his legs as he tried to pull himself up and over.

"Give it up!" Steph yelled. "You'll only end up in the drain." Indeed, now that he'd seen over the top of the fence to what lay beyond, the man gave up his struggle and dropped to the ground. He doubled over, gasping to catch his breath, sweating profusely.

Steph showed him her ID. "Police. There was no need to take off. We only wanted to ask you some questions."

Still panting, the man said, "What about?"

"You were buzzing Cole Burke's place. Is he a friend of yours?"

"He's a mate, yeah."

"When did you last see him?"

"Few days ago. Why? He in some kind of trouble?"

Steph evaded the question. "First things first. What's your name and address?"

The man wiped the sweat from his brow on the sleeve of his shirt. The cuff was torn, and threads trailed in his eyes making him blink. His face was somewhat gaunt, taut, with dry, overstretched skin. The look of a drug addict.

"Shane Watt. Of no fixed abode."

Homeless, then. "Cole Burke was found dead in his flat yesterday," Steph told him.

"Right." Shane rubbed his chin. "That's that then."

"That's what?" Elias asked. Shane looked at him and shrugged. "That's it for your supply of drugs from Burke?" Another shrug.

Elias searched Shane and found nothing on him, other than a few loose coins, possibly from begging. There was no pressing need to arrest him right there and then, but they did need him to give a statement about his knowledge of Burke, and the nature of their relationship.

Steph tried to put him at ease a little. "Look. We're not interested in your drug activities, so I'm prepared to overlook them on this occasion, but we'll need you to come into the station soon to tell us everything you know about Cole Burke and his activities. Is that a deal?" After a moment's thought, she added, "You hungry?" Watt's brow furrowed with surprise and suspicion. "I said we wanted to ask you a few questions. How about we have a chat over breakfast?" Another shrug, followed by a nod.

Shane walked with them back to the High Street and they stopped at the first café serving an all-day breakfast.

"Full English?" Steph asked him, when the waitress came over to take their order. She ordered drinks for everyone. As soon as the food arrived, Shane tucked in as though he hadn't eaten in days. "When did you last eat?"

"Yesterday lunchtime. A woman bought me a burger and chips from McDonald's."

He wouldn't have felt any urge to eat while he was high. For an addict, the need for drugs superseded the accepted hierarchy of basic human needs — food and shelter.

Steph let him eat in peace, guessing that he was currently in a hiatus between one high and the next, where the need for nourishment did have to be satisfied. Only when he'd wiped the last of the egg yolk from his plate, using the last triangle of heavily buttered toast, did she begin to question him.

"Burke was your supplier?"

"I told you already. He was a mate."

"How long had he been supplying you with drugs?"

Shane released a breath through pursed lips, his fingertips brushing against his mouth. If she'd been a smoker, and if the law permitted, Steph would have offered him a cigarette at that moment. Instead, she signalled to Elias to pour him another cup of tea.

"Don't know what you're talking about."

"Come on, Shane. I told you we're not interested in your drug activities. All we're after is some information. Why were you looking for Burke today?"

"He was a mate. I was paying him a social call."

"If you don't mind my saying so, you don't seem particularly upset at the news of your 'mate's' death." Steph waited a moment, then added, "Know anyone who'd have a reason to kill Cole Burke?"

Shane, who had been rubbing his belly in appreciation of a hot meal, looked at her sharply. "You never said someone had killed him."

As if you didn't guess. "You never asked me how he died," Steph said dryly.

Shane looked around him, suddenly jittery. "I gotta go."

He made to stand up but Steph grabbed his arm. "Wait. You said Burke was a mate. Don't you want to help us find out who's responsible for murdering him?"

"I only said he was a mate because I didn't want to say what my real relationship with him was."

"So, he was your dealer?"

"Yes, but I'm off the strong stuff. I want to get clean. I hardly knew him. I only met him a couple of times. He used young lads to do his deliveries."

"Fine, but stay where you are. I have more questions, and you are a suspect."

"Are you arresting me?"

Steph sighed. "No."

"Then you can't detain me."

"Mr Watt." It was Elias, his tone conciliatory. "Please, sit down. Have another cup of tea. This won't take long and then you can be on your way. That tattoo I saw on your forearm when I searched you, *In Arduis Fidelis*, it means 'In Hardship Faithful'. It's the motto of the Royal Army Medical Corps. You're ex-Army?"

Shane stared at Elias for a moment, a look of surprise on his face. Slowly, he sat down, his expression wary but no longer defensive. "Yes. I was a medic in the British Army for five years."

"You must have seen a lot of terrible things," Elias said gently.

"I saw enough." He didn't elaborate.

Steph stared at him and was embarrassed when he noticed.

"Do I disgust you?" he asked her. "How does someone with a background like mine slide into addiction and homelessness? Failed to live up to my motto, didn't I?" He scratched at his right arm, where the tattoo must be.

Steph said nothing. Not even six months ago, he would have been right. She would have been disgusted by his appearance, his fall from grace. All the more so because of the height from which he'd fallen. If you suffered a trauma, you dealt with it and moved on, right? For years after Cal's death, that's exactly what she'd believed she'd done. Now, after a few months of counselling, she was beginning to realise that, far from being strong, she'd been refusing to face up to the extent of her trauma.

Elias returned to the matter of Cole Burke. "So, did Cole Burke have any enemies that you knew of? A rival dealer, perhaps, or a client he'd crossed?"

Shane sighed. "He was a dealer. He would have had enemies, but I don't know who they were. I keep myself to myself." His mug of tea shook in his hand. Elias handed him a napkin to wipe his sleeve.

Steph took over again. "But you must hear things on the street, right? Has there been talk about a takeover by a rival dealer? A gang, perhaps? Have local dealers being warned off their turf? Have you or any of your homeless buddies been threatened with violence for going to the wrong source for your supplies?"

Too many questions. Shane's glance strayed, nervously, to the door. Steph, hoping he wouldn't take sudden flight, pressed on. "Come on, Shane. Talk to us. Burke's killer tortured him before he killed him. It wasn't pretty. Surely you don't want a person capable of doing that to another human being out on the street, do you? You say you saw terrible things in service, well my partner and I saw something terrible yesterday morning, but we're not running scared from it."

Elias shifted in his seat. Steph could sense his disapproval without looking for confirmation. But she was the one in charge, and she didn't have his patience. Killing Shane with kindness wasn't the way to get him to speak. So, she pressed him more. "Because you're looking like a yellow belly to me at this moment. And I don't mean a native of Lincolnshire."

Shane's fingers were interlaced, the knuckles showing white. He prised them loose and clamped them over his juddering leg. "You think I'm afraid to tackle things head on? You know nothing about me. I've told you I can't help you, so piss off and leave me and my 'homeless buddies' alone." He stood up, nodded at Elias. "Thanks for the breakfast, mate."

Steph watched him walk out of the door and turn left in the direction of the town centre. Elias slipped the bill from under the bottle of tomato ketchup and went off to pay. Steph drummed her fingers on the table. She heard the waitress asking Elias if his friend had enjoyed his meal and Elias reassuring her that he must have done, for he'd wiped his plate clean. "Have a good day," she said to him when he dropped some coins in the tips jar on the counter.

They stood in silence outside the café. Finally, Steph said, "Oh, don't be so bloody sanctimonious, Sergeant. Treating him with kid gloves wasn't getting you anywhere."

Elias didn't object that his sensitive approach might have yielded results, had she not butted in, which made Steph seethe all the more, for it made her doubt herself and her decisions.

Had that been Elias's intention — all part of his plan to undermine her belief in her ability to do her job, so that he could get his promotion? Was he biding his time, gathering more evidence against her before he made his move? She looked at him and saw only concern in his gaze.

Steph felt conflicted. It bothered her that she could not make up her mind whether Elias was friend or foe.

CHAPTER SEVEN

Jane
21 May 2019

Jane wondered how long it would take for Warwick to come into Veganbites to question her. Her heart took a tumble when she saw the DI appear in the doorway. *Here we go.* If, as it seemed, fate was intent on throwing them together again, she'd just have to grin and bear it.

She pretended not to have seen Warwick enter, shuffled to the very edge of her seat, as if by doing so she could evade being noticed. Warwick marched straight towards her.

"Special Constable Bell. I believe you were a witness to the incident out there?"

Good morning to you too. Jane looked up to see Warwick's stick-straight figure looming over her. *Why did she have to be so tall?* "Yes, that's correct." She hadn't intended to sound stiff and unwelcoming, and was slightly embarrassed that she did. "Er, would you like to join me?"

Warwick sat down opposite her. She seemed bent on ignoring the niceties, for she got down to business immediately. "Tell me exactly what happened. Take your time and give me as much detail as possible. I've already seen what you told PC Sterne, and it's about as much use as the twaddle the other onlookers came up with. I would have expected your observational skills to be more acute, given that you're a serving police officer."

Before Jane could begin, they were interrupted by Frieda's cheery voice.

"DI Warwick! It's lovely to see you. It's a while since you've been in. You must be gasping for a cup of the best coffee in town."

Warwick gave Frieda a brief smile and ordered a black coffee. Frieda reckoned that Warwick had seemed to enjoy talking to her when she'd last been in the café. Jane found that hard to believe, yet Warwick's default stern expression did seem to soften when she greeted Frieda.

Frieda had once described Warwick as seeming 'vulnerable' and 'lonely', and although Jane agreed with her and Elias about the vulnerability — she'd witnessed it herself in the incident last year — she couldn't help thinking that if Warwick had a less unforgiving personality, it would help with the loneliness.

Frieda brought Warwick's coffee over, then made herself scarce, perhaps afraid of falling out of favour if she lingered.

"You were saying?" Steph said.

"I was about to say that I was waiting at the crossing along with a few other people when it happened. I was aware of the girl before the man grabbed her. Do you know anything about her yet? How—?"

Warwick cut her off. "Nothing at all. So far she's an unidentified female."

"Right. Okay."

"Get on with it, Bell."

"As I said, I was aware of her. She was standing at the edge of the kerb. She caught my attention because she looked so waiflike, you know, pinched and thin. And, of course, I wondered why she wasn't in school."

Jane paused, realising that Warwick's interruption had distracted her from asking the question that had been

45

uppermost in her mind. She tried to ask it now. "Have you heard anything? Is she . . ? Did she . . ?"

"The girl's heart stopped beating in the ambulance. They weren't able to revive her. I'm sorry. I'd forgotten you couldn't have known that." To Jane, the apology sounded rushed, as though Warwick had no time for it.

"I knew it was bad, but I hoped . . ." Jane's throat tightened. She looked at Warwick, not expecting sympathy, but still saddened to see the DI expressing only impatience to continue. She really was hard. As hard as diamonds, with none of their allure.

Jane took a couple of sips of tea to give her a moment to rally, then carried on. "I saw the motorcycle approaching the lights and thought it was going a bit too fast. I think I might even have wondered if it was going to jump the lights, but at the last minute, it overtook the cars already stopped at the crossing and swerved right up onto the dropped kerb.

"There were two men on the bike, the driver and another man sitting behind him. Both were wearing black leathers and helmets. The man on the back jumped off and pulled the girl towards him, almost as if . . . embracing her. Then he just pushed her away from him and got back on the bike. I don't think anyone realised that he'd hurt her at first. She didn't scream. That's odd, isn't it? She didn't utter a sound. Maybe it was shock, and the speed of it all."

"Go on," Warwick said, her tone sounding less harsh than before.

Jane felt a choking sensation in her throat again and pretended to cough. "The girl made a grab for the traffic-light pole, but she missed and staggered onto the road. Then she just folded up and dropped to the ground, right in front of the first car in the queue. My first thought was that she'd fainted. There was so much noise and commotion — the motorcycle engine revving, cars tooting their horns, and then people beginning to react — shouting and panicking when they saw the blood."

Jane took a breath. She had been replaying the scene in her head and was feeling a bit overwhelmed by the full horror of what had happened.

"I believe you took charge of the situation," Warwick said. "Asked people to stay back, preserved the integrity of the scene."

Jane regained her composure. This was as close as Warwick was likely to come to praising her actions. "Yes. My training kicked in. I asked for someone to call an ambulance, while I tried to staunch the blood from her wound. She was struggling to say something to me. It seemed really important to her. It was a name. Nate."

Warwick's keen eyes fixed on her face with undisguised interest. "You're certain that's what she said? Nate?"

Jane frowned. "Yes. Does the name mean something to you?

"No," Warwick said, a little too quickly. "Not at all." But Jane's suspicions were aroused.

"You did get the number of the bike?" Warwick said.

"No. Sorry. As soon as the victim collapsed, I turned my attention to her."

Steph harrumphed. "Just as well someone else had the presence of mind to take a picture. We've already checked it on PNC and ANPR, and it's on false plates, of course. PC Sterne told me you thought the bikers might have been targeting the girl. What made you think that?"

Jane nodded. "The more I think about it, the more certain I am that it must have been deliberate, not just some random attack. The way the bike almost veered right into her. There were plenty of other people standing there, so why pick on a schoolgirl? Wouldn't she be the one least likely to have anything of value?"

"Her bag was snatched. That suggests a robbery," Steph reminded her.

"I know, but again, why pick on her? I was practically standing next to her with my handbag over my shoulder. It makes you wonder if they knew what was in her bag, don't you think? If you ask me, this is probably drug-related. County lines, even."

Warwick gave her a sharp look. Her green eyes sparked with sudden emotion. A flush spread upwards from her neck and spread over her face. Oddly, she said nothing, but Jane would have sworn Warwick had just bitten her tongue until it bled. The DI's reaction only seemed to confirm her suspicion that she knew more than she was letting on about the girl and this Nate. Well, let her be secretive. The girl's story was likely to be all over the media in the coming days.

"I shouldn't need to remind you, Special Constable Bell," Warwick said, "but given your interference in my previous investigation, I'm warning you now not to involve yourself in this one."

Is that what you call it? Interfering? As in saving your goddamn life? Jane bit back her words. Anything she said would only make matters worse. Frieda had told her that Warwick had come into the café last year, full of praise for Jane's courage and her actions in saving her life. If it had been evidence of a potential thaw in their relationship, none of that was on show now.

No doubt Warwick was still furious at her for ratting her out to Elias.

"I hardly need to remind you, either, to contact me if you remember anything else. Or, contact DS Harper. The two of you seem to enjoy putting your heads together. I'm sure that whatever you tell him will be relayed back to me loud and clear."

It was Jane's turn to redden, knowing Warwick had just made an unsubtle reference to her discussion with Elias about whether she was psychologically fit to do her job.

She gave Warwick a polite smile. "Yes. I'm sure DS Harper can be relied upon to do just that."

"I'll arrange for one of our interviewing officers to record a full statement from you. They'll be in touch." With that, Warwick pushed her chair back and with a brisk nod at Frieda, who was hovering by the till, rose to pay for her coffee.

To spare them both the embarrassment of saying good-bye, Jane immediately stood up and made a beeline for the toilets. She made sure she stayed there long enough to give Warwick time to pay and make her exit from the café.

Frieda accosted her the moment she returned. "Did you learn anything about that poor girl?"

"She didn't make it," Jane said in a quiet voice. "Her heart stopped in the ambulance on the way to the hospital. That's all DI Warwick told me. I gave her my account of what happened, and she warned me off getting involved. She's not about to share anything she knows with me either, although she did slip up and react when I told her the only word the poor girl managed to speak was a name, 'Nate'. I'm convinced it meant something to Warwick."

Frieda sighed resignedly upon hearing Jane's next words. "And despite what she says, I'm going to find out what."

CHAPTER EIGHT

Nate
October–November 2018

Nate was surprised to find that his first term at secondary
school wasn't too bad. For the first couple of days, only the
first and the sixth formers were in, so there was time for him
to find his way around without all the noise and bustle of a
normal school day.

His form teacher was called Mrs Brewer. She looked
quite old, but she seemed nice, and she didn't stand for any
nonsense. Nate thought she was the sort of teacher you could
respect because, as long as you behaved, she would treat you
with respect too.

The other kids in the class all seemed to have a couple of
friends from their last school to hang out with. This was what
Nate had been dreading — being the outsider right from the
start. He kept reminding himself that nobody here knew that
his mum was an alcoholic.

A recovering alcoholic, as she called herself now. She
stuck a little yellow smiley sticker on the calendar every day
she went without a drink. She was even talking about getting

a job. Nate had heard it all before, so he didn't get his hopes up. Well, maybe just a bit . . .

His experiences at primary school had made him shy, and wary of other kids. He didn't expect them to treat him well. Charlie and Alfie would probably not have become his best friends if it hadn't been for their mums. Nate was old enough now to realise that they had probably felt sorry for him when they saw him standing all alone in the playground or walking to and from school on his own. Luckily for him, they hadn't been like the other mums and looked down on him. At secondary school, the mums parked their cars further away from the school gates. There'd be no one to notice that he was on his own.

He made friends with another boy in his form but didn't see much of him after registration in the morning. They were in different classes for most subjects. Still, they ate lunch together and sometimes hung out at break times. All in all, things seemed to be going okay. Until half-term, that was. Then, suddenly, everything started to unravel.

The first hint he had that things were about to go down the pan was when he got up one morning during half-term and discovered that his mum wasn't at home. It wasn't unusual for her to sleep late, even now she'd stopped drinking. He didn't worry at first. He made some toast and ate it in the sitting room while he watched telly. Even when she wasn't home for lunch, he assumed that she'd just forgotten to tell him she was doing something that day. But when teatime came around and she still hadn't appeared, he started to feel a bit worried.

He'd poked his head around her bedroom door in the morning, but at six in the evening, he went inside. Now that he was in the room, nothing looked right. There were no bedclothes on the bed. They'd stripped their beds the previous day and put them in the wash. Nate had put a clean sheet and duvet cover on his own bed straight away.

There seemed only one conclusion to be drawn from the unmade bed, and Nate didn't like it. His mum had never gone to bed. He'd last seen her at ten the previous evening when he'd said goodnight and gone upstairs to read in bed. His new friend, Ben, had loaned him two Spider-Man comic books and he was eager to start reading one.

When she was drinking, Angie sometimes used to crash out early in the evening. Often, she never even made it to bed. She'd just sleep on the sofa. Since they'd moved to the new house, she sometimes stayed up really late. Other nights she'd go to bed as early as 7 p.m. Nate had turned his light out at eleven the previous night. He couldn't remember hearing her come to bed.

Nate wasn't sure why he decided to check her wardrobe. It certainly wasn't because he expected to find her hiding inside. Still, he opened the door cautiously, thinking of a book his teacher had read to the class when he was in year five, about some children who walked through a wardrobe right into a magical land full of wondrous creatures. He'd liked that story a lot.

But there were no magical lands at the back of Angie's wardrobe, only bags of empty cans. Nate stared at them, disappointment welling up in him like a fast-acting poison. Angie was drinking again, and by the looks of it, she'd been at it for some time.

There were other signs — the neck of a bottle sticking out from under the bed, one of a dozen empties strewn across the dusty carpet, out of sight. Nate hurled the bottle across the room. It smashed against the wall under the window and landed on the floor in three large pieces and several smaller ones.

"It was supposed to be a fresh start." His cry of anger went unheard.

He slammed her bedroom door shut and went back downstairs. No sense in waiting for her to come home for tea. He'd half-hoped she'd bring back a takeaway since time was getting on. Now he knew that all she'd bring back would be a six-pack of cider and some fags.

There wasn't much in the cupboards. Angie never stocked up. There was a supermarket ten minutes' walk away and she shopped there for essentials every couple of days. In the time they'd been in their new place, Angie had started cooking a bit more, mostly ready meals that she heated in the microwave, but still an improvement on what she'd provided before.

The signs had been there if he'd been observant enough. Angie had been sending him out to buy bread and milk, or other essentials that they'd run out of, more and more often in the past couple of weeks. She'd been trying to hide her drinking by going to bed early or staying up late.

There was no point in wondering what time she'd be home. She must have found some drinking buddies and gone off with them. She'd be crashed out on someone's floor right now, oblivious to everything, including the fact that she had a son for whom she was supposed to be responsible.

Nate looked at the smileys that Angie had stuck on the calendar every day since they'd moved here. Was each and every one of them a lie, or just the most recent ones? He tore the calendar off the wall, lit one of the gas rings on the cooker and held it over the heat until it caught alight. He imagined the deceitful yellow smileys screaming in agony as they burned and turned to ash. Their charred remains ended up in the washing-up bowl, drowned in cold water.

Then Nate emptied all the twenty-pence pieces out of the jar in which Angie had been saving them. There was more than enough for fish and chips from the local chippie.

He felt a chill in the air when he went outside. He hadn't brought a jacket and began walking faster to warm up. Since the nights had begun to draw in, he'd avoided going out in the evenings. He didn't know any of the kids round here, even though a lot of them went to his school. Once or twice, on his way home, he'd been jostled a bit by some of the older boys who lived on one of the blocks near his. Nothing nasty — mostly name-calling but he'd also been

53

pushed and shoved a bit. He'd learned to vary his route home to avoid them.

He'd sometimes see them hanging out in the park opposite the chippie when he passed it on his way to the shops for his mum.

This evening, he spotted them standing in a cluster near the swings, watching his approach. One of them called out to him. "Hey, kid! Where's mummy tonight?" The others laughed. As he drew nearer, they began making crying-baby noises. "Wah! Wah! Wah. I want my mummy."

Nate hurried past, avoiding making eye contact. Besides the chippie, there was a post office, an Iceland, a hairdresser, a couple of charity shops and a Chinese takeaway, but only the Chinese and the chippie were open at this time of the evening, and there weren't many people about.

There was a queue outside the chippie. He joined behind a ginger-haired boy who looked around nineteen.

"They bothering you?" the boy asked, nodding at the kids on the swings.

Nate shook his head. "No." He didn't know if the boy was trustworthy. He could be one of their friends.

"Take no notice." He gave Nate a friendly grin. "So, I'm Wes. What's your name?"

"Nate."

"You live round here, Nate?"

"Yeah. Not far."

"You go to the Academy?"

"Yep. Do you?"

Wes winked at him. "Used to. Got expelled. Anyway, I'm twenty now, finished with school." They talked about some of the teachers. When it was Wes's turn to be served, he asked Nate what he wanted.

"Large fish and chips and a coke, please." Wes ordered two and paid for them both. Nate looked up at the board above the counter to check what he owed and began counting out the twenty-pence pieces.

"Put your money away, bro," Wes said. "This is on me."

Nate hesitated. "Are you sure?" Wes nudged him and showed him a thick, roll of blue notes — all twenties — wrapped in an elastic band.

"I'm sure. Come on."

They took their food outside. The boys in the park had disappeared. Wes pointed to the swings they'd vacated. "Let's eat over there."

"Sure." Nate followed him across the road. After ten minutes, they were joined by another boy of about Nate's age. His name was Drew, short for Andrew.

Wes offered them both a cigarette. Nate hesitated, but he knew he'd look like a little kid if he refused. He took a puff and choked, giving away that he wasn't used to smoking. Wes showed him how to inhale properly, and when he mastered the technique, he felt lightheaded, but not like when you were sick with some virus. This was a good feeling, but it didn't last long.

"Let's try you with one of these," Wes said. He opened a tobacco tin and showed Nate the contents — five or six hand-rolled cigarettes. He lit one, inhaled, then passed it to Nate. Again, Nate hesitated. He knew these weren't ordinary ciggies, but suddenly he didn't care. If his mum was drinking, why shouldn't he do drugs? There was also the temptation. If smoking a bog-standard ciggy made him feel good, then these were going to blow his mind.

"Thanks." At first, there was just the light-headedness, like with the cigarette, but after a few minutes he felt a strange sense of being detached from his body, and it was as though all his worries about his mum and everything else just floated away on a big soft cloud. A few more puffs and he started giggling.

The others grinned at him as though he had passed some kind of initiation test and was now one of them. Nate felt a surge of affection for them, even though he'd only just met them. Wes asked him a lot of questions, and this time Nate felt no hesitation in telling him where he lived and about his mum being an alcoholic. He told them about moving from

Gainsborough and how she had promised things were going to be different this time.

Wes stubbed out the spliff on the seat of the swing, leaving a small burn mark on the rubber — the swing was pock-marked with them. "That sucks, but don't think you're the only one who's got problems. My dad disappeared before I was even born, and my mum abandoned me outside a garage when I was a year old. She fucked off too. I don't know why she thought someone who fixed people's cars for a living would know what to do with a baby. I grew up in foster homes or in care." He rolled up his hoodie to reveal his torso, spotted with red scars. "Some of my foster parents mistook me for an ash tray."

Nate looked at Drew, wondering what horror story he had to tell, but Drew only said, "My mum and dad are dead. I live with my big sister."

Nate had seen marks like the ones on Wes's body before. A kid in his class at primary school had had them all over his arms and legs, and probably in places that couldn't be seen. It made him feel a bit guilty that his only problem was an alcoholic mum.

It was 11 p.m., later than Nate had ever been out on his own. "I best be getting back."

"Wanna hang out with us again tomorrow?" Wes asked. "Sure."

"See you here around two then?" Nate nodded.

He didn't care that the house was empty when he got back. It was better that than be confronted with the sight of his mum sprawled, comatose, across the sofa. He had two new friends. Wes was a lot older than him, but he hadn't treated him like a kid, and he was pretty cool. It felt good to have something to look forward to. He couldn't wait to see them in the park tomorrow.

Feeling suddenly ravenous despite the fish and chips he'd eaten earlier, Nate took a box of cereal up to bed with him to snack on while he read his Spider-Man comic book. He felt perfectly content. Who needed Angie?

In the morning, he didn't bother looking for his mum in her bedroom when he got up. If she'd been on a binge all day yesterday, she'd never have made it up the stairs. He knew she'd come home. He'd heard the front door slam at three in the morning, and Angie had called upstairs to him. He'd ignored her. If she'd been that bothered about him, she wouldn't have started drinking again. She hadn't bothered coming upstairs to check that he was okay, so he'd turned over and gone back to sleep.

She was curled up on the sofa downstairs, turned away from him. Her skirt had ridden up, revealing lumpy white thighs and black knickers. One arm dangled over the side of the sofa, the hand clutching the neck of an empty bottle. For the first time, Nate wasn't moved to pity. He felt only disgust.

He had what was left of the chocolate crisp cereal without milk, because Angie must have been thirsty when she got home and drunk what was left in the carton. She must have been intending to make a cup of coffee, and opted for the milk instead, for the kettle was full of lukewarm water. Nate made himself some tea and sat at the drop-leaf table to read his Spider-Man book.

At one, he made himself a crisp sandwich and another cup of tea. He looked in on Angie on his way to the door. She'd changed position and was now lying on her back. Her top had slipped from her shoulder, exposing a patch of marbled blue and white skin. He considered shaking her arm to rouse her but decided not to bother. Instead, he turned her over on to her side, like one of her ex-boyfriends had shown him to do, in case she choked on her own vomit.

Then he left.

CHAPTER NINE

Steph
Saturday, 27 April 2019

Steph woke feeling rested and reinvigorated after a sleep of nearly eight hours. After months of therapy, she was now going for longer stretches of time free of the nightmares that had plagued her on and off for years. She must remember to postpone the appointment she had with Dr Bryce later.

Postpone, or cancel? If she didn't have to answer to Elias, the answer to that question would be cancel, despite having been cautioned against giving up as soon as she started making progress. But to be honest, she knew that she wasn't ready to stop seeing Dr Bryce altogether.

It bothered her a lot that Elias had this hold over her. As his senior, she should be the one calling the shots. It was infuriating to be beholden to him so that he would keep his mouth shut.

When she arrived at work, she chaired a team briefing to ensure that everyone was up to speed on the various elements of the investigation and to share any new information with their colleagues.

Elias was first to speak. "Burke was renting his place from a private landlord, Fred Cassidy. I contacted Cassidy and he told me that Burke had been his tenant for over a year. He was a good tenant, always paid his rent on time." He paused. "Monthly payments made in cash." Heads nodded, knowingly, around the room. "Apparently, Burke told people he made a living buying and selling stuff online."

"Was any cash recovered from his flat?" Steph asked.

PC Joey Fairbairn answered. "No, ma'am. The assumption is that his killers took whatever they found. His flat wasn't messed up, so it's likely they got him to tell them where it was hidden. Maybe they tortured it out of him. Since his phone still hasn't turned up, it's likely they tortured that out of him too."

"Hmm. What do we know about Burke's friends, girlfriends, other known associates?" Steph listened to the answers and snapped out more questions until she was satisfied that all the bases were being covered.

"Okay. Shane Watt. What do we know about him?

"He's an interesting character," Elias said. "Born in 1985, joined the RAMC aged eighteen, left aged twenty-eight. He worked at QMC in Nottingham for four years, then had eight months off after seriously injuring his back in a car accident. Sadly, he became addicted to painkillers. Upon his return to work, he was caught stealing dihydrocodeine, and the Nursing and Midwifery Council gave him a two-year suspension for gross misconduct. I haven't been able to find any trace of him after he left QMC. He seems to have slipped off the radar. I was planning to task someone with contacting some of his former army colleagues to see if any of them kept in touch."

Steph agreed. "Do that." She turned to Joey Fairbairn. "PC Fairbairn, can you ring round the homeless charities and get in touch with social services to see if he's known to any of them?"

"Yes, ma'am," said Joey.

Steph turned to PC Alice North. "Any luck with tracing the boy Brian Sykes mentioned — Nate?"

"I'm working my way through the local schools, ma'am, and I'm waiting for social services to call me back with some info. Two possible matches in Nate's age group so far, but neither of them have a dia . . . er . . . a gap in their front teeth. There are two possibilities for Wes, one of whom seemed quite hopeful, but he's in his twenties. It's possible Brian Sykes guessed his age wrong, though."

"Keep trying with Nate and send me what you've got on Wes," Steph said. After giving out a few more brief instructions and thanking everyone for their work, she brought the meeting to a close.

About half an hour later, PC North came to her with a result. "Ma'am, I've just spoken to one of the admin staff at the George Boole Academy. They had an eleven-year-old boy by the name of Nathan Price enrolled as a year-seven student last September. He has a gap between his two front teeth. He attended well to begin with, then started being absent for odd days here and there after the October half-term break. His attendance record's been pretty poor since then. In fact, he hasn't been to school at all in the past weeks. They've been in touch with his mum, and she told them he'd had a stomach upset and that he'd be back next week."

"Do you have an address for Nate and his family?"

"Yes, ma'am." Steph gave her a brisk nod.

Elias called after her, "Good work, Alice."

What for? All she did was *make a phone call.* Steph supposed she should have been the one to say it, but she couldn't see why it was necessary to praise someone just for doing their job.

"Meet me outside in five," she said to Elias. "With a bit of luck, we'll find our little truant at home streaming violent movies."

It was a short drive to the estate where Nate lived. Elias pointed at a block of maisonettes. "It's the one on the end."

Elias knocked three times before a voice called through the letterbox. "Who's there?"

"Police. We need to speak with Nate. Is he home?" Elias's mouth was level with the letterbox.

"Has something happened to him?"

Elias pushed his ID through the letterbox. It was immediately snatched out of his hand. "There's no cause for alarm. Maybe you could let us in, and we can explain."

When the door was finally opened, a woman stood in the hall, arm outstretched, Elias's ID flat on the palm of her slightly shaky hand. He took it from her.

"Thanks. Is it okay if we come in?"

"Nate's not here. He's at school."

"Actually, he's not. He hasn't been for a while," Elias said.

The woman just shrugged, showing no sign of concern. They followed her into a sitting room that was light because it faced south and the sun was shining through a door leading to a small balcony, but despite this, it seemed a sorry sort of space, filled with worn furniture and too many signs that the person who lived there had given up. There was evidence to suggest that Mrs Price was an alcoholic. It was ten thirty in the morning and she had a half-empty bottle of vodka on the floor beside the sofa, a half-empty pint glass by its side, which she swept up and emptied in one long gulp.

"You going to tell me where he is then?" Mrs Price asked.

Elias looked surprised. "We were hoping you might know."

Steph fixed the woman with a steely gaze. "Your son has been truanting for weeks, Mrs Price. The school contacted you a few days ago to say that they hadn't seen him in a while, and you informed them he had an upset stomach."

"Not me. I don't remember telling them that." She filled her glass up, belched. "As you can see, I've got a bit of a drink problem. I told Nate it was going to be different when we moved here. A fresh start, I said to him. No more booze. I meant it at the time."

She was wearing a thin cotton dressing gown over a long T-shirt with a picture of Winnie-the-Pooh on the front.

Pooh's paw was in a jar of honey. The word honey was spelled 'hunny'. It made her seem childlike. She was quite attractive, Steph noted, but she was drinking her way to an early death.

"Aren't you concerned about your son, Mrs Price? Do you have any idea where Nate might be when he's not at school? Could he be at a friend's house, for example?"

"I don't know. He started going out a lot when he found out I was drinking again. He was angry. Can't really blame him, can you? I got his hopes up, then disappointed him — again." She sounded resigned, rather than regretful, as if she'd tried her best but it wasn't good enough, and now she'd given into defeat.

"Do you know where he goes when he's out?"

"No idea. He just says he's hanging out with friends."

"Does he ever bring his friends back here?"

"No."

"Mrs Price, when did you last see Nate?"

"I'm not sure. He told me he was going to stay over at a friend's house one time, but I can't remember when that was." She frowned. The pint glass wobbled in her hand.

"Do you know what day it is today, Mrs Price?" Elias asked. His question was met with a vacant look. She shook her head. "I've lost track. Truth is, I drift in and out most days."

"That's all right," Elias said gently. "Would it be all right if we take a look at Nate's bedroom?"

"It's upstairs." Her gaze drifted to an open door through which the stairs were visible.

"He could have been gone for days, weeks even, for all she's aware," Steph said, when they reached the upstairs landing. Elias nodded.

A sheet of A4-sized paper tacked to one of the doors bore Nate's name in red capital letters, surrounded by sketches of superheroes that he must have drawn and coloured himself. His room was tidy, more because he didn't have much than because anyone was cleaning it regularly. The walls were painted magnolia, as in every other room they'd seen. No doubt it had been newly painted by the housing association before Nate and his mother moved in. The fresh walls and white skirting boards showed up the square, unfitted carpet remnant, which definitely wasn't new. Stained and threadbare, it only partially covered the paint-splodged floorboards.

Elias pointed at a clothes rail next to the bed, a neat row of trainers underneath, all in boxes. "Where did he get the money to buy gear like that?"

Steph knew it wasn't a question. There was really only one answer, and it wasn't reassuring. "We need to find this kid."

Elias searched through pockets, while Steph tipped the contents of Nate's schoolbag, a smart backpack bearing a fashionable sports logo, across the bed. There were no surprises, just the sort of items that a year-seven boy would need for school — a pencil case, a cheap calculator, some books and notebooks, and, oddly, another calculator with a cracked screen.

Elias patted down a black puffer jacket. "Something in here." He pulled a small ziplock freezer bag from one of the pockets and whistled. "Fifty quid, looks like,"

"That's a lot of cash for an eleven-year-old kid."

Elias produced an evidence bag from his inside pocket and slipped the ziplock inside, commenting, "Expensive gear, wad of cash. Doesn't take a genius, does it?"

The clear bags reminded Steph, suddenly, of the bag that had been used to suffocate Cole Burke, which in turn triggered a worse memory of a pillow being lowered over her face. She bent over the bed to repack the schoolbag, hoping Elias wouldn't notice she was compromised. At least the pillow hadn't borne an imprint of Cal's mocking face. Things were definitely looking up.

Back downstairs, they found Nate's mother splayed across the sofa, face turned away from them. Her empty glass lay broken into large pieces on the floor.

"Let's leave her to sleep it off," Steph said, but Elias's attention was fixed on the broken pieces of glass on the carpet. Steph followed his gaze, and immediately realised what he'd noticed. "Oh shit!" There wasn't enough glass.

Elias reached her first. He tugged gently on the arm that encircled her waist, the hand tucked between her body and the sofa's yielding upholstery. He pulled harder and a large shard of glass slipped out from the bloody sleeve of her dressing gown. He checked her wrists, sighed in relief. "She's fine. Either she passed out before she could inflict any serious damage, or her heart wasn't really in it. This is a cry for help."

Steph had already called for an ambulance and a police response car, so that a uniformed PC could wait with Angie until help arrived. The ambulance arrived first and Steph watched as the paramedics did their job. Angie was being wheeled out of the house by the time the rapid responsive vehicle turned up. Steph gave the driver a sour look as he stepped out of the car.

The incident had shaken her more than she showed. She'd drunk heavily for a while after Cal. Strength of character had saved her from spiralling into the pit of alcoholism — or so she'd believed back then. Really, she'd only replaced one coping mechanism with another, equally destructive. Disgust for the woman lying on the sofa thawed into a feeling like pity, taking her by surprise. She caught Elias looking at her and before he could say a word, pre-empted him. "Don't ask. I'm fine."

CHAPTER TEN

Jane
23 May 2019

Jane recognised instantly the girl pictured on the front page of the *Lincoln Post*. Her eyes sought out the headline: 'Twelve-year-old victim of fatal stabbing is missing Nottingham schoolgirl Lana Kerr.'

The image of the dead girl's lively, grinning face startled her so much that she dropped the birthday card for her daughter that she'd come in to purchase, along with a bar of chocolate she'd just plucked from the offer shelf near the till. The man behind her in the queue picked them up and handed them to her. Jane thanked him and added the newspaper to her purchases.

She'd arranged to meet her friend and near-neighbour, Allie Swift, at the café on High Bridge for coffee and she was a bit early. She hoped to have time to read the article before Allie arrived.

When she reached the top floor of the café, she saw that Allie was already seated at their favourite window seat, looking out at the view of High Bridge and the River Witham. As she slid into the bench opposite her friend, Jane caught sight of a rolled-up copy of the *Post* sticking out of Allie's handbag. She pointed to it. "Snap. I just got one in WH Smith's."

"That's her on the front page, isn't it? That girl you witnessed being stabbed on Burton Road."

"Yes. I haven't had time to read more than the first paragraph. Have you read the whole article?"

"Yes. You saw her name was Lana Kerr, and she was only twelve? From Nottingham? Okay. Well, she was reported missing by her foster parents when she failed to return home from the pupil referral unit she was attending. Police considered her a possible runaway — she'd run away from two other foster homes in the last three years." Allie shook her head. "Poor kid."

Jane agreed. "Yes. Children get sent to PRUs for a lot of different reasons, but it's usually considered a last resort. It's possible she had emotional or behavioural difficulties. These are often very vulnerable kids. Often children don't attend these schools full-time, meaning they are available at times other kids wouldn't be. All the better for people who want to find and exploit them."

Jane looked out of the window and for a few moments she followed the progress of a group of swans gliding towards the sixteen-metre-high millennium sculpture spanning the river.

The two aluminium and steel figures reaching out to each other from opposite sides of the Witham, their form mimicking that of turbine blades, were intended to evoke Lincoln's rich engineering heritage.

Jane had read that the sculpture represented empowerment. She liked the idea of 'reaching out', but today, the figure stretching upwards from City Square looked like it was trying to catch the other figure soaring through the air before it plummeted into the river. It made her think of Lana Kerr, all the people and services that had failed to catch her as she fell.

Allie eyed her with suspicion. "What are you thinking?"

"Oh, nothing much, just watching the swans."

"You don't expect me to believe that, do you? You feel responsible for this girl, don't you?"

There was no point in denying it. "How couldn't I? She all but died in my arms, Al. I was the last person to hear her speak, and it felt like she was trying to give me a message. This Nate, whoever he is, was important to her. Why else would she struggle to say his name as she lay dying?"

"Have you considered that she might have been naming her killer?"

Jane looked at Allie, surprised. "I admit that never occurred to me, but I think you're wrong. It didn't feel like that. I think she cared deeply about this Nate."

Allie was silent. Jane guessed she was considering her response.

"I know what you're thinking. This is just oh-so-sensitive Jane reading too much into things. I was projecting, and so on."

"You got me," Allie said. "That's more or less what I was thinking, except for adding that I believe oh-so-compassionate Jane has made a deep connection with this girl, and that she won't be able to stop herself from becoming involved."

Jane didn't deny it. She looked back at the river. In her time, she'd seen it in all its hues, the shades of light and dark on its surface altering with the shadows cast by buildings along its banks, or by sunlight or cloud, or by a narrowboat churning up the silt in its depths. Sometimes her own mood seemed to be reflected in the river.

Swans appeared as flecks of white amid the leaves and branches of a mature willow bent low over the water outside the shopping centre opposite City Square. She'd sat in this café at this very table on many previous occasions, appreciating the view. Years ago, she'd come with Sam and the children, and then just the children, when Sam was no longer around. She felt almost as dispirited at this moment as she'd felt coming here alone, in her first weeks of widowhood.

Allie squeezed her hand. "Lana's really got under your skin, hasn't she, Janie?"

Jane gave her a weak smile. "She was so young, and I felt so helpless watching her die like that. I saw that bike begin to overtake the cars stopped at the crossing. I should have realised—"

"Realised what? That the man on the passenger seat was going to jump off the bike and stab her? How could you possibly have foreseen such a thing?"

They had ordered a cream tea for two. It arrived, served by Miriam the waitress, dressed like an extra from an Edwardian costume drama. She chattered away as she laid everything out. She'd served them many times before and always knew without being asked that Jane liked a slice of lemon with her tea instead of milk, and that they both favoured raspberry jam over strawberry.

The *Post* was still sticking out of Allie's bag. Inevitably, Miriam commented on the lead story. "Shocking thing, wasn't it? I don't know what Lincolnshire's coming to these days, with all this knife crime. They reckon it's got something to do with drugs, don't they? County lines, that's what they call it, I think. Gangs sending teenagers to smaller towns to sell their drugs."

Again, Jane was slightly surprised by Miriam's knowledge, acquired presumably from the lead story in the *Post*, or from the BBC's regional news programme, *Look North*.

It was just as well Miriam didn't know about Jane's other identity as a special constable, otherwise she'd probably have hovered longer, trying to prise information out of her. Miriam always seemed to know a lot of gossip, gleaned from her customers as willing — or unwitting — sources.

"Enjoy your scones, ladies," Miriam said, moving on to serve another table.

Allie poured the tea. "Do you think she's right? I thought it might have been a robbery, you know, like what happened to your son Patrick in London when his phone was grabbed that time."

"Unfortunately, she's probably right. Perhaps even more so now that we know Lana wasn't from around here. It's possible she was being held here in Lincoln, in a cuckooed house."

Allie looked puzzled, so Jane explained. "It's the name given to a property that's been taken over by drug dealers. It's becoming more and more common for city dealers to use kids as couriers to transport their merchandise from big cities to small towns, and to place these kids — or sometimes now, local kids — in properties that they've taken over, as a source of unpaid labour."

Allie was buttering her scone. "How awful."

"The worst thing about it is that they set out deliberately to recruit vulnerable people. Children, obviously. But also, people with issues of one kind or another — vulnerable adults — alcoholics, for example, and drug addicts, people with mental health issues or physical disabilities, even lonely older people — anyone they can easily intimidate and exploit.

"They'll visit a town and target places where vulnerable adults hang out. They offer them drugs, alcohol, even love in exchange for using their homes to ply their trade."

Allie laid down her knife. "Love?"

"This is the women, usually. Typically, a male gang member will strike up a romantic relationship with a girl or woman, pretend to be interested in her. She invites him to her home, and he stays. Then he and other gang members might exploit her, use her home as a base for dealing, abuse her sexually and offer her to other men."

"That's not love," Allie said, looking appalled.

"Another obvious tactic that they use is grooming, especially with kids. They'll offer them friendship, drugs, alcohol and cigarettes, nice clothes — anything to gain their trust. The kids think all this is for free, but sooner or later they'll be asked to perform favours in return. The idea is to create a debt bondage backed up with threats of, or actual violence, and intimidation."

Allie shook her head. Jane continued. "A child like Lana can be taken to a town they don't know and forced to work in a cuckooed house. Others are sent out on public transport

69

from the bigger cities as couriers to deliver to the county towns, sometimes with the goods hidden inside them. A practice charmingly known as plugging."

Allie pushed her plate away. "You seem to know an awful lot about this, Jane. Have you been involved in cases like this?"

"Not directly, but some of the officers I've worked with have. It's just something you come across sooner or later if you're a police officer, so I expect I'll have to deal with it eventually in some manner. And I've had training, of course, about the practices and methods employed by county lines offenders. We have to be alert to the sort of things to look out for, signs that a house is being cuckooed, for example. Often, we rely on the public to inform us if something suspicious is going on at a property. We get tip-offs from neighbours, and from people like housing officers and landlords who suspect a house on their patch might be cuckooed. Lots of people coming and going is often an indicator."

"And is Miriam right in saying there's been an increase in knife crime in the Lincolnshire area?"

"Sadly, yes. But it's not all attributable to county lines. A lot of knife crime takes place in domestic settings. Still, there's no denying that county lines involves horrific violence — worse than we've seen related to the drugs trade in the past. There's territorial violence, violence associated with the trafficking of vulnerable people, sexual violence, to name a few."

"Do any of the victims ever get out of the dealers' clutches and go to the police, or seek help?" Allie asked.

Jane took a slug of tea to wash down her last mouthful of scone. "Well, you've got right to the crux of things using the word 'victim'. The thing is, because they've been groomed with gifts, or maybe even paid for helping their abusers, the kids often don't see themselves as victims. And they're not alone in that. Many members of the public would argue that they were willing collaborators, or at least complicit. It can be difficult to prove, even to judges, that they've been manipulated, deceived, coerced, and abused. Which means the victims are afraid to go to the police because they fear they'll be prosecuted. Not to mention they're also terrified of retribution from gang members."

"Is that what happened to Lana, do you think? The gang got to her for something she did?"

"DI Warwick got quite wound up when I suggested as much to her."

"You've seen her since it happened?"

"Yes. She was the SIO at the scene, and I was a witness, so she had to talk to me. Sorry, Allie. I thought Frieda or Karun would have told you by now."

"I've not been to Veganbites for a week or so. Trying to lose weight and I can't resist Karun's carrot cake." She stared bleakly at the crumbs on her plate, all that was left of the extra scone she'd ordered and tried to persuade Jane to share.

"You run a fudge shop!" Jane reminded her.

"I know. I'm surrounded by temptation all day, but I hardly eat any of my fudge, as I've told you before."

Jane suspected that Allie's 'hardly any' would equate to 'quite a lot' in her book, but she didn't say so.

"So, what did DI Up-Herself say?" Allie asked.

Jane smiled at their nickname for DI Warwick. "Oh, you know, she was reticent. Jealously guarding what she knew, lest I should come along and crack her case wide open for her."

"Was Elias with her?"

Jane smiled again. She knew Allie had a soft spot for DS Harper. "Yes, but I only saw him from a distance."

The remark led to an abrupt change in the conversation. "I'm glad we've got tickets for the first night of his new play."

Jane nodded. Elias was a member of a local Shakespeare group that was putting on an open-air production of *A Midsummer Night's Dream* in the grounds of Lincoln Castle. The first performance was to be held on the evening of Midsummer's Day, the twenty-fourth of June.

Jane agreed. "It was kind of Elias to reserve front row seats for us all." By 'all' she meant the members of their book group.

"He'll make a wonderful Puck."

"Er, he's not playing Puck, Allie. He's playing Bottom."

"Of course he is! That's who I meant. No idea why I thought he was Puck."

Jane smiled. Allie wasn't a big Shakespeare fan, but she liked to appear knowledgeable about most subjects.

"Anyway, he'll be brilliant whoever he plays," Allie continued. "He's such a wonderful actor. I've no idea why he wanted to give it all up."

Elias had toured with an amateur group for a year before deciding that the life of an actor wasn't for him. He'd carried on with acting in student dramas while at university, and he enjoyed taking part in amateur dramatics. He now regarded acting as the perfect way to counterbalance the stresses of his police work.

Instead of reminding Allie of this, Jane said, "Thea auditioned for the play, you know, but she wasn't offered a part. She was so disappointed, more so because she was looking forward to seeing Elias at rehearsals. She's had a crush on him since she saw him in *The Winter's Tale* last year."

"Bless her. I've seen her at Veganbites. She's a lovely lass and so fond of you."

"Did I tell you her parents are planning on selling their house and moving to their London property?"

"No. How will that affect Thea?"

"Not sure yet. She's told them she wants to stay here and finish her A levels, then go to Lincoln University. I suppose they'd be okay with that. If they decide to sell the house, she could live in student accommodation."

"Are her parents still cruising the Greek Islands on their friends' expensive yacht?" Allie asked.

"Last Thea heard, yes."

"She does well, coping on her own at her age. Is she still staying over at yours?"

Jane nodded. "Once, sometimes twice a week or so. We watch movies and I help her with her homework, if she needs it. I try to be a bit of a surrogate mum to her."

Their conversation turned to family. No matter how often she and Allie saw each other, sooner or later they'd update each other on how their kids were faring. It was just what parents did.

Jane wondered when Allie would get around to asking her how things were going with Ed. She and Ed Shipley had been seeing each other for over a year now. They were taking things slowly. Surprisingly, Allie didn't ask.

"I'd better get back to the shop," Allie said, looking at the time.

"I thought Tess was minding it for you until one?"

"She is, but I'm worried my delivery will arrive early and I don't want her to have to cope with that and mind the shop."

"I'll walk up the hill with you. I've got a telephone call with one of my distance learners in an hour. It was scheduled for next Monday but I'm doing a school visit then, so she kindly agreed to reschedule. One of the PCs who was supposed to be doing the talk tore his Achilles tendon and I was asked to step in at the last minute."

"You must feel quite at home doing these school visits. What's the talk about?"

"Just what we've been discussing, actually," Jane said, a bit guardedly. "Drugs. County lines. We're stepping up our information programme to raise kids' awareness of what to look out for."

"Can't get away from it, can you?"

"Seems that way." Jane wasn't sure why she'd told Allie that she'd been asked to step in to cover the school talk. She'd actually volunteered for the job as soon as she'd heard about the PC being injured. It seemed the least she could do to make up for failing Lana.

CHAPTER ELEVEN

Nate
December 2018

Nate saw Wes and Drew waiting under the streetlight opposite his house and hurried outside. He'd started hanging out with them whenever he could.

"What we doing today then?" he asked.

Drew shrugged. "Just hanging out, right, Wes?"

"You hungry?" Wes asked Nate. Nate was always hungry. The prawn-cocktail-flavour crisp sandwich he'd eaten an hour ago was now only a rumbling echo in his stomach.

They went to the chippie, as usual. Wes insisted on paying for Nate. "Don't worry about it. You're a mate and I always take care of my mates." Nate noticed that Drew didn't even offer to pay for his meal.

"But how can you afford—?"

"I said, don't worry about it." This time there was a bit of an edge to Wes's tone, so Nate just nodded. Wes could be off sometimes, like a totally different person. To tell the truth, he sometimes scared Nate, the way his moods could change, just like that, from friendly to nasty. Nate was learning not to upset him. He still couldn't believe a cool, older person like Wes wanted to hang out with him, so he put up with the moods and the small cruelties that Wes could dole out as readily as his ciggies.

They stuffed their empty takeaway boxes in a bin near the chippie when they'd finished eating. Wes's litter dropped to the ground, and he didn't bother picking it up. He asked if they'd like to go round to his cousin's place. Drew was up for it, so Nate thought *why not?* He wasn't in a rush to get home. Angie hadn't even texted him to find out where he was.

She'd never change. He'd been stupid to believe it might just happen this time around. It was up to him to change, and he'd started already.

Wes drove them into Lincoln city centre and parked the car in a residential street off the bottom end of the High Street, from which it was only a short walk to his cousin's place. Nate didn't know the area. He seldom had reason to come into town, and when he did, it was usually on the bus with his mum.

There was a bit of banter and a lot of fist-bumping between Wes and his cousin before Wes finally introduced Nate. "So, Cole, meet my new buddy. His name's Nate." A few moments passed before Cole said anything. His eyes bored into Nate's, making him feel uncomfortable, like he was being appraised by a teacher trying to work out if he was going to be trouble. In the end he had to look down, at which point Cole's whole demeanour seemed to change from wary to relaxed and welcoming. It made Nate feel that he'd just passed some kind of test.

They played games and smoked cigarettes. Cole even shared his spliff with him. It was stronger than the ones he sometimes shared with Wes and made him feel sick, but he pretended to like it and after a few puffs the nausea wore off and he started to enjoy the way it made him feel.

At one point, Cole showed Nate into a room at the back of the house that was full of boxes of trainers and brand-new sports gear.

"Take what you want," he told Nate.

Nate started to say that he couldn't afford any of this stuff, but Cole laughed and said he'd be insulted if Nate left his place empty-handed. He selected a box and tossed it at Nate. "Here, these should fit." It was a pair of expensive trainers, the kind that Nate could only dream about.

They fit perfectly. Cole ruffled his hair. "You're part of my family now, Nate, and I always look after my own."

He picked out some other gear for Nate and insisted he try things on — hoodies and sweatpants, and T-shirts. When they went back to join the others, Wes pretended he didn't recognise Nate and made a big thing of asking Cole who his new buddy was. "Who's this? What you done with Nate?" Finally, he stood up and punched Nate playfully on the arm. "You look well good, mate."

Nate swelled up with affection for his new friends. He'd never had kit like this before. It meant a lot, gave him a feeling of acceptance and belonging. He knew they weren't really his family, but they were better than Angie. They looked after him.

Later, Cole ordered pizza. He tossed Nate a can of lager, but Nate asked for coke instead, picturing Angie sprawled over the sofa, hair caked in vomit.

Later still, Wes dropped Nate home, telling him he'd collect him again at the weekend. They bumped fists and Wes drove off, leaving him to face Angie, who accosted him the minute he stepped through the door. "Where have you been? I've been worried sick." Her eyes scanned him from head to foot. "Where did you get those clothes?"

Nate looked at her. Her breath was rank. Blobs of dried vomit still clung to the straggly ends of her hair. "Like you could care less. You haven't been worrying about me. All you're bothered about is your next drink."

Angie started to protest. "I'm going to give up again, after—"

Something snapped. Nate yelled at her. "You're disgusting. You stink and you've got sick in your hair." He pushed past her and ran upstairs to his bedroom, banging the door loudly behind him. When the inevitable ranting began, he covered his ears. He knew it wouldn't last long because it would keep her from drinking.

After that night, he started meeting Wes more and more, staying out until late in the evening. He didn't bother eating at home anymore. They went to McDonald's or the chippie, and Wes continued to pay. Often, they'd end up at Cole's place and he'd order them a takeaway — pizza, Indian, Chinese — whatever they wanted.

His mum stopped demanding to know where he'd been after the first few weeks, proving that she really didn't care as long as she was spared the effort of looking after him.

One day when he went round to Cole's house with Wes, something changed. Drew wasn't with them. They did what they usually did — played games, streamed films and smoked. When it was nearly time to leave, Cole signalled to Wes to leave the room because he wanted to have a quick word with Nate.

"I'd like to ask you to do something for me, Nate. A small favour, that okay with you, bro?"

Nate thought that fair enough. He looked down at his brand-new trainers. Cole had been buying him takeaways and giving him ciggies for weeks. A small favour was the least he could do in return. "Sure."

"Good man." Cole disappeared for a couple of minutes, and when he returned, he was holding a small package. "I want you to deliver this for me. I'll give you the address. Don't worry. It's not far from where you live. You can deliver it in the morning. The man you give it to will give you some money, which I want you to bring back here tomorrow."

He gave Nate that same intense look he'd given him the first time they met, like he was wondering whether he could trust him. "You okay to do that for me?"

Nate wasn't stupid. He knew what was in the package. He understood what Cole was asking him to do. He didn't give it a second thought. Cole had been good to him. He was his family now, and family helped each other out. He held out his hand to accept the package.

Within a couple of weeks, Nate had delivered several packages for Cole, to different addresses, mainly in the northern part of the city, close to where he lived.

The first time, he'd been worried about getting stopped and searched by the police. The pressure of the package in his inside pocket made his chest feel tight, his heart beat faster. It was like being scared and excited at the same time, like he'd felt before he had to say his lines in a school play once.

After he made the drop, a roll of cash taking the place of the drugs, he still felt like a target, as though anyone looking at him could tell he was carrying loads more money than a kid his age had any right to have.

Sometimes Cole gave him ten quid as payment for his work. Nate hid it in a box under his bed. No chance of his mum finding it there. On the odd occasion that she did any cleaning at all, she never did the bits you couldn't see.

He hardly spent a penny of it. By Christmas, he had a thick roll of notes, just like the one Wes had shown him on their first meeting at the chippie. He bought his mum a box of chocolates. He'd sort of forgiven her for letting him down again. He'd read somewhere that alcoholism was a disease, so maybe she couldn't help it. She was sick, that's why she wasn't able to take proper care of him. It wasn't because she didn't love him.

It was up to him to take care of himself now.

CHAPTER TWELVE

Steph
30 April 2019

In 2015, Lincoln became the first city in the UK to use the Antisocial Behaviour, Crime and Policing Act, 2014 to pass a Public Spaces Protection Order banning the on-street consumption of 'intoxicating substances', such as alcohol and legal highs, from the city centre.

A few years later, the council set up a special project in the city of Lincoln as part of its strategy to deal with the various problems associated with drug and alcohol misuse — aggressive begging, rough sleeping and antisocial behaviour.

Steph had asked Elias to arrange a meeting with the coordinator of the team tasked with dealing directly with people on the streets. The team coordinator's name was Kaye Flyte. She greeted Steph and Elias with breezy enthusiasm when they met at her office.

As soon as she introduced herself, Steph had Flyte pegged as the sort of *Guardian*-reading do-gooder-type that someone like SC Bell would get along with. She was middle-aged, annoying, and assertive. Not that Bell was particularly assertive. Unassuming, more like. She just had an infuriating way of quietly and assuredly getting under Steph's skin. As Flyte was doing now.

"Of course, our main objective is to reach out to people and offer them interventions to prevent them from continuing in a cycle of substance abuse and antisocial behaviour. We like to take a holistic approach to helping rough sleepers and those living on the margins of society."

Elias was nodding solemnly. "Dealing with the root causes. The symptoms, not the problem."

"Exactly." Flyte beamed at him, satisfied, it seemed, to have got her message across to at least one of them.

Steph stifled a yawn. Flyte hadn't mentioned that the impetus for the project had been a deluge of complaints by local business owners worried that their customers were being put off by the presence of puddles of urine or even human faeces in their shop doorways.

Nor did she dwell on the fact that as well as existing to provide practical support, the intervention team also had powers to issue community protection notices and criminal behaviour orders to individuals who persisted in exhibiting antisocial behaviour.

"My colleagues will be joining us any minute," Flyte said. There was a knock on the door. "That'll be them."

Two men and a woman entered the room and greeted Flyte, who introduced them to Steph and Elias. "This is Colm Doyle, our mental health outreach worker — he trained as a psychiatric nurse. We're very lucky to have him on the team. Raj Gupta is an outreach worker from the charity We Are With You, formerly known as Addaction."

Steph and Elias nodded to indicate that they were familiar with the charity that offered advice and support to those facing issues with alcohol or substance abuse.

"Last but not least, Mallory Crane is our antisocial behaviour outreach worker."

Steph cleared her throat. "Thanks to you all for agreeing to talk with us. As you know, we're investigating the murder of Cole Burke. Burke has been prosecuted for drugs offences in the past and we suspect that he continued to deal right up until the time of his death. May I ask if Burke was known to any of you?"

Looks passed between the four members of the team before Flyte appointed herself as spokesperson. "We were all aware of Burke, not in person but he was known to us, Inspector."

"He was known to the police." Colm's statement sounded like a criticism. Steph tried not to glare at him. He had fair hair tied up in a topknot and wore an assortment of leather wristbands, like some sort of hipster.

"Yes, he was. But he knew how to keep a low profile," she said.

"By using kids to do his dirty work for him," Mallory said, "so he wouldn't have to show his face on the street for fear of being challenged or arrested. I'm sorry about what happened to him, but I'm not sorry that there's one more dealer off the streets." Mallory's colleagues didn't comment.

"We've heard about some kids, teenage boys, who went to Burke's flat a lot. One of them is called Nate Price. He's disappeared from his home. Actually, you might have come across his mother, Angie Price." Steph looked at Colm. "She's an alcoholic. She attempted to take her own life a few days ago and is currently undergoing a psychiatric evaluation." Steph pictured the white-faced Angie being wheeled out to the waiting ambulance on the day that they'd visited her to talk about Nate.

Colm shook his head. "No, sorry. The name isn't familiar. I've never heard of her son, Nate, either."

Steph turned her attention to his three colleagues, hoping for a more positive response, but three heads were shaking in unison. "What about your clients? People on the streets?"

"We can ask around and get back to you," Mallory said. "But our clients aren't always willing to talk."

Steph nodded. "I understand. The other boy — I should say man, really, since he's around twenty years old — all we know about him is that he's called Wes and has red hair. I can't even confirm whether that's his real name." There were blank looks all around.

Raj raised his hand. "You said that Nate had disappeared from home. What do you think has happened to him?"

Steph decided to share their theory with the team. All would be well versed in the practices of county lines offenders and might be able to offer up some information. "We don't know. We're speculating that Nate might be holed up in a cuckooed house somewhere." No one looked surprised. "Have you heard anything on the streets about a change in the supply chain? Or noticed something that might indicate there's somebody new calling the shots?"

"Our clients don't really care where the stuff's coming from," said Flyte, "as long as their supply doesn't dry up. But there have been rumours."

"What kind of rumours?"

Flyte looked at Raj. "Tell them what you heard."

"I had a drink with one of my colleagues a few weeks back. She told me that a couple of dealers in the area had been persuaded to move on. The rumour was that they'd been beaten up pretty badly, and that customers were being given new instructions about how to obtain their gear.

"One of my colleague's clients confided that he'd been contacted out of the blue by an unknown dealer offering him crack. This was a surprise as he hadn't purchased anything for a couple of months after coming to us for help kicking his addiction. This wasn't his usual supplier. It was a stranger who'd somehow got hold of his contact details. When he tried to contact his old dealer — who wasn't your man, incidentally — he got a message telling him the number was no longer available."

"The list of contacts on the dealer's phone would have been acquired as part of the takeover," Steph said to Raj.

She thought of Cole Burke's missing mobile phone, which could possibly have been taken by his killer to obtain his list of customers. Was that really why Burke had been tortured before they killed him? Had he been stupid enough to resist handing over his phone? If so, he'd way underestimated the kind of people he was dealing with.

"They offered him a special introductory price and explained that they often had special offers." Raj shook his head as though in disbelief. "Bogof deals and discounts for bulk purchases, that kind of thing, as though what they were selling was no different from the sort of everyday shopping items you'd buy in a supermarket. Incredible."

Steph nodded. "County lines gangs are organised, and they know what they're doing. They borrow techniques from the world of marketing to sell their stuff. It gives them an edge over their competitors and helps keep their customers loyal. Giving discounts for bulk orders means that users can group together and pool their money to keep the cost to individuals down. Did your client obtain any information from his caller?"

"No. He explained that he'd been in rehab, wasn't interested anymore."

"How did Cole Burke die?" Mallory asked quietly.

"He was suffocated," Elias said, giving Steph one of his concerned looks.

"That's bad enough," Raj commented, "but I've read about some killings by members of these gangs being unsparingly brutal and violent."

"You've obviously never been suffocated." Steph's comment earned her another look from her DS. "Oh, and he had several of his fingers hacked off. *That brutal enough for you?*"

There was a bit of a silence, broken by Colm. "Look, if your plan is to talk to rough sleepers and people with alcohol and substance abuse issues, I feel an obligation to point out that these are very vulnerable individuals. They don't trust the police. They're not likely to open up to you. They don't always trust us either. Our role is to be proactive. We offer help and support, but at the end of the day, everyone knows that this team's remit is also to clear the streets of what certain people regard as undesirables and their perceived anti-social behaviour. Speaking for myself, I'm unwilling to risk betraying the trust I've built up with my clients by playing police informer."

Mallory groaned and rolled her eyes. "You're not about to go off on one of your rants, are you, Colm? Come on. We'd never get our job done if we spent all our time obsessing about what our *real* role in the overarching social structure is. Let the politicians debate the big issues that inform policy — or don't, as the case may be. We're the ones with our feet on the ground providing practical support, picking up the pieces—"

"With puny resources," Colm said.

His remark coincided with a good-humoured dig by Raj. "Mal. Who's the one having the rant now?"

"Sorry, everyone." She gave Colm a pleading look. "Forgive me?"

"Only if you make me some of your excellent millionaire's shortbread."

"It's a deal. I'll bring some in on Friday."

"We often have debates about stuff," Raj explained. "We all like to play devil's advocate sometimes, but basically we all believe the same thing."

Kaye Flyte nodded. "We've been given a budget and we do what we can to help people. That's the bottom line for us, never mind whether we get the money because certain people don't like visual reminders of the fallout from the austerity measures that they support, or because of a genuine impulse to help society's most vulnerable. Mallory's power to enforce the law is always a last resort."

Steph considered that they had wandered off track and decided to rein this rather vocal team in. "Thanks. I'm aware of the remit of your team. We were also hoping that you'd be able to give us some information on a man called Shane Watt. He was hanging around Burke's flat the day after he was killed, looking to score. He bolted when we stopped him, but we caught up with him. Unfortunately, we didn't get much out of him, despite buying him a standout breakfast."

"I met someone called Shane Watt," Colm said. "I looked after him for a bit when he first moved to Lincoln from

Nottingham. He was sleeping rough and was brought to the county hospital one morning after suffering a seizure outside Primark. It turned out to be a reaction to something he'd taken. The A & E consultant asked for a psychiatric evaluation. I was involved in that. Watt was discharged after being offered support for his addiction. I believe he moved to Norfolk to stay with a family member."

"We know that he was in the Army Medical Corps, and that after that he worked at Queen's Medical Centre in Nottingham. The Nursing and Midwifery Council gave him a two-year suspension for gross misconduct after he was caught stealing pain-killing medication — dihydrocodeine. He'd become addicted after being prescribed the medication for an injury."

Colm nodded. "He also received a suspended sentence from the judge who heard his case. Two hundred hours of unpaid work in the community."

"Yes," Steph said. "Well, we've seen him in Lincoln recently, so maybe he changed his mind about going to Norfolk. He told us he was sleeping rough."

"Maybe he's staying with an old army buddy?" Kaye suggested.

"Most likely he's moved on again, to another town," Colm suggested, obviously put out that his theory about Watt being in Norfolk had been dismissed so brusquely.

"I appreciate your time and comments," Steph said.

Flyte looked at her watch. "It's nearly time for today's walkabout. Is there anything else we can help you with?"

"Not right now," Steph said. "Thanks for fitting us in."

Elias was quiet until they left the building. "You know they're probably right about their clients not trusting the police. Kaye Flyte said they don't even trust her and her colleagues a lot of the time."

Steph had a hunch she knew what he was going to suggest.

"What we need is someone they know they can trust because he's one of them."

"Bet you wish you were trained to take part in covert activities, Sergeant. Give you a chance to put your acting skills to good use for a change."

"I can just see myself infiltrating a criminal gang or something. I'm sure I could be pretty convincing. It's the sort of thing a method actor would do to prepare for a role."

"Since when have you been a method actor? I can't believe you needed to immerse yourself much in that drippy character you played in *The Winter's Tale*. All you had to do was prance about swooning over that stupid girl. And your next role won't require much research either. You're playing an ass, aren't you?"

"Hee-haw," Elias said.

"See. You're a natural." Steph thought for a moment. "It's a good idea, though. An undercover operative. I'll find out if covert tactics are an option."

CHAPTER THIRTEEN

Nate
24 February–April 2019

Early in the new year, Nate began staying at Cole's place more and more. He also started skipping school — a day here and there at first, then days at a time. Cole wrote notes for him to explain his non-attendance, but it wasn't long before his teachers started asking questions. "That's two bouts of ton-silitis you've had in three weeks, Nate," Mrs Brewer, his form teacher, pointed out when she saw what was on his latest note. "Has your mum taken you to see a doctor?"

"Yes, miss. I'm taking antibiotics."

Nate always had an answer ready, usually an explanation that Cole or Wes had suggested. One day towards the end of January, he found an official-looking brown envelope amid the assorted menus for pizza and other takeaways, charity bags, and junk mail lying in a pile on the floor under the letter box. Angie barely looked at the post these days.

But this letter looked sort of important. Nate ripped it open and read the contents. It was from his school. They wanted Angie to come in to discuss his frequent absences. He decided to take it to Cole's place. Cole told him not to worry about it, he would deal with it. After that, the letters stopped coming.

In the last week of February, the weather turned exceptionally cold, and he woke up one morning to find that it had snowed lightly in the night. From his open bedroom window, he watched kids on their way to school trying to scrape up enough snow to make snowballs. It looked like fun and he found himself wishing that he could join them, but he had a few drops to make for Cole that morning, and he was already running a bit late, having forgotten to set the alarm on his new phone.

If it snowed all day, there would be enough to make a snowman, perhaps even enough to take out the sledge that he'd found in a skip outside a house in Gainsborough last Christmas. Nate wondered what his old friends Charlie and Alfie were up to these days, and for a moment he felt sad, remembering the good times he'd spent playing with them in the park in the snow.

He also felt a stab of guilt, for he'd promised to keep in touch with them, but since he'd started hanging out with Wes and Cole, he'd spoken with them less and less. They'd be surprised if they knew what he was getting up to these days. What would Alfie's mum think? He thought of the ruler set and dinosaur erasers she'd given him as a going-away present and felt a bit choked.

Pull yourself together. This is your life now. He set off in a gusty wind that drove wet snow against his face. He wasn't cold. Thanks to the favours he did for Cole, he'd been able to afford a brand-new, down-filled, black puffer jacket. It was the first coat he could remember wearing that hadn't come from a charity shop. Life wasn't so bad.

The weeks passed. Angie was seldom sober now. She'd made some new drinking pals, and sometimes she'd disappear without warning for a couple of days. Off drinking at some other drunk's house, or on the streets. Nate didn't want to know. The sympathy he'd felt when he discovered that she had a disease had thinned into something vaguer, a mixture of pity for her and sadness for himself.

One day in April, he did a series of drops, then walked to Cole's place. He'd skipped breakfast and was feeling famished. With luck, Cole would probably order in pizza for lunch.

There was no answer when he pressed on the buzzer to Cole's flat. Nate stepped back on the pavement, straining to look up at his living-room window. The curtains were fully drawn. That wasn't unusual. It was to keep the light off the screen when Cole was lying on his big leather sofa, gaming, as he did most of the time.

Luca emerged from his barber's shop and lit up. Nate remembered what Cole had said to him about being polite to Luca. "Don't do anything to attract attention or make him suspicious. I told him you're my little cousin."

Luca called out to him. "Hey, kid! Off school again? What is it this time?"

Nate pointed to his throat and rasped, "tonsilitis."

Luca nodded. "Painful. Had mine whipped out when I was a toddler. Better that way. Never had any trouble since."

Nate nodded, grimacing as he swallowed for a bit of authenticity, even though he knew Luca was just playing along with him. He pressed on the buzzer of the old man who lived across the landing from Cole and waited. It would take Brian a while to answer, if he'd even heard. He wasn't much of a walker.

"Who's there?" Brian's rasp put Nate's to shame.

"It's Nate, Mr Sykes. Cole's cousin. Can you let me in, please? Cole's not answering."

The buzzer sounded and the door clicked open. Nate waved to Luca and went inside. As he expected, Brian Sykes was standing at the open door of his flat when he reached the top landing.

Cole had told Nate to be polite to Brian too, so he stood and chatted to the old man for a few minutes. He knew he was probably the only person Brian had spoken to all day, so he didn't mind. Nate knew what it was like to feel lonely and anyway, he liked the old man. At last, Brian shuffled back inside his gloomy hall, closing the door behind him.

There was no answer when he knocked on Cole's door. It didn't sound like Cole was gaming. Usually, with his ear to the door, as it was now, Nate would hear some noise from within. He knocked again, louder this time.

The door opened. A stranger stood in the hall regarding Nate with unfriendly eyes. Everything about him, from his shaved head and tattooed scalp to the skull with red-jewelled eyes hanging on a heavy chain around his neck, and the fire-breathing dragon on his black T-shirt screamed at Nate to run away. He stood his ground. "Where's Cole?"

Before he knew what was happening, the man's beefy arm shot out, fingers grasping the collar of Nate's jacket to pull him up to within an inch of his face. "Who wants to know?" he snarled.

"N . . . Nate Price. I'm his cousin."

"Are you now?" The man laughed. "Better come in, *cuz.*"

Nate lost his balance as he was released, roughly. He staggered against the wall, like his mum did when she was too full of booze to stand upright.

"In there," the man barked, shoving Nate in front of him down the hall to Cole's living room.

"What the fuck's this? You were supposed to send whoever it was packing." The other man's voice was deep, like the tattooed man's. He looked like him too, except this man was even scarier. Taller, hairier, built like a tank, with cold, staring eyes like a vampire.

"Nate!" Cole's voice sounded thick and slow. Nate hadn't noticed him when he was shoved into the room, the other stranger having caught his attention first.

"Says he's Cole's cousin." There was an edge of cruelty to the first man's laugh that would have set Nate's nerves jangling had his attention not been focussed on the shocking sight of Cole. He was slumped on the sofa looking like his two hefty visitors had knocked him around the ring between them.

"'S'all right, mate. Worse'n it looks." Nate knew Cole meant to say the opposite, which made him worry that Cole's brain was in as big a mess as his face. Looking down, he saw that Cole had his right hand wrapped in the bottom of his T-shirt, from which blood was dripping on to his jeans.

"Had to take a couple of fingers, I'm afraid," the man without the tattooed head said. Nate followed his gaze to a glass on the coffee table containing what looked like two sausages dipped in tomato sauce. His eyes widened. He thought the man was having him on, that it was a couple of those fake fingers you got at Hallowe'en.

"Cole's not in a talkative mood, but that'll change when I take a couple more."

Nate's legs wobbled as the truth hit home. He felt sick. He looked back at Cole, but Cole's eyes were closed, his head had rolled sideways and was resting on his shoulder like it was on a broken hinge. Nate felt a lump in his throat. He bit back tears. No way was he going to blubber in front of these bullies.

Cole's respite was short lived. He coughed and choked, spitting blood. Nate saw a gaping hole where one of his top teeth had been. He opened one eye a slit and pleaded with the men. "Let the kid go."

"I'll decide when he goes," said the second man. He took a swipe at Cole's face — as if it were possible to inflict more damage.

He then turned to Nate. "Know where your big cousin keeps his personal phone? He claims he can't find it."

Nate shook his head. Tattoo patted him down and found his own phone and the money he had collected from the clients he'd visited that morning. Nate made a grab for the phone. "Hey! That's mine!"

"Not bad. How much of this were you going to hand over, Burke?" Tattoo's voice was full of menace. "Because this is quite a bit more than what we'd normally collect from a routine drop."

Cole attempted to protest, but second man silenced him with a vicious blow. Then he closed in on Nate. "You work for us now, sonny. Cousin Cole's just gone out of business."

Nate looked from him to Cole in confusion. The man shoved him over to Tattoo. "Take him to the house. Careful not to attract attention when you're leaving the building. I'll be along later. I just need to finish up here first."

Nate kicked Tattoo in the shins. "No! I'm not going anywhere with you!"

Tattoo's face was ugly with rage. He pulled Nate towards him. A knife materialised from nowhere and was pressed against Nate's face, the tip of the blade angled so that it nicked his cheek. Nate panicked, feeling a thin trickle of blood run down over his lip and into his mouth. He ran his tongue around the inside of his mouth to feel if it was real, and it tasted the way it did when he lost a tooth, leaving him in no doubt.

"No!" Cole made to rise from the sofa, but he was slapped back down.

Tattoo kept the blade pressed against Nate's cheek. "Do as you're told, lad, unless you want my friend over there to rip Cousin Cole wide open and spill his guts over the carpet right in front of you."

Nate's eyes slid to Cole, whose pulpy face looked like it was already smeared with his innards. His voice trembled, but he managed to look Tattoo in the eye.

"Fine. Just — don't hurt Cole again."

Tattoo released him and pocketed the knife. "Smart kid. Blow your cousin a kiss, and let's go."

Nate walked numbly to the door, leaving Cole alone with the other man. As Tattoo marched him down the stairs and out of the building, all he could think of were the chilling words, *I just need to finish up here.*

CHAPTER FOURTEEN

Jane
24 May 2019

Jane and her colleague PC Harry Simpson arrived at George Boole Academy in plenty of time for the school talk. They began to unload from the car the equipment and props they'd brought with them to accompany their hour-long presentation on county lines to year seven.

At the school reception desk, they were each issued with a visitor's pass on a lanyard in the school colours of maroon and gold and asked to wait. In less than five minutes, a man and a woman greeted them. The man, tall and thin with a bald head buffed to a shine, shook hands with them, introducing himself as Mike Short, head of year seven. "And this is my colleague, Diane Howard."

They followed Diane and Mike down a long corridor to the school hall. On the way, Jane admired the students' framed artwork on the walls, thinking how wonderful it was that the children's work was celebrated and displayed so prominently. What a boost to their confidence!

"Here we go." Mike showed them into the school hall, where rows of chairs had been laid out in readiness for the children arriving. "You can set up over there in front of the stage if you like. I hope that's okay?"

"Yes, that'll do nicely," Jane assured him. Harry was looking at the rows of chairs, his lips moving as if counting aloud.

"One hundred and sixty," Diane Howard informed him.

Harry thanked her. "Just checking we've brought enough leaflets from the car."

Jane got to work setting up her PowerPoint presentation on the laptop, while Harry assembled the whiteboard and unpacked pens and flip-chart paper. They had both done these talks before, though not together, and had discussed who would do and say what on the drive to the school. When Harry learned that Jane was an ex-teacher, he seemed happy for her to do most of the talking, which she didn't mind. She'd had years of practice after all.

It was too big a group to make the session very interactive. It would be up to the teachers to do follow-up sessions with their forms in PSHE lessons, where they could incorporate activities and discussion. Today's objective was to raise awareness and get as much information over to the kids as possible in the time allotted.

Their audience began filing in at five minutes to the hour, and despite a lot of noise and shifting of chairs, they were settled in time to start. Form teachers stood watch at the side of the hall, ready to swoop on any troublemakers.

When they were completely quiet, Jane introduced herself and Harry. She explained that if anyone was affected by the issues they'd be covering, they should talk to their form teacher, or to a responsible adult. She did a quick scan of her audience and saw the usual expressions, ranging from bored to keen interest.

Jane began by explaining how organised criminal gangs in the big cities used dedicated mobile phone lines to set up customer bases in country areas, and how they often used children to transport drugs for them.

Some of the content was quite hard-hitting, covering issues of violence, child criminal exploitation and modern slavery. She also showed them some scary statistics about how many children it was thought were being exploited by county lines gangs. The point being that it could happen to any one of them.

Then she showed them a drama-documentary about a thirteen-year-old boy being groomed to take part in criminal activity. Though she'd now seen the film several times, Jane never failed to be moved by his story, which she knew was based on a real-life case.

The film showed the boy accepting gifts and drugs from gang members. Jane paused the film and explained how these gifts were used to groom children into doing favours in return. Sometimes, the gifts might be expensive clothes, sometimes drugs, which the children thought were being given for free. She explained, "Don't be fooled. Nothing's for free. Sooner or later, the gang will demand payback. They'll force you to work for them for nothing to repay what you owe. This is called debt bondage."

Jane paused to scan the rows of attentive faces. Some of the children looked a little anxious, which Jane regretted, but she had to give them the facts to keep them safe. She restarted the video.

In one particularly harrowing scene, the boy was beaten up and the money he was carrying from a drop stolen from him. When he reported his attack, he was held personally responsible for the loss of the money, leading to another beating and further debt bondage. There was an audible gasp from the hall when it was revealed that the attack and theft of the drugs had been staged by the gang.

Jane was careful to explain that the boy in the film, and all other children treated in this way, were victims, not willing participants. They were not to blame for the violence and abuse inflicted on them, and this was true even if they believed themselves to be complicit because they'd willingly accepted gifts or other rewards for taking part in criminal activity.

She went on to emphasise that adults who coerced or manipulated children under the age of eighteen into engaging in criminal activity were guilty of child criminal exploitation. They were the ones who carried all the blame.

Jane paused a moment to let that sink in before moving on to talk about cuckooing — lots of laughter over the word until she described that it involved taking over the homes of vulnerable people, often through the use of violence and intimidation.

"The cuckooed house is a base for storing, cutting and distributing drugs," she told her audience. Then she spent a few minutes talking about human trafficking, explaining that children were often brought from other areas of the country to work in cuckooed houses in towns they didn't know. The accompanying slide showed a house that any of the kids present might have lived in.

There was then some legal stuff to cover to hammer home that possessing and selling drugs was illegal, before Jane moved on again. "Which brings us to the violence associated with criminal gangs and drug dealing."

A noticeable frisson of excitement shuddered around the hall, and some of the students seemed to sit up straighter and pay more attention.

"Gang members often carry weapons — knives, or even guns — to protect themselves from rival gangs, or because of other dangers associated with what they do, or to intimidate and control reluctant recruits." She showed them a slide of some weapons of choice, followed by statistics relating to the growth of knife crime, then one of a section of a torso with a long, stitched wound that had been inflicted by a knife. This prompted the predicted responses of gasps and nervous laughter.

The final few minutes were used to tell the kids how to spot the signs that a friend or family member might be involved in county lines, and what to do about it.

In summing up, Jane gave information on how to seek help if they or anyone they knew became involved. She held up a copy of the leaflet that Harry was distributing along the rows, giving contact details for the police, charities and other agencies, some of which offered confidential advice and support.

A quick glance at her watch showed that their time was up. Jane would have liked to end with questions and discussion, but no time had been allocated for this. She watched as the kids stood up and began to file out of the hall, their silence and sombre faces at the end of the talk soon giving way to smiles and chatter. She could only hope that some of what she'd tried to put over had been absorbed.

Mike thanked them for their time and hurried off.

Harry congratulated Jane. "Well done. You held their interest brilliantly. I usually send them to sleep. Only other time I've seen them that engaged was when we brought the sniffer dogs along."

"Thanks," Jane croaked, her voice hoarse. Her mouth was parched after speaking for a full hour. No one had thought to leave out water for her, and she'd left her own water bottle in the car. "I just hope we got through to them."

They packed up and carried their equipment back to the car.

Just as she was about to get in, Jane noticed a boy hurrying across the car park towards them. He kept looking over his shoulder, as if worried that he was being followed. "Hang on," Jane said to Harry. "I think this lad might want to talk to us."

He had been in the front row, Jane realised when he drew nearer, and she could see his face clearly.

Ignoring Harry, the boy looked at Jane. "Please, miss, can I talk to you?"

"Of course, but have you got permission to be out here?" It wasn't break time.

"I asked if I could go to the toilet," he answered. "It'll be okay for a bit."

Not fully believing him, but reluctant to put him off, Jane accepted what he'd told her. "All right, then, but if we need longer than a couple of minutes, maybe my colleague could go to reception and just let them know you're talking to me. Would that be okay?"

The boy nodded. "It won't take long."

"What's your name?" Jane asked.

His eyes focussed somewhere just above Jane's chest, he said, "Caleb Moss. You know what you were saying about how you could tell how someone might be getting groomed by gangs?"

"Yes. Are you worried about one of your friends?" Jane asked.

"There's a boy in my form called Drew Wilson. He was in my class at primary school too. We weren't really friends then, but because we got put in the same form here, we sort of got friendlier." He looked Jane in the eye for the first time.

Jane nodded. "Go on, Caleb."

"Drew was okay for most of the first term, but then, just before half-term last October, he started acting weird. He started taking days off school a lot and when he was here, he didn't want to do any of the stuff we used to do, like playing football and going to clubs. He told me he didn't want to be my friend anymore because I was a stupid little kid. He said that after he offered me a cigarette one time and I said no, because it gives you cancer."

"Good for you, Caleb. Had Drew ever smoked before that time?" Jane asked.

"I don't think so. He didn't say he did, and I never saw him with any before then. He told me he got them from his new friend. He said he was older than us, but he didn't treat him like a kid, and he gave him stuff." Caleb looked down at his hands. "Expensive stuff. Like trainers."

Jane felt a tug of sympathy for him. He was small and looked young for his age, and, she thought, not really ready for secondary school. She imagined he'd lived a slightly sheltered life. His parents probably worried that he'd be bullied. She hoped he'd have a sudden growth spurt sooner rather than later.

"Did Drew tell you the names of his new friends? Are they students here?"

Caleb shook his head. "He just said they were older and that they were really cool. I don't know what school they go to, but I don't think they go here, 'cause he'd probably have hung out with them if they did."

Jane wondered if older boys hung out with year sevens and decided they'd probably consider it uncool, but she didn't say so to Caleb. "Is Drew at school today? Was he at our talk?"

"No."

"Do you know when he was last in school, Caleb?"

"I don't know. A few weeks, maybe?" He tossed his head back. Then, he said, hesitantly, "Miss, I heard my parents talking about that girl who was stabbed the other day. They were saying it had to do with county lines." His eyes on the ground, he mumbled in his boyish treble, "Do you think that'll happen to Drew too?"

His question took Jane by surprise. Her mind flashed back to the horrific moment when she'd seen Lana Kerr drop to the ground, fatally wounded, and she was unable to answer for a moment. Her instinct was to reassure Caleb. He was just a child, a fact that his grown-up shirt and tie and oversized maroon blazer failed to disguise. But the truth was, if Drew was mixed up with county lines offenders, he could be in a lot of danger.

"Let's hope not, lad." Jane was grateful to Harry for butting in and resolving her dilemma of how to respond. His cheery tone seemed to banish some of Caleb's anxiety.

Jane added, "You've done the right thing telling us about your concerns for Drew, Caleb. PC Simpson and I will look into it." She was pleased to see Caleb's face flush with pride. "Now, you'd better get back to class before you're missed."

"Yes, miss. Thank you, miss," Caleb piped, before spinning round and darting off to the school entrance.

"Great little lad," Harry commented. "Hope he doesn't get into trouble for being out of class so long."

Jane hoped so too. She left Harry waiting in the car while she went back to the reception desk to obtain more details about Drew Wilson. Unfortunately, Drew's form teacher and his head of year were taking classes, but the receptionist agreed to ask one of them to get in touch with Jane when they were free.

"You'd better write this up in your report," Harry said. "Make sure someone looks into it."

Jane nodded. She looked out of the window as Harry reversed out of their parking space. She was thinking of Caleb's question about his friend. Harry was right. She would have to pass the information on.

Jane had recognised the name of Harry's form teacher, Geoff Smith. He had taught at Ollie Granger's a few years back when she was still there. Looked like he'd changed schools. After Sam died, Geoff's attentions towards her had bordered on harassment. He'd often made inappropriate comments, though nothing outrageous. He'd always stopped just short of causing offence, but after Sam's death he'd been a bit too eager to console her, slipping his arm around her and pulling her into a hug as though their friendship warranted such unsolicited behaviour. She'd regarded him as a bit of a rogue, annoying, but harmless. She should have challenged him over it. *We live and learn.*

It wasn't her job to investigate Caleb's claims any further. She would pass the details on, and the matter would be referred to someone else.

Then again, it couldn't do any harm, could it, for her to renew her acquaintance with an old colleague? She felt invested in Drew's welfare. Having witnessed the tragedy of Lana, a child almost certainly mixed up with county lines, she felt duty-bound to do whatever she could to save Drew Wilson from meeting a similar fate.

CHAPTER FIFTEEN

Steph
1 May 2019

Steph hadn't expected great results from her interview with Kaye Flyte and her team concerning Shane Watt. Her expectations were fulfilled when Flyte contacted her after a few days to confirm that she had nothing for her.

Officers in Steph's team, who had been checking in with local charities that provided support to rough sleepers and others in need, had also drawn a blank. One or two interviewees thought they recognised Watt from his description, but none were able to provide reliable information on his present whereabouts. Steph suspected an unwillingness to blab to the police.

"Maybe we should focus our energies elsewhere for a bit, boss," Elias suggested. "Even his old army buddies don't seem to know where he could be."

Steph disliked the polite, quiet manner in which Elias sometimes questioned her priorities and decisions. It felt like a challenge to her authority, a threat even. When she'd mentioned this to her therapist, Dr Bryce had suggested that Elias was simply behaving as any colleague might — expressing opinions, testing theories, offering a different perspective.

Moreover, she hinted that Steph's attitude to Elias asserting himself in their partnership might stem from her need to be in control. As someone who had once been the victim of a controlling and ultimately murderous boyfriend, Steph's default position towards other people was now one of suspicion and distrust. She was assessing everyone she encountered for the level of threat they posed.

Dr Bryce's words had given Steph food for thought. She knew that she was no longer the person she had been before Cal, but neither was she a complete stranger to her former self. She'd flinched that time when she'd overheard two female PCs describing her as 'hard and uncompromising', but one part of her had taken the criticism as a compliment.

Sometimes it seemed as if there were two versions of herself, and they were continually at variance.

She'd admitted as much to Dr Bryce. "It's like I'm at war with myself. Take, for example, the way I relate to other people. Sometimes what I really want to say to them, or how I really want to interact with them comes out all wrong, the opposite of what I intended."

Dr Bryce made a few observations, including some that Steph had expected from her own research on the effects of traumatic experiences — many of which, she'd concluded, didn't apply to her. Post-traumatic stress was something that often happened to soldiers or victims of abuse or torture who'd experienced unimaginable horrors. She wasn't like them. Her symptoms weren't as severe either. Sure, she had nightmares and the odd moment when she saw Cal transpose himself onto the faces of other people, but apart from that, she was functioning pretty well. *Wasn't she?*

One of Dr Bryce's comments had made a big impact on Steph — the suggestion that trauma could lead to changes in brain chemistry, which in turn could affect personality.

For Steph, this had been a shocking revelation. It caused her to reflect on her feelings of anger and hostility, her distrustful attitude towards people and the world in general.

There were some positives to being the way she was now. She'd toughened up, stopped placing her trust in individuals without question, become more assertive, and emotionally independent. Not to mention that she was doing a job she once thought she would never have the confidence to do. If all that meant people didn't like her much, and she had to suffer the odd nightmare, she deemed it worth the sacrifice. She wasn't interested in winning popularity contests, and at least it meant she'd never be a willing victim again.

Curiously, Dr Bryce had not disagreed when Steph explained this to her. She'd pointed out that additional caution, awareness of danger and mistrust of strangers would have been useful attributes for our ancestors to protect them from danger from predators and other dangers. But she also hinted that in order to move forward, Steph needed to accept that she'd been transformed by her trauma, but that it needn't define her and that hiding behind her hard persona was not acceptance but denial. *And so on. And on. And babble, babble, babble.*

Dr Bryce also seemed confident that it would be possible to balance the negatives and the positives. "We'll work to integrate the two aspects of your personality that are currently in conflict."

"You mean mess about with my brain chemistry again?"

Her comment had prompted raised eyebrows and a recommendation that Steph continue with the medication she'd been prescribed, as well as with the therapy. Not a scenario she was happy with, but it was reassuring that Bryce seemed to have faith in her ability to make significant progress.

With all this in mind, Steph resisted having a dig at her sergeant for telling her what her priorities should be.

Encouraged, Elias said, "I've had a look at the results from the house-to-house enquiries. The officers spoke with everyone living or working near Cole Burke's place of residence — neighbours and shop-owners who might have been well-placed to see any comings and goings to the property. One or two seem quite interesting."

"Go on."

"A Mrs Agnes West lives above the nail bar Nails & Beauty, almost directly opposite Cole's flat. She doesn't get out much and spends a lot of time sitting by her window. She described seeing a couple of boys entering and leaving the street door to Cole's building on a number of occasions. The day before Cole's body was discovered, she saw a young boy leaving Cole's building in the company of a 'suspicious-looking man with a tattooed head'. She thought the boy was being manhandled."

"Okay. We don't know if this was Nate, but go on."

"She said that they turned left down the High Street, whereas when she'd seen the boy leave previously, he'd always turned right, and she thought he looked scared."

Steph raised an eyebrow. "How the hell could she tell that from across the street — there're four lanes on the High Street at that point, aren't there? Did she have a pair of binoculars trained on them?"

"The PC asked her that question and she said that the boy kept looking over his shoulder, as if he wanted to go the other way. Every time he did so, the man seemed to drag him forwards 'as though he had him by the elbow'."

"That doesn't sound good. If this man was Cole's killer, he might have abducted the boy and taken him to a cuckooed house somewhere in the south side of the city, where he's possibly been ever since. How far have we got on checking any CCTV footage from the days before Cole's murder? If we're lucky, we might be able to work out where Nate was taken. If it was Nate."

"PC Fairbairn's been working on that," Elias said.

"Let's see what he's got for us."

Quite a bit, as it turned out. "I was about to contact you with what I've got, ma'am. I think you'll find it interesting. When DS Harper told me that a neighbour had spotted a young lad and a man leaving Burke's place and turning south down the High Street, I concentrated on that area in the hours before and after the time of death we have for Burke. This is what I found."

He showed them a man and a boy walking closely together. Definitely close enough for the man to be propelling the boy along by the elbow, or even holding a weapon against his side. The man was bulky, the top of his head dark, and the image wasn't clear enough for them to determine whether he had a tattoo or just short, darkish hair.

"Here they are again passing St Katherine's church. We were able to access footage from the security cameras mounted on the front and side of St Katherine's, so we can confirm that the man and boy turned right into Colegrave Street, but unfortunately there's nothing after that."

"That's a residential area. A lot of houses," Elias said. "There's a charitable housing association that owns a fair number of properties in the Park Ward area. They specialise in providing accommodation for vulnerable adults, including people recovering from substance abuse. I, er, contacted them earlier, and the manager, Sue Valentine, is happy to speak with us."

Steph made herself recognise this as initiative rather than an attempt to upstage her. "I suppose you've made an appointment for us to interview her as well, have you?"

"Not exactly. Well, she is available this morning, from eleven until one."

"Good. Contact her and tell her to expect us at eleven."

They set off for the housing association's offices at ten forty-five. A woman on the reception desk announced their arrival to Sue Valentine. She appeared a few minutes later to escort them back to her office.

After introductions had been made and Sue had informed them that tea and coffee were on their way, she asked, "How can I help you? Usually when the police turn up, they're either looking for someone or there's been some trouble involving one of our properties."

"Does the term county lines mean anything to you?" Steph asked.

Sue looked slightly offended. "Of course it does."

"Then you know what a cuckooed house is?"

"Absolutely." Sue fished in her drawer and took out a leaflet which she handed to Steph. Steph recognised it as the familiar Crimestoppers pamphlet. "We've posted these to all our tenants. We also have the Home Office poster displayed prominently in our reception. Didn't you spot it?"

Steph shook her head. She wondered how many of Sue's tenants bothered to look at the leaflet.

Sue looked worried. "Are you concerned that one of our properties might be cuckooed? Because we house vulnerable adults? We've had no complaints from anyone living in properties neighbouring ours about unusual activity or lots of visitors. We know the signs to look out for."

Just in case Steph and Elias didn't know the signs, Sue proceeded to list them. "An unusual number of callers, signs of drug use, an increase in litter and antisocial behaviour, an increase in the number of cars and other vehicles parked outside. Have the police had complaints?"

"No. Sergeant Harper and I are investigating the death of a known drug dealer and we believe that his murder might be connected to a county lines gang that's taken over his patch. We also have reason to believe that the gang is exploiting at least one child against his will and forcing him to live and work in a cuckooed house." Steph explained about the footage from the security camera on the side of St Katherine's. "What we're hoping is that you might be able to identify for us those tenants you think might be most at risk of being exploited."

They were interrupted by the arrival of the tea and coffee. "Thank you, Marisa. Marisa is our apprentice." Marisa looked embarrassed and practically ran for the door. "She's very shy," Sue commented unnecessarily. She invited them to pour themselves tea or coffee according to their preference. Steph reached for the French press.

"To return to what you were just saying, information on our tenants is held electronically, but I suppose we can release it, given that we'd be cooperating in a murder investigation and because our tenants could be at risk. It shouldn't be a difficult task to identify those most likely to be targeted. We only have a few properties in Park Ward and some of those are shared houses, which we can probably eliminate."

Steph and Elias waited while she consulted her tenancy records. It took only a few moments for her to come up with a list of five tenants who were living alone. Their addresses were scattered around the streets of the area known as St Catherine's, which was bounded on one side by the South Common, on the other by the River Witham.

"Here we go. Bear with me a moment while I buzz Marie Kemp. She's the housing officer for those properties and should be able to give you more information than I can about the tenants. She doesn't start work until one but I'm sure she'll come in if she's somewhere nearby."

Marie arrived five minutes later, breathless and a little dishevelled. "I was in the central library and ran over as quickly as I could." Sue introduced her to Steph and Elias and filled her in on why they were there.

"I know our tenants quite well," Marie said. "Some of them need a lot of support, especially after first moving in. I help them fill out forms and sort out their bills as well other things not necessarily housing related.

"Our housing officers are a bit like social workers," Sue commented.

Marie perused the list of names, finally saying. "I could put these names in order of most likely to least likely of being targeted by the kind of people you've been talking about."

"That would be very helpful," Steph said.

"Okay. So, I'd say first on the list would be Mr Cooke. Bobby Cooke. He's twenty-seven. On methadone to aid his recovery from heroin addiction. I read that people on methadone can be targeted outside pharmacies where they go to collect their medication. Appalling, isn't it?" No one disagreed.

"Then there's Eleanor Field. Eleanor is seventy-five. Her daughter, Katie, lives with her. Katie has a mild learning disability.

"The other three I would classify as less vulnerable but perhaps at some risk of exploitation. There's John Lyndon, forty-two years old. He was referred to us after becoming homeless when he lost his job and his partner kicked him out. He drank heavily for a while, but he's now joined Alcoholics Anonymous and he's doing well. Unfortunately, he contracted an infection and developed sepsis during his time on the streets and his right leg had to be amputated.

"Then there's Kaz Fisher, mid-thirties. Kaz was about to become homeless when she was referred to us by the council. She's an ex-addict and was on the game for a bit. Last, but not least is Kelvin Norgrove, fifty-one. Kelvin gets himself into trouble for antisocial behaviour every now and again. He was recently diagnosed with an autistic spectrum disorder." Marie looked at Steph. "Would you like me to accompany you when you visit these tenants?"

Steph thought for a moment. Like Kaye Flyte's clients, some of these tenants might not welcome a visit from the police. "Actually, it might be better if you pay them a call without us present. Sound them out and let us know your thoughts. If there is something going on at one or more of these houses, we'll need to organise surveillance on them to gather appropriate evidence. But I don't want anyone entering any of these properties. No one should be put at risk."

Sue regarded Marie with concern. "How do you feel about that, Marie?" Before Marie could answer, Sue turned to Steph. "I don't want my staff putting themselves at any sort of risk either."

"I understand," Steph said. "And we would never ask a member of the public to put themselves in danger." She looked at Marie. "Do you know your tenants well enough to spot whether they might be afraid, or anxious, or hiding something, for example?"

Marie seemed to think for a moment. "I think so, but some of them have a social worker. You should speak to them too."

Steph nodded. She had already considered this possibility. Marie continued, "I guess I could call on them all under the pretext of doing some sort of doorstep survey?" She looked at Sue.

Sue agreed. "Yes, that might work. A tenant satisfaction survey, or a questionnaire of some kind, but with only a couple of quick questions. That's the sort of thing we do from time to time."

Steph nodded approvingly. "Thank you. I appreciate your help."

"Oh, believe me, Officer, if there's any exploitation of vulnerable persons going on in our properties, we want to flush it out just as much as you do," Sue said.

"I'd be grateful if you would give this matter priority. The boy we told you about is probably being held against his will and forced to work for his captors, not to mention the danger to your tenant."

"We'll be in touch in a day or two," Sue said, while Marie nodded.

Marie accompanied Steph and Elias back to the reception area. Steph sought out the government poster on county lines and spotted it, displayed prominently on the wall behind the desk, just as Sue had claimed.

Out on the street, raising her voice to be heard above the roar of lunchtime traffic on Broadgate, Steph instructed Elias. "Get someone to contact social services and find out which of the tenants on that list has a social worker. Get them to ask if they know of any other vulnerable people in that area who might be easy targets for exploitation. And contact the Park Ward Neighbourhood Policing Team. Find out if they've had reports about any suspicious behaviour in their area that might suggest a cuckooed property. If we want to set up surveillance, then we need to have an idea of where to concentrate resources, otherwise we're unlikely to get approval."

"Yes, boss." Elias sounded enthusiastic.

Steph hoped this wasn't a wild goose chase. She knew better than to get excited. They had no guarantees that after turning alongside St Katherine's church, Nate — if it even was Nate — had been taken to one of the many residential properties in the vicinity. For all they knew, he might have been whisked away in a car to who knew where.

CHAPTER SIXTEEN

Jane
27 May 2019

Jane summoned a smile for the man perched on a stool at the bar in the Red Lion.

"Bloody hell! Jane Bell! Look at you!" he exclaimed. "You look amazing."

Jane doubted it. She'd made no effort to look anything more than presentable.

"Looking pretty good yourself, Geoff. The beard suits you."

Geoff stroked his chin, then patted the top of his head where his hairline had receded cruelly. "You've got a new job, I hear."

Geoff had contacted Jane following her request to speak with Drew Wilson's form teacher and head of year. Predictably, he'd asked her to meet him socially.

"I'm a volunteer, actually. I don't get paid. Tutoring's my bread and butter."

Geoff moved on quickly. "Look, the grub here's not bad. Why don't you join me, and we can have a little chat

111

about the good old days? Oh, and I can tell you what you want to know about the Wilson boy."

Jane would rather have switched Geoff's priorities around so that she could come up with some excuse to avoid 'a little chat about the good old days' once she'd pumped him for information on Drew. She felt guilty for still feeling slightly repulsed by him. *Stop feeling guilty. Remember when he groped you at the Christmas party that time, then pretended he'd lost his balance and stumbled against you.* He'd grabbed hold of her boob, the first thing to hand, apparently.

Jane was conscious of him staring at her chest now, as she tried to attract the bartender's attention. Geoff might have a trendy beard, but he evidently hadn't caught a whiff of the change in the air regarding behaviour of that sort towards women in the twenty-first century. She hoped his younger female colleagues didn't put up with it. Her daughter Norah was right. Women should never have put up with it.

Geoff drained his glass and placed it on the bar. Jane remembered that he'd always been the last one to stand a round, hoping, no doubt that a lot of people would be on soft drinks by the time he had to put his hand in his pocket. "Same again?" she asked.

"Oh, go on then, Jane."

"How's Barbara?" Barbara was Geoff's wife.

Geoff patted his paunch. "Oh, you know. Not getting any slimmer. Not that I can talk. Now you, Jane, you're as trim as ever."

Jane had never considered her pear-like proportions to be trim. Still, she smiled, indulging him. She needed him in a good mood. "Thanks, Geoff."

Geoff leaned closer, "It's nice when a woman appreciates a compliment. Not many do these days. I'd be more likely to get a slap in the face than a thank you if I told a lass she had a pretty face. And that's just my daughter." He laughed uproariously at his own joke. Jane smiled, despite herself. Geoff was a dinosaur, but she remembered that he could also be quite self-deprecating at times.

They moved into the dining area. Over the meal they covered all the usual catch-up topics of family, old colleagues and past times.

Jane tried to think of an appropriate segue into a discussion about Caleb Moss's concerns for his friend, Drew. The opportunity arose when Geoff started a conversation about her special constable role. "Well, you're full of surprises, Jane. I can't imagine my Barbie going off and doing something like that."

Then, unable to help himself, he made some predictably suggestive jokes about handcuffs and truncheons, after which, he covered her hand with his, briefly. "Only joking, but you know that, don't you, Jane? No offence intended."

Resisting the urge to roll her eyes, Jane extracted her hand and picked up her wine glass.

Geoff then said, "I heard everyone was impressed with your talk on county lines. Apparently, you held their attention for the whole session. That's no mean feat with a bunch of eleven- and twelve-year-olds."

"I just hope they took something away from it." Before Geoff could respond, she added, "So, what can you tell me about Drew Wilson?"

Geoff frowned. "Drew. Ah, yes, Andrew Wilson. I forgot he goes by Drew. He appears as Andrew on the register, of course, and that's what I always call him." He gave a short laugh. "Or maybe I just forgot who he was altogether, as he's hardly ever at school. Is that why Caleb's worried? Because of Andrew's persistent absences? Perhaps he's concerned his friend's got some sort of serious illness."

Jane was momentarily confused. Then she realised that Geoff had missed the connection. "Actually, I think he's worried that his friend might be caught up in county lines."

Geoff pretended he'd understood that all along. "Yes, of course, that was my initial thought really. It just seemed so implausible. Why would he think that?"

Jane told him what Caleb had said about Drew smoking and hanging out with older boys, about the expensive trainers and the fact that he got on well with Caleb at first, then considered him too immature to associate with. "It sounds very much like Drew was being groomed by this older boy he was meeting."

"Let's bloody hope not," Geoff said. "They reckon that young lass who was stabbed recently was mixed up in all of that county lines business. Shocking thing."

Jane weighed up whether to tell him she'd witnessed Lana's murder, but opted not to bother. "Yes. That was very shocking. Caleb had heard about it. I think that, together with my talk, made him worry about Drew."

"Poor kid. Andrew lives with his older sister. She gave up the chance to go to university to get a job so that she could look after him after their mum died." He looked at Jane. "Actually, you might remember her. Shelby Wilson? She used to go to Ollie Granger. I taught her maths. Bright girl. Could easily have studied maths at university. Perhaps she'll go back to it." He took a slug of wine.

Jane thought for a moment. "I remember her. I taught her in year eight. She was good at English too." Even as she said it, Jane made up her mind to find out where Shelby lived and pay her a call. On a sudden impulse, she asked Geoff, "I don't suppose you've come across a boy called Nathan, or Nate, in any of your classes, have you, Geoff?"

Geoff laughed. "Only half a dozen or so. It's a popular name these days. Do you have a surname?"

Jane shook her head.

"How old? Is he in trouble too?"

Jane sighed, realising the impossibility of what she'd asked. "I don't know. To both questions."

Jane hoped to make her getaway after they'd finished eating, but Geoff insisted on buying her a drink. It was an offer she couldn't refuse, even though she knew he'd only offered to stop her rushing off. Besides, she felt she owed him a little more of her time in return for using him as an informant. Not that she'd learned much. She managed to get him back on topic with another question.

"Caleb mentioned that his friend Drew was hanging out with some older boys. Did you ever see him with older lads at school?"

"No, but as you probably remember, the kids tend to socialise within their own year group."

"Do you know of any older kids at your school who've been in trouble with the police over drugs?"

"You really are taking this special constable role seriously, aren't you?"

"Oh, it's just that I know this detective who's investigating the stabbing of that girl you mentioned. Any information that might have a bearing on that incident would be welcome."

Geoff gave her a suggestive look. "Seeing him, are you? This detective?"

"It's a she."

"So?" Geoff said with a lewd glint in his eye. Jane was about to say that she wasn't seeing anyone when she remembered that wasn't quite true.

"I am seeing someone but he's not a detective. He's a blacksmith."

"Well, I suppose Sam would have approved. He was a builder, wasn't he? A practical man. Not a boring intellectual like me."

It was news to Jane that Geoff was an intellectual, but she didn't say so. She stuck up for Sam. "Sam was a clever man." As was Ed. He was an artist who designed and crafted beautiful objects. But she didn't want to mention Ed's name to Geoff.

Geoff looked at her. He was slightly drunk. Who knew how many beers he'd downed before she arrived? To her dismay, he grabbed her hand and said, "I had a bit of a thing for you back in the day, Jane. But you know that, don't you? I thought, after Sam . . . you know . . ."

Cringing, Jane withdrew her hand and spoke to him sternly. "Geoff, I think you've had a bit too much to drink. And to be honest, you had a bit of a thing for anything in a skirt back in the day, didn't you?"

To his credit, he roared with laughter. "I was a bit of a rake, wasn't I? Truth is, I'd never do anything to hurt Barbie. I'm all bluster."

"Hmm." Whether that was true or not, Jane doubted George would behave this way with his female colleagues nowadays. He still hadn't answered her question. Then, he did.

"Come to think of it," George said, "I saw Drew talking to an older boy called Wes at the school gates a couple of times when I was on bus duty. Don't ask me for his surname because I can't remember it, but I can get back to you on that. I noticed Wes because he was in my form once upon a time. He ended up getting expelled after being arrested for some sort of drug-related offence in town. No idea what happened to him after that — Pupil Referral Unit, maybe. Right little scrote, he was. He must be nineteen or twenty by now. I had words with young Drew about talking to him, but it sounds like I didn't get through."

"Wes." Jane spoke the name aloud. "Thanks, Geoff." She gulped down the rest of her wine and felt immediately lightheaded. "I'd best be off now. Thanks for the catch-up." Before he could act first, she gave him a quick peck on the cheek and stood well back to say goodbye.

"Let's do it again sometime," Geoff said.

Jane smiled. "Yes. We must." *Not.*

Ever hopeful, Geoff called after her, "You know where to find me."

CHAPTER SEVENTEEN

Nate
22 April 2019

After leaving Cole's flat, Nate was jostled down the High
Street by Tattoo. He had no idea where he was being taken,
only that it couldn't be anywhere good. He thought of Cole
and was scared for him. What would be left of him by the
time the Vampire was done? A shiver juddered through him,
but it wasn't the cold. The tug of Tattoo's hand on his sleeve
was a terrifying reminder that under his own sleeve, Tattoo
was concealing a knife.

Nate was now in strange territory. He'd never been further down the High Street than Cole's flat. It was important
to pay attention to his surroundings so that he could find his
way back. The cathedral was behind them, solid and constant
amid all the uncertainty.

Ahead was a roundabout, and they were nearing a junction dominated by a large church. A sloping field stretched
into the distance on the other side of the roundabout. Nate
supposed it must be the South Common.

At the church — St Katherine's according to a board
outside — they turned right down a street lined with houses

on both sides. At the end of that street, they turned left, then left again and then again, three times in all, or was it two? Tattoo stopped abruptly outside a house facing the river, opened the gate, and half-pushed, half-dragged Nate up the path to the front door.

The house had looked okay from the outside, but the hall they stepped into was almost impassable owing to the amount of unopened post, crushed takeaway boxes, empty bottles and cans littering the floor. Whoever lived here must never take their rubbish out. Yet, behind the squalor, the walls looked clean and freshly painted, the carpet newish.

Nate could hear voices coming from a back room. When Tattoo pushed open the door, he saw two kids around his own age sitting on a sofa. Another, older person was sitting at a table, with his back to him. He was wearing a baseball cap. The younger kids were reading comics, the older person was looking at his phone. There was something familiar about him.

One of the younger kids was a pale-faced girl with greasy brown hair reaching to her waist. She reminded Nate of a zombie, but even so, she was quite pretty.

The other was a boy with a purplish-red birthmark covering one side of his face. His fair hair was parted to the side and flopped over the blemish, partly covering it and wholly concealing his left eye.

The older, taller boy looked over his shoulder. Nate gasped. "Wes!" He hadn't seen Wes in over a week. "What's going on?"

"He works here," Tattoo said. "That's all you need to know."

Nate was silent, stung at the way Wes had turned back to his phone without a second glance. "Wes?"

"Ouch!" Nate's cheek stung. He flinched as Tattoo made to strike him again using the back of his hand. Wes must have heard, but he didn't even turn around. Why was he acting like this?

"Everything all right, Wes?" Tattoo asked. "Everybody behaving?" He turned his cold stare on the boy and girl."

"All good, Shark."

Nate stared at Tattoo. What sort of name was Shark?

"No trouble from upstairs?"

"I've given her something to make her sleep. Where's Wolf?"

"Taking care of business."

Not a vampire then, a wolf. Nate had a sudden, terrifying vision of Cole being ripped apart.

The boy and girl had carried on reading throughout Wes's and Shark's exchange, but Nate could tell they were taking everything in. He'd caught the girl glancing at him over the top of her comic.

Wes used to work for Cole, but now he worked for Shark and Wolf. He seemed to have willingly transferred his loyalties to them, but the two younger kids — they weren't here willingly. Their faces looked pinched and scared. Nate shivered and eyed the door. Those kids were prisoners here, and now he was too.

"I'm going upstairs," Shark announced. He pushed Nate towards Wes. "Make sure he understands his position here."

Nate waited until he heard Shark's footsteps on the stairs. "What's going on, Wes? Why are you acting like we've never met? Have you any idea what they've done to Cole? They've hurt him *really* bad."

He noticed the younger boy looking at him through his slanting fringe. The girl too raised her eyes, though her head remained still.

Wes grunted. "If you know what's good for you, you'll forget about Cole. We don't work for him now. And I'm not pretending I don't know you. It's just things are different now. I've got responsibilities here, and I don't want you messing things up. So, do what I tell you, or whatever they did to Cole, I'll do to you. Understand?"

Nate didn't understand. The old Wes had bought him chips and given him cigarettes. Sometimes he'd been a bit offhand, but this Wes was a stranger. This Wes was threatening to pulp his face, or worse. "Yes," he lied softly.

Wes cupped his ear with the palm of his hand. "What was that? I can't hear you."

"Yes." Nate's voice shook with anger.

"Good." Wes pointed at the girl. "Give him a comic, Lana. Dex, I want to know if he so much as thinks of leaving the room." The boy nodded.

Wes gave Nate a final warning look before leaving the room himself.

Lana passed a comic to him. "Best do as he says."

Nate pushed it away. "What's going on here?"

"You really don't know? You were working for Cole before, weren't you?"

Nate was confused. "Working for him? No, I just liked hanging out with him. Wes took me to see him. They're cousins."

Lana and Dex stared at him like he was an idiot. Suddenly the idea of Cole and Wes being cousins seemed as unlikely to him as it clearly did to them. "Well, Wes told me they were."

"Bet they gave you ciggies and drinks and other nice stuff too, didn't they?" Lana said. Nate looked down at his new trainers.

"They were grooming you," Dex said.

Nate knew what the word meant, but he didn't think it applied to him. "No. They were my mates."

Dex shrugged. "Have it your way."

"Did Cole ask you to do stuff for him? Illegal stuff?" Lana asked.

Nate thought about the drug drops. He'd been aware that what he was doing was against the law, but it had seemed harmless enough. The people who bought drugs from Cole were normal, not like the addicts you saw around town. They lived in nice houses. "Cole was good to me," he said. "Sometimes he gave me money."

"He was using you," Lana said. "He didn't want to be caught in possession of Class A drugs himself, so he got you to run around for him. Police are less likely to stop a kid." Nate stared at her, knowing she was telling it how it was.

"Look, it sounds like this Cole treated you okay, but the people you're going to be working for now aren't like that. They're really bad people. If you don't do what they say, you'll get hurt. Bad."

More afraid now, Nate asked. "Are you their prisoners? How long have you been here?"

"A few weeks. We never stay at any place for long. The neighbours start to get suspicious, so we move on to another house. The woman who lives here is a prisoner too. Shark got her to trust them by pretending he was interested in her. Now she's locked in her room."

"Have you ever tried to get away?"

Lana's eyes widened. "You heard what Wes said. Do as you're told, and things won't be so bad. You can't get away, ever. When they find you, they hurt you, maybe even kill you — and they always find you." She looked Nate in the eye for the first time, and her terror showed.

Not me, thought Nate, and was about to say so when Dex spoke up. "Shhh! He's coming back."

Wes came and stood behind Nate for a few moments before sitting down on the leather sofa and taking out a pack of cigarettes. He didn't offer them round like he used to. He turned on the TV and began watching a movie. After a while his breathing altered. His pursed lips made a whistling sound when he breathed out. Some of the tension in the room seemed to ease.

Lana spoke in a low whisper. "Wes was recruited by Wolf and Shark. That's what they do — come to a place, find out who's dealing. They recruited Wes weeks ago, and Cole, too, but Cole's crossed them somehow. And they don't think he's given them a full list of his customers. Wes told us they were going round his flat today to teach him a lesson. Which means kill him, case you don't get it. They don't give people chances. You do as you're told or . . ." Lana drew a finger across her throat.

"Wolf and Shark — that's not their real names — they're not the ones in charge. They're members of a gang based in

Nottingham, but they're in charge of us. Them and Wes, but only Wes is here all the time. Wolf and Shark come and go. They're all the boss of us and we have to do what they say. If we don't, they'll beat us up. Show him, Dex."

Dex lifted his T-shirt to reveal a flourish of colourful bruises blooming across his pale torso. Lana said, "That was for pinching one of Wes's cigarettes. One he'd already smoked, nearly down to the end."

There was a sound from the sofa, but it was only the leather squeaking as Wes turned over.

Nate looked at Wes, then at the door. "We could get away while he's asleep."

Lana and Dex exchanged a look. "You still don't get it, do you? We just told you. They'll kill you. Or they'll kill your mum, or your sisters or brothers, if you have any."

"They don't even know where my mum lives. I bet—" Nate broke off. He remembered walking past the block where he lived, pointing out his bedroom window to Wes and Drew, and his voice faltered.

"If I try to get away, they're going to shank my little brother, then me," Dex said. "Shark showed me a picture he took of him outside his primary school, so it's not just me I have to worry about."

Nate pictured his mum, drunk, opening the door to Shark or Wolf, inviting them inside. They'd only need to give her a bottle of vodka to gain her trust. Then they could take over her house, keep her a prisoner too. He began to appreciate the seriousness of his situation. "I'm going to get away. I don't care if they try to kill me. I'll get away and I'll see they don't get to my mum. I'm not staying here to be their slave."

Lana shrugged and went back to what she was doing. Dex shook his head. "You don't get it because you're new. You'll learn soon enough."

"No I won't. You'll see. I'm going to get away from here."

From the sofa came the sound of harsh laughter. Wes. He was awake. How long had he been listening?

"You should listen to your new mates, Nate. Cole's dead, by the way. Wolf called when I was upstairs, told me he'd got a bit carried away."

It was a shock, even though Nate had feared as much when Wolf had talked about 'finishing up'. He'd meant Cole. It was Cole he was going to finish.

What was more shocking than the news that Cole was dead was Wes's lack of concern. He'd been Cole's friend, or so it had seemed.

Nate thought of the glimpses of a different Wes that he'd seen peek out from time to time. He realised that he was seeing him properly now for the first time.

CHAPTER EIGHTEEN

Steph
8 May 2019

Marie Kemp contacted Steph a week after their conversation at the housing association headquarters.

"DI Warwick? I think I've got some news for you. I visited all five of the tenants we discussed when we met last week, and you were right that one of them has a story to tell. Kaz Fisher. Turns out Marisa, our apprentice, had taken a couple of calls from neighbours about this property, but she hadn't passed the information on to me. She said she thought the neighbours were just being nosey."

"What kind of complaints?"

"Marisa remembers three calls in all, over a two-week period. One about rubbish piling up around the side of the house. Another about kids being seen entering and leaving the house during school hours. Another was from a woman who claimed to know Kaz Fisher, saying she'd been turned away from her door by a young man of around twenty, claiming to be Kaz's cousin. He claimed Kaz was in bed with a cold."

When Steph and Elias had discussed who was most likely to be cuckooed, they'd guessed Bobby Cooke, with his history of drug abuse, but really, it could have been any one of the five.

"I take it the house is no longer cuckooed, given that you were able to speak with Kaz?" Steph said.

"Yes. Poor Kaz. She was in a terrible state. She had no idea what to do. She was a prisoner in her own home for a whole month. Now she's asking to be rehoused somewhere far from Lincolnshire."

"That's understandable."

"You should probably hear the story from Kaz herself. She didn't want the police coming to her house, nor does she want to go to the station, for obvious reasons. I've asked her if she'd be willing to come here to our offices, and she agreed."

Steph was grateful for Marie's proactiveness. She glanced at her watch. "Can you contact her now and see if she's able to come this morning? Tell her to take a taxi. I'll refund her fare."

"I'll get back to you," Marie said.

Steph barely had time to fill Elias in before she received a text from Marie, confirming that Kaz would be at the housing association offices in half an hour.

They set off immediately, arriving only a few minutes late. Marie showed them into a meeting room furnished with steel-framed, blue vinyl stacking chairs and an oval beech table.

Kaz arrived twenty minutes later, bringing with her an odour of unwashed skin and stale breath. Steph glanced at her sideways, resisting an urge to cover her mouth and nose. Marie opened a window, tactfully pretending to be warm.

Kaz seemed wary, guarded in the way of people who have reason to mistrust the police and other authority figures. Steph had expected her to be subdued and anxious after the ordeal of being held prisoner in her own home. Who knew what abuses she must have suffered at the hands of her captors? So it was almost disconcerting to watch her almost swagger across to the table and greet Marie with a high five. Putting up a front? It was impossible to tell.

Marie did the introductions. Steph suddenly had an uncomfortable sensation of being under scrutiny. She looked at Kaz properly and gave a start.

"Oh, so you do recognise me, do you, Stephie? I was wondering when the penny was going to drop."

The voice, though huskier than she remembered, was unmistakeable. Kaz's face was one she'd seen almost every day of her life for years. But how could it be? She'd never known a Kaz Fisher.

"Karen?" She searched the face, knowing she was right.

"Yeah. It's me. I was Karen Cutler when you knew me. I got married to Paul Fisher. Remember him? Complete tosser. I left him after two years."

"I heard you went to London."

"Yep. Worse thing I ever did. Got in with a bad crowd." She gave a shrug. "Should have listened to your advice and gone to college to redo my GCSEs, Stephie. Might not have made such a mess of my life."

She smiled, showing the kind of nightmarish teeth that would make a dentist weep. "Never mind. It is what it is. Been back in Lincoln nearly five years now, as it happens. Was staying with my mum up until last year when she passed away, bless her. The bloody council wouldn't let me take over her tenancy, and I thought I'd be put out on the streets until this lovely lady came to my rescue."

"I can't take the credit," Marie said. "Kaz was referred to us by the council."

Steph had noted Elias perk up when he heard that she and Kaz were acquainted. It was pathetic how needy he was for any scrap of information about her past.

"Karen — Kaz — and I were at secondary school together," she explained.

"You left out the bit about us being best mates for a bit." Kaz affected a hurt look.

A flush swept up from Steph's neck, engulfing her face. An image presented itself of Karen Cutler the last time she'd seen her. It bore little resemblance to the woman sitting across the table from her now.

"Thought you got a job at the bank?" Kaz said. "When'd you change your mind and join the police?"

"A little later. I needed a career change." Steph felt hot and flustered. The meeting was not going to plan.

Karen's husky voice softened suddenly. "I heard you got attacked, Stephie."

There was a silence. *Who told you that?* Steph hadn't kept in touch with anyone from the old days. The atmosphere in the room was suddenly leaden. Steph baulked at acknowledging Kaz's comment, fearful of the emotions it might evoke.

Instead, she cleared her throat, detached herself and turned a clinical eye on Kaz. "I think we need to focus on the reason we're all here today. Perhaps you'd like to begin by telling us how your home came to be cuckooed?"

Kaz shrugged, turned to Elias. "Your partner never used to be so serious, you know. Stephie was a little ray of sunshine back in the day, so easy-going and friendly." She frowned, caught Steph's eye. "Bit shy, but still fun. We had some great laughs together. And not all of them legal." Steph stiffened. Kaz went on. "Seems like I'm not the only one who's changed. What the hell happened to you, *DI Warwick*?"

I was attacked, remember? You just said it.

Marie cleared her throat. "Kaz, I don't think DI Warwick meant to sound unfriendly. She's investigating a murder and time is of the essence."

Kaz yawned. "Whatever. Yeah, I know about that murder. Cole Burke."

"Did you know Cole?" Elias asked.

"Used to."

"You bought drugs from him?"

Kaz shrugged. "Might've done."

"When did you last see him?" Elias said.

"Not sure."

Steph let Elias take the lead. It was a relief, in a way, not to have to speak too much, because she was still reeling from Kaz's comments.

He pressed Kaz to be more precise. "Around the time you got mixed up with the county lines gang?"

Kaz's eyes narrowed. Marie offered reassurance. "I don't think the police are here to charge you with anything, Kaz. They just want information." She looked at Elias, who nodded.

Steph found her voice again. "It's likely you'd be regarded as a victim, if anything." Not every judge would see it that way, she knew, but didn't say.

Looking at Elias, Kaz said, "A man came up to me on the street. He told me Cole's patch and all his customers were under new management, so to speak. I was clean by then, hadn't been using for a while. He must have got my details from Cole. I told him I wasn't interested, but he asked me along to the pub and we got talking. He came home with me and soft-talked his way inside my house.

"I didn't mind, not at first. He seemed genuinely interested in me, and, yeah, we had sex. More fool me. Next thing I know, he's turned my place into a trap house. Can't say anything, really, can I though? It was me who let him in. Next thing I know he's drugging me up. Nothing bad, just something that made me sleep a lot."

"He deceived you," Elias said. "Led you to believe he was romantically interested in you, then used your home as a base for dealing drugs. You were exploited."

Kaz gave a snort. "Romantically interested? That's one way of putting it. I should have known. I mean, look at me. Not much of a catch, am I?"

Elias looked embarrassed. Marie pressed Kaz's arm. "No one's judging you, Kaz."

"Did he tell you his name?" Steph asked.

"He told me everyone called him Shark. I'm guessing that wasn't his real name. His mate, 'Wolf—" she rolled her eyes — "came along within a couple of days. He brought some kids with him. A boy and a girl. Never saw them much after that. I was locked in my room most of the time. They'd bring me something to eat, chips or sandwiches and a cup of tea. I was asleep most of the time, so I didn't need much."

Elias looked at her sharply. "Were you ever threatened, or beaten?"

Kaz shrugged. "Only when I kicked off."

"Did you carry on having sexual relations with Shark?" Steph asked.

"From time to time."

"Was it consensual?"

"I didn't get much say in the matter."

"No, then." Steph was grim-faced. "Can you describe Shark and Wolf to us?"

"They were white." Kaz ran her palm over her scalp. "Shark had a tattoo on his head. A black web-like pattern."

Elias and Steph exchanged a look.

Kaz was sharp. "What? Do you know him?"

"Your description matches one we were given recently, in connection with Cole Burke."

"Did he kill Cole?" Kaz asked.

Elias shook his head. "We don't know. What about Wolf?"

"Big, bushy beard." She frowned. "That's all. I can't get a picture of him."

"The kids. What can you tell us about them? For example, how many were there? Did you learn their names?" Steph asked.

Kaz picked at her sleeve. "Can't tell you much. I wasn't allowed out of my room a lot, remember? I think there were just two of them at first, a boy and a girl, then more recently, another boy. Other kids came and went, I think, sometimes with Shark or Wolf, sometimes on their own. And there was another man too, with a young-sounding voice. Wes. Shark and Wolf were in and out, but he was there most of the time, from what I could tell." She gave a sniff. "Then again, I was doped to the eyeballs a lot, as I said, so who knows what was real or not?"

Her voice had seemed to soften when she mentioned the children. Steph was slightly shocked to hear the reason why. "I had a kid once. In London. She was taken off me because

129

I couldn't look after her properly. Best thing for her. She's with a nice family now. If she'd stayed with me, she'd have probably ended up like those poor kids."

Steph had a sudden memory, of Karen in a science lesson when they were in their first year at secondary school. The teacher had left the room and a couple of boys had gone into the big walk-in cupboard behind her desk and taken one of the rats from its cage. They'd held it up by its tail and dangled it in front of everyone. Most of the class shied away, but Karen marched up to the boys, grabbed the terrified creature and held it to her, comforting it before returning it to the cupboard. Karen, who had really been quite brave and fearless about most things, who'd been all heart, how had she ended up like this? A person who couldn't even be bothered to wash, and who smelled bad? A person who'd had her child taken from her.

Steph didn't want to remember things about Karen, because it might lead to complicated emotions that she didn't have the time or the inclination to deal with. She particularly wanted to avoid feeling pity for her. Pity, as Steph reminded herself constantly, was like love. It made you drop your defences.

Karen, or Kaz, as she had become, had dropped her defences for the promise of love when she met Shark. Look where that had got her. Look where falling for Cal had . . . *Stop it!*

It would have been a small thing to offer some words of comfort to Kaz, then, but Steph left it to Marie and Elias to make the appropriate noises and gestures.

The session ended soon after that. Some useful facts emerged. Kaz had had a TV in her bedroom and so was able to keep track of time. She was thus able to tell them when the third boy had joined the others in her house. It matched the date of Cole Burke's murder, making it more likely that the boy was Nate. If her testimony could be believed, of course.

It also helped them establish when the offenders had left Kaz's flat. A wakeful neighbour or someone in the area might have seen something. Nate — if it was him — had spent just over two weeks at Kaz's house, but the house had been cuckooed for longer than that.

It was a tense walk back to the station. Steph expected an interrogation of some description from Elias and was surprised when he walked beside her in silence for most of the way, his eyes on the road ahead. Then, as they turned into the street leading to the station, he began humming. It took a moment for Steph to pick out the tune, and when she did, she flushed with annoyance.

Dee dee dee DEE dee. Dee dee dee DEE dee — You are my sunshine. My only sunshine.

"Don't."

Elias looked all innocence. "Would you—?"

"I said don't. It's none of your business. What that woman said—"

Elias pointed at the café across the street. "I was only going to ask if I could get you a coffee, but since you brought it up, you're right. It's not my business whether you've undergone a personality shift since Kaz knew you as a little ray of sunshine."

He regarded her with uncharacteristic chilliness. "But it is my business if it interferes with your ability to do your job. I meant what I said about keeping an eye on you. You can't afford to let your personal issues threaten another investigation."

Steph was about to unleash her fury on him, when his expression softened. "You know, you should understand that by keeping an eye on you, I also mean watching out for you. Having your back. I'm not your enemy."

"I don't need you or anyone else watching my back."

Elias shook his head and, seeing a gap in the traffic, stepped out into the road.

Steph watched him, experiencing a dizzying flux of emotions. For a split second, she considered calling out after him. She wanted to tell him she was sorry, that he was right, he wasn't her enemy.

Except she was afraid of what that might mean. For, if not her enemy, what did that make him? A friend? Someone she could trust?

Muttering an oath, Steph turned, quickening her pace. She didn't have time for this.

CHAPTER NINETEEN

Jane
28 May 2019

Jane swallowed. *Here goes.* She stepped up to the door of the house on the Cathedral Estate where she'd established that Drew Wilson lived with his sister, Shelby. Glancing over her shoulder, she waited for someone to answer her knock, but no one did. She wondered if Shelby would have recognised her if she'd been at home. A good few years had passed since Jane had taught her at Ollie Granger's.

Jane leaned on the wall for balance and tried to peek in the window. As she did, she heard the door of the neighbouring house squeak open.

"Shel's not there. They've both gone away." The voice belonged to a woman in her mid-to-late-twenties dressed in the uniform of an upmarket local supermarket. "You from social services?"

"No," Jane said. "I'm an old acquaintance of Shelby's. Do you know when she'll be back?"

"Not a clue."

"Has her brother Drew gone with her, do you know?"

At once, the woman's eyes narrowed with suspicion. "Why do you want to know about Drew?"

"No reason. I just wondered if she was still looking after him." The woman was curious, but also wary. How could she obtain her trust? "I'm Shelby's old English teacher. She loved English when she was in my class at Ollie Granger's."

The pinched face relaxed. "What's your name?"

"Jane Bell."

"Mrs Bell! You should have said. Shelby's always talking about you and saying what an inspirational teacher you were."

Jane was genuinely touched. "Really? That's lovely. Just the sort of thing an old teacher loves to hear."

The woman tutted. "You're not old. Shel's always reading, you know. She lends me books but I don't always read them. It's a shame you've missed her."

"Is she all right? And her brother?" Jane was keen to keep the woman talking. She sensed that she knew more than she was saying.

Suspicion returned to the woman's eyes at the mention of Shelby's brother, but this time it didn't seem to be directed at Jane. She looked up and down the street. "Look, do you want to come in? I've just got home from work, and I've got an hour or so before I pick my Jessie up from nursery."

"Thank you," Jane said. *Mission accomplished.*

"I'm Faye Crowther," the woman said, showing Jane inside. "Grab a pew while I put the kettle on."

Jane sat down on a cream faux-leather sofa opposite one of the biggest TVs she'd ever seen. Much too large for the size of the room. There were several plastic boxes tidied up against the wall under the window, overflowing with children's toys, the predominant colour being pink. Jane hoped little Jessie would one day escape the mould of little princess. There was nothing in the room to suggest a male presence in the house. Either it was all upstairs or Faye was a single parent.

Faye handed Jane a mug of tea and sat down beside her. "Saw you admiring my telly. Shel loves it too. She often comes round to watch something with me when Drew's at school and Jessie's asleep, or at nursery." Her eyes rested on the TV.

"You must miss her company," Jane said.

"Oh, yes. She's lovely, Shel. Never complains about having to look after Drew either, though it's not been easy for her lately." There was a pause.

Jane held her breath, hoping she'd won Faye's confidence sufficiently for her to feel comfortable confiding in her.

Faye sighed. "Drew was a lovely, bright little boy until he went to secondary school last September — actually maybe it all started a bit before that. During the summer break he started going out for longer and longer during the day. When Shel asked him what he was up to, he'd tell her he was playing football, or hanging out with his mates. A few times, he stayed out until late in the evening, and when Shel challenged him over it, he got angry and said she couldn't tell him what to do. She wasn't his mum. Poor Shel, that really upset her after she'd tried so hard to make up for them losing their mum."

Jane nodded. "That is very sad."

"I told her it must be his hormones — to cheer her up, even though we both knew he was a bit young to be turning into a rebellious teenager."

"It must have upset her a lot."

"Yes. The school started getting on to her too, complaining about Drew's behaviour and all his absences. That was news to Shel. She'd had no idea he was bunking off. She told the teachers he was sick and that she'd forgotten to write him a note. She was scared they'd take him off her otherwise."

Jane noticed how Faye had become hesitant as she spoke. Was it because she was concerned that she was saying too much, or because she wanted to say a lot more but was holding back?

Wary of sounding pushy, Jane said, "Such a worrying time for her."

"You don't know the half of it." Faye stared at the blank TV screen.

135

"Look. Tell me it's none of my business, but I can sense something's wrong. Do you want to talk about it?" Jane said.

"I . . . I said I wouldn't tell anyone."

Jane squeezed Faye's arm. "You can trust me, Faye. I promise."

Faye was astute. She said, "You didn't just decide to look up your old student, did you? Why did you really come?"

It seemed best to tell the truth. "I gave up teaching full-time a few years ago and now I do part-time tutoring. The year before last, I applied to become a special constable. I recently gave a talk about drugs at George Boole Academy, and afterwards a young lad came up to me to say that he was worried about his friend."

Faye nodded. "He was talking about Drew."

"Yes."

"Why didn't you just tell me from the start that you're police?"

"I'm sorry. I was genuinely interested in Shelby when I heard that her life hadn't worked out as expected. I'd always assumed she'd go to university. So, when I heard she was looking after her brother, I really did want to check that she was okay. I wasn't just here on police business."

Faye leaned forwards, resting her elbows on her knees. "Everything isn't okay."

"Go on."

"Shel was going out of her mind trying to deal with Drew's behaviour. Things kind of came to a head one evening when he confessed to Shel that he'd been going to a drug dealer's place with some boys he'd been hanging out with. He admitted he'd 'delivered a couple of packages' for him. Shel was terrified. She got some advice from a . . . a friend of hers, and he said the best thing would be for her and Drew to go away for a while until things settled down."

She closed her eyes and made a pained face. When she opened them, she didn't look at Jane as she had done before but stared down at the carpet.

"I . . . I don't know all the details. Sorry."

136

Jane said nothing. Again, she had the sense that Faye was holding back. It seemed to her unlikely that Shelby would just up and leave her home like that. She must have really trusted her friend to take his advice. And why on earth hadn't she gone to the police if she suspected Drew might be in danger? Was it because Drew had been involved with the drug dealer and she feared he would be charged with something? That she feared she'd be considered unfit to look after him? She really needed to speak with Shelby.

Faye fell into silence. Jane asked, "Where did Shelby and Drew go, Faye?"

"She didn't want me to know. She said if I didn't know I couldn't tell people where they were if they came after her and Drew. She called it 'plausible deniability'. That means—"

"I know what it means," Jane said. "It also means that she is a good friend who wouldn't put someone she cared about in danger."

Faye bit her lip.

"I know you can't tell me if you don't know, but maybe you have an idea about where she might have gone. Was there a friend or relative she visited from time to time? Or maybe she mentioned a place where she'd been on holiday? A place where she'd felt safe?"

Faye cast her eyes downwards. "I . . . I'm not sure." She frowned. "No, wait. Maybe I do know where she might have gone. Once when we were chatting, we discussed maybe going on holiday somewhere with the kids. She said she had a friend who had a caravan in the Wolds. He'd offered to let her rent it cheaply if she wanted to get away with Drew any time. She was going to ask him if we could go there this summer."

"Did she tell you her friend's name?"

Faye frowned again. After a few moments, she shook her head. "I'm sorry. She did tell me, but I can't remember. All I know is that he used to give her piano lessons. She plays the piano really nicely, but she had to give up taking lessons when her mum died."

A music teacher. It would take a long time for one person to locate and talk with every man who taught piano in the area. "Well, that's something to work with. Thanks, Faye."

"I'm glad you're not proper police," Faye told her. "That way, I haven't broken my promise to Shelby not to speak to the police. I don't think she'd mind me talking to you."

Jane smiled, not in the least minding Faye's comment about proper police.

"What will you do now?" Faye asked. "Will you try to find Shel and Drew? Can you help them if you do?"

"Yes. I intend to try."

"If you do, will you let me know if they're okay?"

"Of course. And if you remember the name of Shelby's piano teacher—"

"I'll let you know."

Jane suddenly remembered what else she should ask Faye. "Faye, did Drew or his mum ever mention a boy called Nate?"

"No, not that I remember." Faye looked at the time. "I have to go and collect Jessie now. Shall we exchange phone numbers?"

Jane nodded. They went to the door together, Faye carrying her daughter's scooter. Jane waved to her a moment or two later as she drove past.

She still had a niggling feeling that there was something Faye hadn't told her.

CHAPTER TWENTY

Nate
May 2019

Nate lay awake in the middle of the night wondering at the swiftness with which his life had unravelled. There'd been nothing for it but to try to adjust to the situation.

Along with Lana and Dex, he was locked in a bedroom every night at the same time and let out at whatever time Wes cared to get up, usually mid-morning, by which time all three of them were beyond hungry.

Breakfast — any meal, in fact — wasn't a given, and there was no such thing as regular mealtimes. There never seemed to be enough food. Mostly, their diet consisted of carbs — microwavable meals or takeaways — endless bags of greasy chips, or pizza, never enough portions to go around, so that their hunger was never quite satisfied.

Much of the time, they were put to work weighing and bagging crack and heroin. Lana and Dex showed Nate what to do. The drugs arrived twice a week, brought by kids, some of whom looked even younger than Nate. They only ever spoke to Wes, who took them upstairs as soon as they arrived.

Nate felt sick to his stomach when Dex explained how the drugs were often transported inside their bodies.

When they weren't busy with the drugs, there wasn't much to do except watch TV or read the same comics over and over.

Nate wasn't allowed out, presumably in case someone recognised him, but he knew that wasn't likely. He hardly knew anyone in Lincoln, and even though he would be missed at school, he doubted anyone would be looking for him. Kids like him went missing all the time, almost like it was expected of them.

Dex and Lana carried out a lot of the local deliveries, mostly in the mid-afternoon or evening so nobody would question why they weren't at school, but also whenever a client got fed up waiting.

Nate never saw the woman whose house they were occupying. She never came downstairs. She was as much a prisoner as he, Dex and Lana. Sometimes she banged on her bedroom door for attention. Wes would have to respond in case the neighbours complained about the noise. He soon shut her up.

Most of the time, Nate felt angry and on edge, jumping whenever he heard the door in case it was Shark or Wolf, either of whom would turn up without warning at odd hours of the day or night, sometimes bringing another kid with them. A man travelling in a car with a child on board was less likely to arouse suspicion.

It was all Angie's fault. She should have taken proper care of him. Drinking meant more to her than her son did. Served her right if she was worried about him. Mind you, she probably hadn't even missed him. He'd been staying over at Cole's place more and more often before Wolf took him, and she probably assumed that's where he was now, if she thought about him at all. *Alcoholism's a disease. So what? She still could have gone to AA or something.*

Maybe the 'authorities' would start asking questions. His mum would have to answer as to his whereabouts and if she couldn't, they'd have to start looking for him, but he doubted he'd be on the news like those kids from good homes that the police search for, leaving no stone unturned.

Nate sighed. He looked around the bedroom he shared with Lana and Dex. Both of them were fast asleep on their mattresses on the floor. Lana's was under the window. Light from a streetlight seeped from under the blackout curtain, illuminating her pale, sharp features. Nate studied her, absently, for a bit, noticing the way that her long eyelashes fluttered as her eyes moved rapidly under her closed eyelids. He hoped she was dreaming about something nice.

His own dreams made him restless and fearful. Time and again he'd woken with a start, not always able to recall the content, but knowing with absolute certainty that it hadn't been sweet. He'd wake with his T-shirt soaked through, a crushing sensation of dread gripping his chest, making it hard to breathe.

"Pretty, isn't she? Bet you fancy her, don't you?" Dex's whisper made him start.

A beat too fast, Nate said, "No!"

Dex shrugged. "Whatever." He turned his back on Nate, pulling the thin cover over his head.

Nate's gaze shifted back to Lana. With a sting of embarrassment, he saw that she was awake and looking at him. Had she heard Dex's remark? Nate took his cue from Dex and rolled on to his side so that Lana couldn't see his face. His cheek burned against the mattress.

The following morning, he avoided looking at Lana. To his surprise, Dex didn't make any snide remarks to him about her. Maybe he'd been too sleepy to remember.

There was nothing to do that morning while they waited for the latest delivery. Wes was streaming a film about gangsters that Nate found hard to follow. It was all swearing and violence as far as he could tell. He, Lana and Dex were lounging around, rereading comics, as usual. They were interrupted by the sound of banging from upstairs.

Wes jumped up, his right hand already balled into a fist. "Bitch never learns. I'll smash her ugly face in." He left the room.

After a few minutes, Lana said to Nate in an urgent voice. "I heard Wes talking to Wolf on his phone. We're moving to a new place tomorrow. This one's getting too hot."

"Right." Nate avoided looking at her, still conscious of what Dex had said in the night.

"Wolf or Shark will come to drive us there. Whatever you do, don't upset them, especially Wolf. You haven't been around Wolf much. You don't know what he's like."

"Yes, I do," Nate said. He told her about Cole. The fingers in the glass.

Lana nodded. "Yeah, well. I've seen the way you look at Wes and how you want to get away from here. Me and Dex want to get away too, but we're not stupid. We know we can't. You don't get that yet, but you need to learn 'cause me and Dex don't want you bringing us more trouble. So if you're thinking tomorrow's move will give you the chance you're waiting for, forget it. Whatever you do, it won't work, and we'll all be the worse off for you trying."

Nate didn't appreciate the way Lana prodded him in the chest as she neared the end of her speech. "Remember what I said."

Dex backed her up. "She's right. Don't do anything stupid. You're not the only one who'll suffer if you wind Wolf up."

Nate just looked across at the window, picturing himself ripping apart the permanently-drawn curtains and smashing through the glass — only one of the fantasies of escape he envisioned a dozen times a day. He knew what Lana and Dex wanted him to say but he remained stubbornly silent.

All that day his head swirled with ideas and fears. He got why Lana and Dex didn't dare run away, why they were so scared he'd try. No one wants to be responsible for bringing harm to their loved ones, or to themselves, but it didn't stop him wanting to make the attempt.

Later, in the small hours, locked in the bedroom for what might be his last night in this house, he was still conflicted. Angie wasn't the best mum, but she'd done her best.

142

Alcoholism was a disease, he reminded himself yet again. It wasn't her fault she'd caught it. She didn't deserve to be beaten or killed because he'd got himself into this situation in the first place.

He'd known all along what was in those packages he delivered for Cole. He could have just walked away. It wasn't as if Cole had ever cared about him, that much was obvious now. Cole had used him to save himself from getting caught in possession of Class A drugs.

Nate understood how stupid he'd been. *Stupid. Stupid. Stupid.* There was a word for what adults did to kids like him. It was called 'grooming'. The police had come to his primary school to warn the kids about it.

"These people will pretend to be your friend, but they're not." Nate had only been half-listening. The rest of his mind had been occupied with reconstructing the football game he'd watched at the weekend. He should have listened more attentively. Then he might have seen through Wes and Cole. Maybe Cole had never really been his friend, but Nate still felt sorry for what had happened to him.

He pulled the cover up around his face and closed his eyes. Lana's mattress creaked as she turned and turned, trying to get comfortable. The mattresses were old and stained, and if you rolled onto the wrong part, you could feel the springs jabbing you. Bugs bit him in the night. His body was covered with little red swellings. If the amount of scratching Lana and Dex did was anything to go by, they had the same problem.

We're like those neglected kids you see in pictures from books about the olden days, he thought. Thin because they didn't get enough to eat, or ate the wrong things, itchy and unwashed.

They all smelled bad. Except Wes. His clothes were clean and smelled fresh. Every so often he'd disappear for a couple of days and Shark, or another man, would take his place. When Wes came back, he wore different clothes and he always brought a bag with him, crammed with clean gear and luxuries from the outside world.

Lana was awake. He could tell by the way she was breathing. If he could tell she was awake, she could probably tell that he was too. He wondered what she was thinking about, whether he was the cause of her wakefulness. Was she lying there worrying what he might do the following day, the danger he might put them all in if he tried to escape during the move? He felt a shiver of guilt.

He must have drifted off to sleep eventually, for the next thing he knew, Wes was kicking the side of his mattress and shouting at him to get up.

Wes looked at the three of them, startled out of sleep, but already bolt upright and alert. "Get your shit together. We're moving out today. And be quick about it."

He left the room.

What shit? Nate had no possessions to pack, and he hadn't seen Lana or Dex with any either.

Everyone was nervous about Wolf and Shark's arrival. You could have cut the tension with a knife.

Wes prowled the room, or sat, watching the telly and smoking. Every now and again, he jumped up, drawn to the gap in the curtains by the sound of an approaching car.

Lana chewed her fingernails. Dex kept making trips to the toilet. Nate's left leg juddered against his right.

It was late evening when a car stopped outside the window. "Here we go," Wes said, as Dex jumped up and made as if to go to the toilet again. "Where the hell d'you think you're going, Short Arse? We don't keep Wolf waiting, remember?"

Within moments, Wolf strode into the front room, casting his gaze around, taking in the assembled people, the empty cans and pizza boxes and dirty mugs and plates. "What a shithole."

Wes bent to pick up a discarded can, making Wolf snort. Then, he growled. "Leave it, man. I don't give a shit how you like to live. We good to go?" He looked around again. "Where's our hostess?"

"Upstairs. She's wasted, man. No need to worry about her."

Wolf nodded. "Get them in the car."

Wes glared at the three of them. "You heard him. Let's get going. And no noise, all right?"

Outside, Nate took a last look at the house where he'd been imprisoned for who knew how many weeks. He gulped in the fresh night air. It made him feel lightheaded, but not for long. A hand clamped down hard on his head, guiding him into the back seat of the car after Dex and Wes.

Lana was in the front seat next to Wolf, sitting so stiffly straight she might have been one of the carved stone statues set in the recesses of the cathedral's walls. Nate was in the back, Wes between him and Dex, watching them. He'd already shown them the tip of a knife concealed up his sleeve.

Nate recognised the streets he'd been marched along on his way to the trap house, weeks ago. The big church on the corner, St Katherine's, he remembered. It seemed like a lifetime ago. He recognised the barber's shop under Cole's flat as they drove past and shuddered, remembering Cole the last time he'd seen him, bruised and bloodied, his severed fingers in a glass on the table in front of him.

Soon, Nate saw another familiar sight, the cathedral, high on the hill, softly floodlit. It made him think, suddenly, of his old friends Charlie and Alfie, and of things that were grounded and safe. The lump in his throat made it hard to swallow.

Another few minutes and they were alongside the cathedral, the car slowing to stop at the lights. A couple of oncoming cars filtered through a stone arch a little way ahead. Wolf swore, impatient at the delay.

A couple of pedestrians turned a corner, walked towards them. "Everybody behave," Wes warned, eyes on the couple until they were safely past.

When the car began to move, Nate gazed after them. Would they have turned their heads if he'd hammered on the window? Even if they had, they'd have thought he was just some stupid kid messing about.

The car stopped again, just minutes later. More lights. Wolf punched the steering wheel in frustration. Nate knew he wouldn't dare run the lights. It wasn't worth the risk of being stopped by the police. There wasn't a soul about. The only cars in sight were far away at the opposite side of the junction.

Suddenly and without warning, Lana sprang forward in her seat. There was a clicking sound. She threw herself at Wolf, screaming, "Go, Nate!"

It took a split second for Nate to realise that she'd just deactivated the central locking. He moved fast, unbuckling his seatbelt, lunging against the door. He tumbled out onto the road, Wolf's roar booming after him. "Get him! For fuck's sake! Get him!"

A rush of adrenalin helped him to his feet, and he was off, charging along the pavement, Wes close on his heels.

If only some moron hadn't left that stupid bag of rubbish on the pavement — Nate crashed to the ground.

Wes was on him in a beat, pulling him — surprisingly gently — to his feet, putting his arm around his shoulders, dusting him down in apparent concern. This would have seemed confusing had Wes not kept up a running commentary. "I've got a knife. Get up. Pretend we're mates larking about. Start walking towards the car, then get in."

Nate glanced sideways at Wes as they walked back to the car. All he could see was the tip of Wes's nose sticking out from the side of his hood. It dawned on him then. They were acting out in case there were security cameras.

Lana was staring straight ahead when he passed her window. He caught sight of her pale, strained face, her bloodied mouth. But it was the look of sheer terror in her eyes that made his blood run cold, because it told him that Wolf hadn't even begun to take his revenge.

CHAPTER TWENTY-ONE

Steph
15 May 2019

Steph's request for authorisation to use a Covert Human Intelligence Source, a CHIS, was granted by the superintendent. She'd read the CHIS's file with interest. His name was Alec Healey, born and bred in Livingstone, a West Lothian town lying between Glasgow and Edinburgh.

Healey had served time for drugs offences but was now a reformed character. Steph didn't know whether she trusted him. Post Cal, she was wary of relying solely on her own judgement to gauge a person's character. What she did know was that Healey had successfully infiltrated a drugs ring operating in some of the coastal towns of Lincolnshire, leading to many arrests and major disruption in the supply chain. Far better to judge people by their actions and experience than by her own subjective feelings towards them. Gut instinct was often unreliable.

She wasn't permitted to meet Healey in person because of the need to maintain a 'sterile corridor' between the investigating officers and the covert operative, so Steph spoke with Healey by phone, his handler Greg Boyce listening in.

"I'd like to run through the brief and fill in some of the minor details with you. That okay with you, Alec? I know Greg's been through it with you already."

He responded in a broad Scots accent. "Aye. Fire away, hen. Sounds like the kinda thing I've done before."

Steph nodded. "What we're asking you to do sounds straightforward enough — speak to the people on the streets and obtain information — but it's part of an ongoing investigation into the murder of a young man, Cole Burke, who was tortured prior to being killed. I mention this because I don't want you going into this thinking there are few risks involved just because you're not going to be penetrating a gang and dealing directly with the bad guys. You need to be aware of who and what we're dealing with here."

"Where drugs are concerned there's always risk factors, hen. I'm no stupit."

Steph raised an eyebrow. She told him in more detail about the circumstances of Cole's death, about Shane Watt's disappearance, and about Nate, whom they feared might be holed up in a cuckooed house against his will.

"Obviously, locating Nate is a priority. While he's being held captive, his safety can't be guaranteed. We had been hoping that Shane Watt might be able to give us some pointers."

Healey responded without hesitation. "Leave it to me."

They spent some time discussing how Healey would go about establishing himself in the city without raising suspicion. A backstory had been put together to explain his presence in Lincolnshire. They ran through it, tweaking it until everyone was happy.

Healey was to pose as a Scot who'd come to Lincolnshire looking for work, bringing his drug habit with him. He'd managed to find some seasonal work in the fields and in the seaside towns. Now, he'd come to Lincoln to try and find a more permanent job. He was renting a bedsit in the St Catherine's area of the city.

"You'll be asking questions on the street, finding out where you can get your fix. We're hoping to get approval for surveillance, which might, eventually lead us to the cuckooed house. We've asked the superintendent for specialist support from EMSOU but for now, you're our best bet."

"Fine by me. As I said, I've done this sort of thing before," Alec said.

After a little more discussion, they agreed a time and place for Healey to speak with them again, and Steph ended the call.

It wasn't the first time she had worked with a CHIS. The shadowy world of covert policing was something that she had equivocal feelings about. A CHIS was commonly someone with a criminal past, or even still engaged in criminal activity, perhaps seeking leniency from the courts by cooperating with the police in their investigations. Some were like Healey, looking to atone for past crimes. Others were seeking revenge. And, of course, some were police officers working under cover.

The use of Covert Human Intelligence Sources wasn't without controversy. One of the issues was how far they should be allowed to go in order to maintain their cover. There were well-documented cases of covert officers engaging in criminal activities to maintain their secret identity. In some instances, the activities were justifiable — after all, a person couldn't infiltrate a drugs gang, then refuse to shift drugs — but other cases were more of a grey area. Steph thought of the undercover officers who had entered into sexual relationships with female activists as part of their cover. This was the kind of thing that made her feel uncomfortable.

There was no doubt that CHIS played a big role in the fight against criminal activities such as terrorism, child sexual exploitation, drugs and organised crime. Infiltrating groups enabled them to access intelligence that could not be obtained by any other means. But at what point could it be said that police and other authorised agencies had crossed a line? Should they, for example, be allowed to get away with murder? Clarification on these matters was desirable, particularly as the level of violence committed by drugs gangs had escalated in recent years.

Steph didn't concern herself with the politics. It was up to politicians and lawmakers to argue the legal and moral issues thrown up by the use of CHIS. Healey was unlikely to have to resort to anything more criminal than buying a few grams of crack.

She briefed Elias on the conversation she'd had with Boyce and Healey. He nodded but seemed distracted. By now Steph was beginning to recognise when he was troubled about something. "What's bothering you?" she asked.

He gave a heavy sigh. "I was just thinking about the kids caught up in all of this. Even with all the safeguarding precautions that are in place these days — the multi-agency cooperation and information sharing — kids like Nate still fall through the net."

"There are some explanations for that. Nate's mum was late in enrolling him at secondary school in Lincoln. The school has confirmed that there was a delay in his records being sent over from his previous school, and anyway, when the records did arrive, they didn't flag up any serious issues. Maybe Angie Price was good at covering up her alcohol problem. Nate wouldn't have been on their radar immediately. Then there's the fact that Nate was transitioning from primary to secondary school. Form teachers have a lot on their plate. They're not always going to notice when a kid's got issues out of school. Add in the fact that he was in a new, unfamiliar neighbourhood, an environment where he hardly knew anyone. He went out on his own and got targeted by someone looking out for kids just like him. When you take all that into account, it's not so strange." Elias nodded. "His frequent absences were noted, but he always brought a letter signed by his mother to explain them. Four bouts of tonsilitis in a three-month period. We now know that it wasn't Angie writing those letters. Guess the school didn't look into it in any depth because they believed his mother was backing him up. Well, he's on our radar now, and the PVPU will be working with us to obtain a better outcome for him. He'll be brought to the attention of social services, and they'll assess his needs and devise a child protection plan for him. I know it sounds a bit like locking the stable door after the horse has bolted, but with the best will in the world, some kids just won't be picked up before something bad happens to them."

Steph was aware that her words weren't particularly encouraging, but she preferred to be realistic about these things. The truth was that the numbers of children put at risk by county lines could seem overwhelming.

The PVPU — Protecting Vulnerable People Unit — was a specialist department within Lincolnshire Police, the remit of which included the protection of children and vulnerable adults, as well as the investigation of sexual abuse and domestic abuse. The unit was made up of detectives, uniformed officers working in plain clothes, and police staff. Steph had already liaised with a DS from the unit to alert them to Nate's case.

She'd had to admire the efficient and calm way in which the DS had listened, commenting only when necessary. Working for the PVPU could be harrowing. It wasn't for everybody. Coming into contact with the most vulnerable victims and the most dangerous offenders on a daily basis took its toll. Rigorous support measures, such as regular meetings with Force Occupational Health, were in place to address staff wellbeing.

Elias remained sceptical. "I read about a fifteen-year-old just the other day. His situation was different from Nate's — he had nurturing, clued-up parents, but once he fell under the influence of a drugs gang, it was as if he moved beyond help. He was so terrified that the gang would kill him or a member of his family that every time they summoned him on his burner phone, he went back. He'd disappear for days at a time, and his parents had no idea where he was. They enlisted help from the police, social services, all of whom got involved — but whatever they did, it wasn't enough. You know, all that kid had to look forward to in the future was a prison sentence. That, or being knifed by one of the gang." He gave a deep sigh. "If we find Nate, who knows what shape he'll be in? Who knows if he'll be beyond help too?"

Steph raked her fingers through her hair. Elias's negativity was beginning to grate. "*When* we find him, Sergeant. He's safe as long as he does as he's told and they have a use for him. There's even a possibility they're treating him okay. County lines tactics are evolving all the time. There are some gangs who've cottoned on that fear and intimidation aren't the best way of retaining a loyal workforce. Some of them are reputedly paying the kids generously for their work now, offering them the opportunity to rise through the ranks."

"After seeing what they did to Cole, I'm inclined to believe the people we're dealing with are the type who would favour an economic model that relied on coercion over reward and promotion." Elias looked downcast. "Apologies if I'm sounding like the voice of doom. It's just . . . kids, you know. I can't stand the thought of them suffering. Always gets to me. I don't know how anyone can specialise in that area of police work."

"Well, none of us can stand cases involving kids. They're the worst. But you need to toughen up, Sergeant. You'll never make it in this job otherwise. You're one of the noble people who join the force to help people. I get that, but how can you help anyone if you're sponging up all the emotional pain and anguish around you? You'll end up just wallowing in misery, no use to anybody—" Steph stopped abruptly. "Too much?"

Elias smiled. "Maybe should have stopped a few sentences ago. Right before you accused me of being an emotional sponge. I can't help it if I soak everything up. I'm an actor."

"You're a police officer. A detective," Steph reminded him. "Unless you're thinking of jacking it in and going back on the stage."

Steph was surprised to discover that the thought bothered her. She'd grown accustomed to having Elias as her sergeant, even though she didn't completely trust him.

"Would you miss me if I did?"

"It would be tiresome to have to train up your replacement."

"Good to know I'm appreciated."

CHAPTER TWENTY-TWO

Jane
29 May 2019

Jane passed Mr Kendrick on her way to the counter in Veganbites and smiled at him. He nodded in return. Mr Kendrick was a regular at the café. He always sat at the same table near the window so that he could watch the world go by on Burton Road. At his side was his constant companion, not a dog but his violin in its worn case, lying flat on the wide windowsill. Jane had never seen him without it.

All she really knew about Mr Kendrick was that he had taught at Ollie Granger's before her time there. She'd heard the story about him walking out on his class one day and sitting in the staffroom playing his violin and refusing to budge until his wife came to coax him home. He'd never returned to the school. It was said that he'd suffered a mental health crisis, what Jane's grandmother would have called a nervous breakdown. Nowadays, he was often to be seen busking in the Bail, or somewhere on the High Street, his open violin case full of copper and silver.

To Jane, he didn't seem like someone who had lost his wits. He seemed to radiate a sense of serenity that had a calming effect on her whenever she spotted him sitting there alone, sipping his tea. Frieda often chatted to him. She thought he was lonely. Frieda often confused sitting alone with loneliness — she'd said the same about DI Warwick. Jane was of the opinion that Warwick sat alone out of preference. She seemed the type who was irrationally irritated by other people in her vicinity.

Frieda spotted her from the open door of the kitchen. "Hi, Janie. I'll be with you in a mo." She was as good as her word.

Jane looked over her shoulder. "Where's Thea?"

"On a break. She's gone to do some errands in the Bail."

"I see Mr Kendrick's here again."

Frieda looked across at him with fondness. "Bless him. He's such a lovely man. So courteous. And so talented. A real maestro. He played for the London Philharmonic as a young man, you know, but he suffered from stage fright and had to abandon his career as a musician. So tragic."

Jane nodded. She'd heard Mr Kendrick play and had often been struck by how good he was. He always drew a big crowd on a warm day. "That is sad. Teaching stressed him out too. I wonder why he doesn't give private tuition." Jane had a sudden thought. "Oh!"

Frieda looked at her sharply. "What's up?"

"Nothing. I just thought of something that Mr Kendrick might be able to help me with. Do you think he'd mind some company?"

"I think he'd be quite pleased. No one ever talks to him except me and a couple of old ladies who come in for coffee and bring their own cake. They think I don't notice, but you'd have to be wearing blinkers not to see what they're up to."

Jane laughed. "Perhaps if you started serving cakes with butter and real cream, they'd be more tempted."

Frieda took her order, and Jane made her way over to an empty table next to Mr Kendrick. He looked up and nodded at her again as she pulled out a chair, then turned his attention back to the world beyond the window.

Jane let a few moments pass before she spoke to him. "Excuse me. It's Mr Kendrick, isn't it? I've seen you in here often enough, so I thought it was about time I introduced myself. I'm Jane Bell. I don't know if you know, but we have something in common. We both escaped from Ollie Granger's."

Mr Kendrick turned his serene gaze on her. She hoped she hadn't offended him. "You've probably heard about the manner of my leaving then."

"Er . . . yes. I'm sorry. It was insensitive of me to refer to your old school."

He waved a hand to show it wasn't an issue. "It doesn't matter. I wasn't cut out to be a teacher in any case. I'm afraid I blundered into it and stayed in the profession far too long. I should have realised the effect it was having on my mental health."

"I think I got out just in time," Jane said.

Frieda approached with Jane's coffee. "I told Jane that you once played with one of the big London orchestras, Mr Kendrick. I hope you don't mind. She'd just been saying how well you play."

Mr Kendrick nodded, emanating serenity and good humour. When Frieda moved away, he said to Jane, "I expect you've heard about the manner of my leaving that profession too?"

"Stage fright. I'm so sorry."

"Don't be," Mr Kendrick said. "It's all a long time ago now."

"Not so very long, surely?" Jane said. She hadn't really thought about Mr Kendrick's age. He did have grey-white hair, which he wore in a ponytail, but his face was relatively unlined.

He didn't answer, but he didn't look away either, which Jane took as a positive sign. "I still do a bit of teaching. Tutoring, to be specific. Much less exhausting, and I can work as much or as little as I please. Have you ever thought of giving private music lessons?"

"It never appealed to me, and I don't need the money. I was fortunate enough to receive an inheritance from my mother."

"And there's your busking," Jane said.

Mr Kendrick smiled. "I'm not about to get rich that way, but I've found that now there's no pressure on me to perform, I quite enjoy having an audience. I play the fiddle in a little folk group too."

Jane was glad he had found an outlet for his talent and said so. Then, she asked the question that was on her mind. "I'm trying to track down a piano teacher. He used to give lessons to a young woman called Shelby Wilson. I was wondering if perhaps you had some contacts in the music world around these parts? Maybe you could ask around and see if you could find out his name for me? I know it's a bit of a long shot. I do know one other thing about him — he has a caravan somewhere in the Lincolnshire Wolds."

"Are you asking in your role as a police officer?" Mr Kendrick asked.

Jane was a little surprised that he knew about that. Perhaps Mr Kendrick was more aware of the conversations going in the café than anyone gave him credit for. Or one of her friends had been blabbing.

She opted for honesty. "Actually, yes. I think someone I'm looking for might be staying in his caravan. She's the Shelby I mentioned. She has a brother called Andrew — Drew for short." She added hastily, "Neither of them is in any trouble with the police."

Mr Kendrick smiled. "I think Giles Brimble might be your man. Another retiree. Taught music at Horncastle Grammar for years and now he gives lessons. He's a good friend of mine, and he happens to have a caravan on a farm somewhere in the Wolds. Near Somersby, I think."

"Well, I'm glad I asked," Jane said. "I don't suppose you have his contact details to hand, do you?"

Mr Kendrick reached inside his jacket and pulled out a small notebook with a picture of a treble clef on the cover.

He thumbed through pages of what looked like illegible pencilled notes. "Ah. Here we are." He extracted a small pencil from the spine of his notebook, wrote down some details, then tore out the page and handed it to Jane.

Jane nodded. Giles Brimble lived on Massey Road, a residential side street off Nettleham Road, where she'd sometimes parked on shopping trips to Lincoln when she'd lived out of town. "Thank you so much, Mr Kendrick."

"Now that we're acquainted, you may call me Merlin."

Jane smiled. "Like the wizard?"

Merlin rolled his eyes. "My mother was obsessed with Arthurian legend. I suppose I should be grateful that her passion wasn't *The Lord of the Rings,* or I might have ended up as Gandalf, or, God help me, Bilbo." He shrugged. "Though I suppose I would then have become plain old Bill."

"Like me. Plain Jane," Jane said. They both smiled.

Merlin returned the notebook to his pocket and reached for his violin case. "Time to go if I want to get my place on Castle Hill before that dreadful chap with the ukulele shows up." He gave a little bow, and Jane reciprocated with a wave.

"Merlin's actually quite chatty, isn't he?" she said when Frieda came to offer her a refill. Frieda looked blank.

"Do you mean Mr Kendrick? That's his name?" Frieda sounded injured. "He never told me. Maybe it's because you're a police officer."

"What's that got to do with it?"

"Well, you know — people might feel they have to confide in the police," Frieda said.

If that was true, Jane thought, a police officer's job would be a whole lot easier.

CHAPTER TWENTY-THREE

Nate
7–8 May 2019

Lana's thin shoulders shuddered as the car drew to a halt. Nate could hear her teeth chattering, though it wasn't cold. He wished he could lean forward and touch her on the shoulder, take away some of her fear.

Nate was scared too. He'd seen what Cole looked like after Wolf and Shark worked him over. Maybe Lana had seen Wolf and Shark do worse than that. Maybe even to someone close to her.

He looked at Dex. He was white-faced and tight-jawed — and he hadn't even done anything.

Wolf stopped the engine and snarled at Wes. "Get them inside."

Wes got out of the car after Dex and came round to Nate's side. He signalled to him to get out. Lana was next. There was no manhandling, no rough treatment. People could be watching.

Wolf came around from the driver's side and pushed past them to walk up to the front door of the house, casually checking left and right before inserting the key. Nate hoped that a nosey neighbour might be hiding behind a curtain somewhere, taking note of the late hour and wondering at the arrival of this odd little group.

Wes ushered them to the door and inside. He was nervy, checking left and right, but with none of Wolf's subtlety. He should chill out a bit if he didn't want to look suspicious.

At least the other place he'd been taken to had been clean, if messy. This house was filthy and smelled foul. Nate gagged. Bad smells always made him do that. It earned him a slap on the face from Wolf.

The slap wasn't a punishment for gagging. It was the overture to a thrashing, while Wes held Nate still, covering his mouth with his hand to stop him crying out.

Wolf kicked him in the shins, punched his arms and torso again and again, grabbed his balls in his fist and twisted them until Nate squirmed in agony, his shrieks stifled by Wes's smothering hand.

At last, Wolf stepped back, wiping the back of his hand over his face, leaving streaks of red that gave him a savage, inhuman look.

Half-senseless, Nate wobbled. He gave Wolf a defiant look.

"Kid's got spunk, I'll say that for him." Wolf's iron fist shot out again, only this time, grinning, he slammed it into his palm at the last moment. Then he spun around to face Lana.

Nate bit down on Wes's hand, drawing blood. Wes yelped. Nate yelled, "Leave her alone!"

Wolf spun back to Nate. "Oh, we have a gentleman, do we?" He launched himself on Nate again.

Nate's whole body was numb by the time Wolf stopped. He wasn't even sure if he was in pain. The sight of his own blood streaked over Wolf's fists and face made him giggle hysterically.

His head reeled and darkness began closing over him. Just before he blacked out, he caught sight of Lana at Wolf's back, tears in her eyes as she silently moved her lips, "Thank you." That was enough to make it all worthwhile.

When he next opened his eyes, the first thing he saw was Lana, which made him think he'd only blacked out for a moment, until he saw that they were in a different room, and Wes and Wolf were no longer around.

Lana spoke in a hushed voice. "They're not here. We're locked in."

Prisoners again. In a near-replica of their last prison. Three squalid single mattresses in an otherwise empty room. Dex was sleeping on one of the mattresses, snoring lightly. Of course, it must be the middle of the night.

"Does it hurt?" Lana asked.

He moved tentatively, tried to sit up. "Whoa." He tested his limbs one by one, breathing in short, quick gasps. "Yes. Everywhere."

"Can you make it to the mattress if I help you?"

"Not sure. Give me a minute." Then, "I can try."

It took long, agonising minutes, prompting Lana to ask, "D'you think anything's broken?" When he shook his head, she said, "It's gonna hurt like hell tomorrow."

Nate didn't have the energy to tell her it hurt like hell already.

"Thanks for, you know, saying what you did and distracting him from me," she said. "He'd have laid into me for sure otherwise. I still can't work out why he didn't. The only thing I can think is that beating the shit out of you must have tired him out." Lana's anxious face twitched into a strained smile.

Nate closed his eyes against the pain, thinking, again, that it had been worth it.

"Then again," Lana continued, her words chilling, "He did warn me that next time either one of us stepped out of line, he'd kill us both."

"Why did you do it?" Nate asked. "You'd just warned me off trying anything."

Lana shrugged. "I don't know. It just seemed . . . I don't know—"

"It might have paid off," Nate said. "Next time it will." Lana didn't answer.

Lana was right about him feeling worse the following day. He lay on the soiled mattress all morning trying to move as little as possible, while Dex and Lana hovered nearby, checking on him every so often. Around noon, he raised his head. Lana was by his side immediately. "Any better?"

Nate winced. "It's not so bad."

She unscrewed the top of a bottle of water and helped him drink. His face was numb from the nose down and he dribbled like a baby.

"They haven't given us anything to eat," Lana said. "I'm starving."

Dex's stomach growled loudly. "Me too."

Nate nodded. They were in a smallish square room, bare walls, a plastic bucket in one corner.

Lana saw him look at it. "We're not even allowed to use the toilet." Nate was glad he seemed to have lost his sense of smell.

"Where's Wes?" he asked.

Lana shrugged. "We haven't seen him since we arrived."

Dex moved to the edge of his mattress. "We've heard voices. Wes and Wolf talking, nothing much from the man who answered the door last night. I think he might be locked in another room, 'cause we heard Wes knocking on the door opposite this one, asking if he wanted anything."

So, Wolf hadn't gone yet. Was he going to stay this time? Nate gave an involuntary shudder.

"This is all your fault," Dex said. "The two of you." He glared at Lana. "You should have known better."

Nate didn't have the energy to argue with Dex, but Lana said, "Leave it, Dex. Nate hasn't been with Wolf and Shark long enough to lose all hope of ever getting away. Remember what we were like in the early days?"

Dex sniffed. "Sooner he learns, the better it'll be for all of us. And you were the one encouraging him by opening the doors." He stood up, paced the room, relieved himself in the plastic pail, then, there being nothing much else to do, sat back down on his mattress and began picking at a thread on the hem of his hoodie.

"Well, I've changed my mind," Lana said. "What I did last night was stupid, but it's given me hope again. Imagine if Nate'd got away. He could have given the number of Wolf's car to the police." She looked anxiously at Nate. "You did memorise it, didn't you?"

Nate reeled off the registration number.

"See?" Lana gave Dex a fierce look. "He's actually not stupid. She turned back to Nate. "What we need is a plan."

"Here we go again," Dex said. "You're the stupid one. You finally learn how things are after your last crazy escape bid, then lover boy here comes along and all of a sudden, you're all for going back to making plans again. Well, count me out. I don't want to end up with a shank in my belly." He looked at Nate. "You're lucky all you got was beaten up."

Nate ignored Dex's warning. He'd heard only one thing. He looked at Lana, eager to hear more. "You tried to escape before? What happened?"

For all her new-found enthusiasm, Lana went silent, her face strained and white.

Dex had a self-satisfied smirk on his lips. "Go, on then, Lan," he said. "Tell him about Minnow."

At the mention of the name, Lana burst into tears.

CHAPTER TWENTY-FOUR

Steph
17 May 2019

Following discussions with Steph's DCI and the superintendent, it was agreed that the investigations into Cole Burke's
death and Nate Price's possible abduction by a county lines
gang could best be served by working closely with the East
Midlands Special Operations Unit.

The EMSOU was a specialist, collaborative unit that
provided support to the five East Midlands counties of
Derbyshire, Leicestershire, Lincolnshire, Northamptonshire
and Nottinghamshire. Its areas of expertise spanned major
crime, regional organised crime, counterterrorism and forensics, among other things. The unit was staffed by officers
from across the five regions it represented.

Collaborating across borders in this way enabled indi-
vidual forces to share specialist skills, expertise, capabili-
ties and intelligence. It also meant that financial and other
resources could be focussed where they were most needed
and allowed the police to be more proactive in planning for
and responding to threats.

What began as a small unit set up in 2001 to facilitate undercover operations across the region had quickly gained recognition nationally for its successes, but, perhaps more importantly for those with their hands on the purse strings, the venture made good sense financially.

Steph had worked with members of the EMSOU on previous occasions. She was pleased to attend a meeting via video link with DI John Sulley and DS Terry Munks, both of whom worked in the EMSOU's Regional Organised Crime Unit, or ROCU. John was seconded from the Lincolnshire Force, Terry from Nottinghamshire. John and Terry had been briefed in advance and they got down to business immediately.

"Morning, DI Warwick. I understand you're requesting our help with a possible county lines case," Sulley said.

"Yes. It's in connection with the murder of a local dealer and the possible abduction of a minor."

Steph explained what they knew so far about the change to one of the local supply chains and the suspected involvement of a county lines gang. She noticed how beleaguered John and Terry looked, as if they'd heard it all too many times before.

The pair had recently been involved in a highly successful county lines operation in the south of the county involving multiple arrests, the seizure of assets and, importantly, a disruption in the supply of Class A drugs that had been flooding into the county from Sheffield and Leicester.

There had been arrests from the top of the chain to the bottom, and the success of the operation meant that it had been widely reported locally and nationally. It had done much to bring the evils of county lines offenders to the public's attention.

"Do you have any ideas, thoughts, clues as to where the drugs might be coming from?" Terry Munks asked.

"Only rumours that it's a Nottingham-based gang," Steph admitted. She cleared her throat. "We have a possible identification of one of the minors involved — although we know there are several. A possible gang member was seen leaving the victim's — Cole Burke's — premises with a boy of around twelve."

Terry shook her head. "Why am I not surprised?"

Steph nodded. "We have a witness who thinks coercion was involved. We believe the same boy was held at a cuckooed address along with at least two other minors before being moved on to another, currently unknown, address."

"Burke would have been offered the opportunity of working for the new boys or getting out of town," Sulley said. "He must have crossed them in some way. Refused to give up his territory. If so, he had no idea of the brutality of the people he was up against."

Terry nodded. "Or, he might have been cheating on them in some way. Was your witness able to describe the man who led the boy away from Cole's property?"

When Steph mentioned that he had a tattoo on his bald head that looked like a spider's web, Terry and John exchanged a joyless smile.

John filled them in. "Michael Dodd, aka Shark. Most recently convicted of a drugs-supply offence in Thailand. He got sixteen years but, unfortunately for us, he was released early. Sounds like his spell in prison out there hasn't made a new man of him."

"What else can you tell us about Dodd?" Steph asked.

"I expect you don't need me to tell you he's dangerous — and ruthless," Terry said. "He's forty-eight years old. He's done time in this country too for serious criminal offences — drugs, assault. Suspected of involvement in at least one murder. Since he returned to the UK, he's been living in Nottingham with his brother, Tommy, commonly known as Wolf." She rolled her eyes at yet another absurd moniker.

"It'd be a challenge to decide which of the two is the bigger thug, but there are some stories about Tommy that would make your toes curl — psychopath's a word that often crops up when his name's mentioned. I can tell you one thing though. Neither Michael nor Tommy are the ones running this operation. They don't have the brains to head up something like this."

Steph nodded. She'd guessed as much from the fact that Michael Dodd had been seen leaving Cole Burke's building. The people at the top didn't show their faces anywhere near a crime scene.

It would be nice to think they could get all the way to the top of the chain, but it was more realistic to hope they could achieve some disruption of the supply.

"What help do you want from us?" Terry asked. "We can offer surveillance, beginning with Tommy's place? Monitor who goes in and out, track the brothers' movements. It might lead us to your cuckooed house, or at least to the gang's contacts in Lincoln. We can set up surveillance in Lincoln too, soon as you give us some details. Could probably offer you a crime analyst and see if we can get approval for some additional resources from Serious and Organised Crime. We also have financial investigators who can identify assets and produce detailed financial profiles of your main players."

Steph would take any help she could get. She'd have to clear every last detail with the superintendent, of course, but she was confident of gaining approval.

"Thanks. I know it could take time." She grimaced, thinking of how the brothers had dealt with Cole Burke, keen to make fast inroads to prevent further carnage.

When the video conference ended, the room fell into silence. Steph considered her next moves. It was a relief to know that they could count on additional operational and tactical support, possibly even more detectives to assist with the investigation into Cole's murder. All very heartening, but her earlier thought still niggled.

There would always be a small number of individuals sitting safely out of reach, while below them a network of minions scurried around doing their bidding, ready to take the fall.

CHAPTER TWENTY-FIVE

Jane
30 May 2019

The path to Giles Brimble's front door was bordered on either side by overgrown tufts of fragrant lavender, just coming into flower. Its heady scent infused Jane with a sensation of wellbeing. From somewhere in the house's interior came the sound of vivacious piano music, giving her spirits an additional boost.

It took a few minutes for Giles to answer her knock, not on account of any mobility issues, but because he obviously considered completing the piece of music he was playing a higher priority than answering his door.

He apologised for the delay. "Sorry for keeping you. I was so nearly at the end. I knew that if it were important, my caller would wait."

Jane smiled. Giles Brimble was dressed in a crisp white shirt, a waistcoat, bow tie — and a pair of rumpled khaki shorts. "I'm Special Constable Jane Bell. I called earlier. Mr Kendrick said you might be able to help me with something."

Giles looked about him as though worried someone might be listening. "Ah, yes. You'd better come in."

Jane followed Giles into a large back room that housed a polished grand piano as well as an assortment of other instruments, only some of which Jane recognised.

Giles must have noticed her look of curiosity as her eyes fell on an instrument that resembled a wooden chopping board overlaid with fork handles of differing lengths. "Lovely little thing, isn't it? It's called a kalimba. It originates from specific regions of Africa." He picked it up. "Really, it's like a finger piano." He played the instrument by plucking the tines with his thumbs. To Jane's surprise, the music produced was both haunting and beautiful.

She listened, entranced, clapping when he stopped playing. "Bravo. That was lovely. It reminded me of a harp, only it was more ethereal, and sort of enchanting."

Giles nodded enthusiastically, evidently pleased with her reaction.

"Collecting unusual musical instruments is a hobby of mine. When my musician friends come round, we create some weird and wonderful music." He put the kalimba down and picked up a stringed instrument.

"That's a lute, isn't it?" Jane said.

"A baroque lute." He turned it over to show her the instrument's smooth, bulbous back, which he stroked lovingly as though it were a cherished, elderly pet. It was a rich, reddish-orange colour that made Jane think of autumn leaves. "Beautiful, isn't it? These ridges are called ribs. They're made out of strips of flame maple. Our mutual friend, Merlin, plays the lute like an angel."

He laid the instrument down carefully. "Merlin tells me you're seeking information on the whereabouts of a certain young person of my acquaintance."

Jane was now in no doubt at all that Merlin Kendrick had called Giles ahead of her arrival.

Giles invited her to sit down. Jane got straight to the point. "I believe that Shelby Wilson and her brother Drew are staying at your caravan somewhere in the Wolds."

There was a moment's silence before Giles said, "The neighbour?"

"Faye. Yes. I told her I was Shelby's old English teacher. That's the only reason she trusted me."

It was Giles's turn to sigh. "Let's hope so. I'd hate to think she's telling all and sundry. Still, you are police. I tried to persuade Shelby to go to the police in the first place, but she and Andrew were terrified that the gang would come after them if they did. I hoped that they'd change their minds once they were safely at the caravan."

"So, you know why they had to get away?" Jane said.

"Yes. Shelby rang me to ask about the caravan, saying she thought it would be nice for Andrew to have a holiday. I was slightly puzzled that she was thinking of taking him out of school in term time. I didn't answer straight away when she asked, so she must have thought I was going to say no, because all of a sudden, she burst into tears. Then it all came out in a torrent. Andrew was truanting and getting into trouble at school, and outside. It wasn't until I went round to her house to see them that I began to appreciate how serious the situation actually was." His features hardened. "Potentially life-threateningly serious, in fact."

Jane nodded. "Yes." She told him about Lana, an example of the fate of another child caught up in the world of county lines.

Giles closed his eyes for a brief moment. "I read about her, poor child. I'm glad Shelby and Andrew are safely installed in my caravan for the time being."

"I need to speak with them," Jane said.

"May I ask why?"

Jane considered the question. "I was with Lana Kerr when she was attacked. I held her while we waited for the ambulance to arrive. There was nothing anyone could do. Lana died on the way to the hospital."

Giles looked shocked. "My dear, I'm so sorry."

Jane swallowed. "While I held Lana, she whispered something to me. A name — Nate. Whoever this Nate is, I could tell he meant a lot to her. I've been unable to get Lana — or Nate — out of my mind since. I feel I owe it to both of them to find the truth about what happened to them." Jane took a breath. "I have no real reason to believe that the drug dealers Drew was mixed up with were the same people Lana was involved with. I don't know whether Nate was connected at all, but I have a sort of intuition that he is."

She didn't reveal to Giles that the source of her intuition was DI Warwick — her expression when Jane told her that Lana had mentioned Nate's name. Warwick knew something about Nate. She was sure of it.

Giles frowned. "And you think Andrew might be able to help you locate Nate?"

"Yes," Jane said. "But my primary reason for wanting to speak with Shelby and Andrew is to check that they're safe and to try and persuade them to speak with the police. If that leads to information on Nate's whereabouts, fine, but, as I said, I have no reason to make a connection between Nate and Lana, and Andrew. Except that I suspect they have all been exploited by drug dealers. I just don't know if it's the same ones."

Giles seemed to come to a decision. "I'll call Shelby on my landline — there's a phone at the caravan site office. We decided not to communicate by mobile, just in case. If she's happy to see you, I'll give you the address."

Jane gave a sigh of relief. "Thank you."

As he got up to use the phone, Giles asked, "Is it customary for a volunteer special constable to conduct interviews like this? I thought that would be a detective's role."

Jane was uncomfortably aware that she wasn't in uniform. Giles smiled, impishly. "Don't look so alarmed. I can tell you're the sort of person who has an enquiring mind and can't let go of a puzzle until you've solved it." He went off to make the call.

Jane approved of his description of her as a problem solver. It had a better ring to it than 'meddler' or 'interfering busybody', which was how DI Warwick had described her on more than one occasion.

She waited a little anxiously for Giles to come back. To calm her nerves, she picked up the kalimba and plucked at the tines the way Giles had done, but the sound that ensued from her attempt at making music on the intriguing little instrument bore no resemblance to the magical sounds Giles had coaxed from it.

"I could teach you how to play it if you like." The sound of Giles's voice startled her, and she set the kalimba down quickly, feeling like a child caught touching a valuable ornament in a stranger's house.

"I think that would be a complete waste of your time. I have no musical ability whatsoever."

"I doubt that's true. We humans are naturally musical."

Jane scanned his face. "She agreed to speak with you and could meet you this afternoon," Giles said.

"Thank you so much for persuading her. I know she trusts you absolutely."

Giles nodded. He crossed to a mahogany desk and removed a notepad and pen from a drawer, scribbled for a moment or two, then handed the torn-off sheet to Jane.

"It's near Somersby. Where the poet Tennyson grew up?"

"Yes, I've been there," Jane said. "Tennyson is one of my favourite poets."

"Our caravan is on a nearby farm, owned by my sister and brother-in-law. My wife and I go there at weekends when the weather's fine. We don't normally rent it out, but I'd offered it to Shelby before all this happened. I thought she could do with a holiday."

Jane thanked Giles, promising to come along to the pub where he and Merlin played one evening soon. As she closed the door behind her, she heard the first notes of a sombre Chopin nocturne coming from the back room. Giles had returned to his music, but it seemed that his mood had altered following their conversation.

It was almost midday. Somersby was just under an hour's drive from Lincoln, so Jane decided to set off immediately. It was a familiar route, one she'd driven many times with the kids on trips to the coast or countryside. She reached the busy market town of Horncastle within forty minutes and turned off the A158 soon afterwards. From there, it was a pleasant fifteen-minute drive through the undulating Wolds countryside to Somersby. Jane glanced at the Georgian rectory where Tennyson was born as she drove past. It was now a private house.

The farm where Giles Brimble's relatives lived took a bit of finding as it was located a mile or so distant from the village itself, down a single-track lane, a perfect hiding place, Jane thought. The sort of place you wouldn't find unless you knew it existed.

It wasn't a proper farm, as she soon discovered, more a beautiful house and outbuildings in a lovely spot, enveloped by rolling hills. Jane couldn't help wondering what Drew and Shelby did all day out here in the sticks.

Giles's caravan was encircled by a fenced, wooden veranda on which stood a selection of planters overflowing with pansies. Jane parked in the space alongside the caravan. Before she could step up to the veranda, a young woman appeared at the door.

"Mrs Bell! I can't believe it's you. You haven't changed a bit."

"Hello, Shelby. It's lovely to see you again. I just wish the circumstances were better."

"Me too, but I feel safe here, and Drew does too. We're so lucky Mr Brimble — isn't it a funny name, like something out of Beatrix Potter — let us stay here."

Jane looked around. She didn't see Drew and assumed he must be in one of the bedrooms. To her surprise, Shelby said, "He's out helping Barry, Mr Brimble's brother-in-law. He and his wife Iris are so lovely. They let Drew help with the animals, and Barry also lets him help with other work around the farm. I help out too. It's the least we can do. Barry and Drew get on so well together. It's really helping Drew."

Jane smiled. It was good to see that something was going well for them.

"Drew knows about you coming. I asked him to come back around now. Would you like a cup of tea?"

"Yes, please. I'm parched. I didn't think to bring any water with me."

"How weird is this?" Shelby said, "Me making tea for Mrs Bell."

"I'm sorry your plans for your future didn't work out," Jane said as she watched Shelby put the kettle on and line up three mugs on a tray. There was the slightest pause before Shelby answered.

"It's okay. My plans are on hold, that's all. I couldn't have lived with myself if I'd let Drew be fostered or taken into care. The supermarket's been really good and I've made a friend for life in Faye.

"I'm glad to hear that, Shelby."

Shelby gave her a radiant smile. She looked over Jane's shoulder. "Here's Drew now. Just in time for a cuppa, as always."

Drew gave Jane a quick glance, but he was bursting with news for his sister. "Dory's had her pups. Barry and Iris let me see them. They said I could have one if you were happy about it."

"Iris and I discussed it and the answer's yes," Shelby said. "As long as you appreciate that looking after a dog is a big responsibility."

"I know. I'm up for it. There's one pup in particular. It's—"

Shelby cut him off. "We'll talk about it later, Drew. I'd like you to meet my English teacher from Ollie Granger's, Mrs Bell."

Drew turned to look at Jane with obvious reluctance. "Hi."

"Hello, Drew. Lucky you. A puppy. Your sister's right, though, a puppy is a big commitment."

"I know." He grabbed one of the mugs of tea and sat down at the table. "I know why you're here too. Shel says you know about the stuff I was mixed up in back home." His gaze was on the geometrical pattern on his coaster, and Jane could see how tautly he held himself, straight-backed in the chair, cradling his mug of tea.

"Is it all right if I ask you some questions, Drew?"

Shelby nodded at her brother. "We can trust Mrs Bell, Drew. I promise."

"Sure," Drew said, eyes fixed on the coaster.

"Can you tell me how you got involved with drug dealing, Drew?"

"It was through a mate. Someone I met in the park on the Cathedral Estate. I'd been hanging out with a friend from school, but he had to go home early, and this older boy started talking to me. He bought me chips and we talked for a while. I started hanging out with him, and eventually he asked me if I wanted to come round to his cousin's house to play games and stuff."

"What was the older boy's name?" Jane asked.

"Wes Savage. His cousin lived in town. Down the High Street, in a cool flat above a barber's shop. He was called Cole Burke."

Wes was the name of the boy Jane's former colleague Geoff Smith had told her about, the one he'd seen talking to Drew at the school gates. Jane frowned. "Cole? Was he a dealer?" The name stirred a memory but she couldn't place it.

"Yeah. Cole Burke." Drew looked up from the coaster. "You heard what happened to him, right?"

Jane frowned, her mind grappling for an elusive memory.

Drew enlightened her. "They killed him."

"It was in the papers a few weeks back," Shelby said. "He was tortured and murdered in his flat. The police still haven't got anyone for it."

"I know who you're talking about now," Jane said. "The name Cole threw me."

Drew shrugged. "It's what his mates called him. The papers gave him his full name, Nicholas."

Nicholas Burke. Jane recalled the killing now in all its gory details. His killers had cut off four of his fingers and beaten his face to a pulp before suffocating him using a plastic bag. There had been plenty of talk about it in the station. Her colleague Tim Sterne had heard a first-hand account of the murder scene from one of the PCs who'd been on duty at the time. No wonder Drew and Shelby had been afraid.

Was Warwick investigating Burke's murder? Had Nate, like Drew, been involved with him? That would explain the flicker of recognition in Warwick's eyes when Jane mentioned Nate's name. She must have connected Lana's death with Cole Burke's murder right there and then. She wondered if Warwick had questioned Drew. Her mind bubbled over with questions.

"How long have you been staying here?" she asked.

"Since the middle of April," Shelby said. "I can't believe it's been that long, but we daren't go back."

"Cole was murdered in April. Did you work for Cole after Wes introduced you to him, Drew?"

Drew stared at the coaster again. "I ran some errands for him."

Shelby gave a sigh of exasperation. "Oh, come on, Drew. Mrs Bell's a police officer now. She knows what that means."

Jane nodded. "You delivered packages for him — drugs. What did he give you in return? Gifts? The odd tenner?"

Shelby butted in again. "He was grooming you, Drew. That's what he was doing." Jane imagined they must have had this conversation many times.

Drew nodded. Jane was impressed that he showed no hint of defiance or denial. She thought, he's glad to be out of it. He'd appreciated the danger he'd brought upon himself and his sister, and he was relieved to be here, safe from it all. Unlike Lana, and possibly Nate, who had not been so lucky.

"Do the names Nate and Lana mean anything to you, Drew?"

Drew thought for a moment. "Nate, yes. Lana, no. Me and Wes were in the park near the chippie where I met Wes. Some older boys were bullying Nate, and Wes had a go at them. He paid for Nate's fish n' chips, and Nate started hanging around with us. I saw him at Cole's house too." He looked at Jane. "Who's Lana?"

"Lana was a twelve-year-old girl from Nottingham. Nine days ago, she was approached at some traffic lights by two men on a motorbike. One of them stabbed her, and sadly, she died." Jane cleared her throat. "I was a witness. Before she died, Lana mentioned Nate's name. I'm trying to find out who he was and what happened to him."

Shelby gasped. She turned to her brother, white-faced, her voice cracking. "That could have happened to you."

"I'm sorry," Drew mumbled. Then, "Cole wouldn't have done something like that. He was a decent person. I know he was a drug dealer and all, but he wasn't violent. It's the ones who killed him that's violent."

"That doesn't mean it was okay being involved with him," Shelby said.

Drew looked down. "I know that now. I just got all swept up in it for a bit."

"What happened next, Drew?" Jane asked quickly.

At a nod from his sister, Drew told his story. "I found out that Cole had got involved with some drug dealers who wanted to take over from him, and that they were really bad people, and that they might hurt me and Shelby if we didn't do what they said." Drew's bottom lip quivered.

"That's when Drew told me what was going on," Shelby said. She looked at Jane. "I know what you're thinking — why didn't we go to the police? I thought about it but I was scared the drug dealers would hurt Drew if they found out." She looked down. "Also, I didn't want Drew to get taken from me if the authorities found out he'd been doing something criminal. And . . . and I didn't want him going to prison."

Jane didn't reproach them. It was obvious that the siblings' primary concern had been for each other's safety.

Drew had begun to cry. Shelby slipped an arm around his shoulder. "I'd read about county lines. I knew these people carried out their threats. I couldn't risk Drew getting hurt. That's when I got in touch with Mr Brimble. We were scared one of the gang members would come round the next day, so we left in a taxi and stayed at Mr Brimble's overnight. He and his wife Anne were so kind. They drove us here early the next morning."

Jane noticed that Shelby had omitted a detail. "Faye told me you contacted a friend and that he advised you to go away for a while. Who was this friend? Why did he advise you to go away? Did he have experience of this sort of thing?"

Drew and Shelby exchanged a look. Shelby hesitated a moment before coming to a decision. "He wasn't a friend as such. He was a client of Cole's. When Drew said he found out about the drug dealers taking over from Cole Burke, it was from this client, not Cole himself. Drew delivered a package to him. He warned Drew he'd heard a rumour that Cole was working for a dangerous drug gang from Nottingham, and that he should stop going to Cole's place, stop working for him immediately."

"I think Cole didn't tell me about the gang before because he didn't want me to worry," Drew said.

How considerate of him. "Cole Burke put you at risk by not telling you he was involved with a dangerous criminal gang, Drew. He wasn't the person you thought him to be."

She gave Drew a moment to absorb her comment. Something niggled. Why had Cole's client taken it upon himself to warn Drew that he might be in danger if he carried on working for Cole? Puzzled, she asked Shelby, "What I don't understand is why you got in touch with Cole's client and asked his advice. I understand why you didn't want to go to the police, but why take advice from a virtual stranger?" Another question occurred to her. "And how did you know how to get in touch with him?"

When neither sibling answered, she added, "And why would this man take it upon himself to give you a warning? I'm no expert, but I'd have assumed addicts aren't in the habit of scaring off the people who deliver their fix."

Jane became frustrated with their continuing silence. "Do you know where this man lives, Drew? I'd like to talk with him."

Another look passed between the pair. It was obvious that they were both holding back. Could this 'client' be someone with a personal connection to one of them? Jane appealed to Shelby. "You know you can trust me. Was the man someone you already knew?"

Shelby looked straight at Jane and gave a deep sigh.

"I . . . suppose it won't help to keep it from you. I promised Faye I wouldn't tell anyone about it, but other people might be in danger, and I don't want to be responsible for anyone coming to harm."

Jane waited, feeling a tingle of excitement.

At last, Shelby said, "Yes. We knew him — sort of. His name is Shane Watt, and he is — was — my neighbour Faye's partner. He's little Jessie's dad." She let her words sink in before adding, "He used to be in the army. After he left, he got a job at a hospital in Nottingham. They were looking for a house in Newark so he wouldn't have so far to commute, but then one day Shane dropped a bombshell. He told Faye he'd lost his job because he'd stolen some drugs — strong painkillers — from the hospital. He'd got addicted to them after being injured some months earlier. After he lost his job, he got into other drugs. Things at home went from bad to worse. Faye's mum looked after Jessie so that Faye could work more hours to make ends meet, but Shane got hold of Faye's bank card and withdrew all her money to buy drugs. Eventually, Faye asked him to leave. Shane promised her he'd get himself sorted out."

Jane thought of Faye. How untroubled and positive she'd seemed. It would never have occurred to her that she had been through so much. *When will I stop being surprised that anyone can have a grim backstory?*

"Does Faye know where Shane is now?" Jane asked.

Shelby sighed. "I don't know. I would guess he's probably hiding out somewhere because of his own connection with Cole."

Drew looked troubled. Evidently, he'd been mulling something over. "That girl, Lana. If she knew Nate, do you think they killed him too?"

Jane had no answer for him. "I don't know, but I'm determined to find out what happened to him. Do you know what school he went to, Drew?" Drew shook his head. "One more thing, Drew. Can you describe for me what Nate looks like?"

"Well, he's pretty ordinary-looking except he's got a gap between his two front teeth. It's the first thing you'd notice about him if you met him."

"Thank you, Drew." Jane wasn't sure how Shelby and Drew would react to what she knew she must say next. "Look, I know you feel safe here, and that you're scared of going to the police, but I'm going to have to pass on what you've told me to the detectives who're investigating Cole Burke's murder."

To her relief, Shelby, who was holding her brother's hand now, nodded. "I know it's what we should have done all along, and I'm glad that you know now, Mrs Bell. I'm sure you won't let anything bad happen to us."

Her words reminded Jane of the huge responsibility invested in her as a police officer. She knew it was a responsibility that she couldn't bear on her own shoulders. It was time to speak with DI Up-Herself.

CHAPTER TWENTY-SIX

Nate
8–20 May 2019

"Who's Minnow?" Nate asked, turning his gaze to Lana.

Dex corrected him. "You mean who *was* Minnow?"

Ignoring him, Nate waited for Lana to speak. Instead, she hurled herself at Dex, pummelling him with her fists until he managed to throw her off.

"Get off, Lana. It's not my fault she's dead, is it?"

"She's not dead, you moron. I don't know what happened to her."

"Was she your friend?" Nate asked.

Lana sniffed. "Yes. Minnow was a nickname, because she was so tiny. She never told me what her real name was. I met her one afternoon when I was hanging around the Victoria Centre in Nottingham. This girl came up to me and asked me if I had any ciggies. I didn't, but I had some money on me that I'd pinched from my mum's purse, so I offered to buy us some. I ended up hanging out with her for a bit. She was funny. I thought she was much younger than me, but it turned out we were the same age."

To begin with, Minnow's story sounded a little like his own, except that Minnow had run away from home because her stepdad kept trying to get her to give him a blow job whenever her mum wasn't around.

"Minnow lived in Birmingham. She didn't want her mum's boyfriend to find her, so she stole some money from him when he was asleep and bought a train ticket with it. She wanted to go to London, but then she met a woman at the station who talked her into going to Nottingham instead. The woman told her she'd look after her. She'd seemed okay, but she wasn't. The next day she took Minnow somewhere else." Lana looked around the room. "Somewhere like this. Minnow stayed, because where else would she go? At that point, she thought she could leave whenever she wanted to. She acted as a courier, taking packages all over the place. One day, after she'd done a drop, she was on her way back when two older kids grabbed her and pulled her into an alleyway. They beat her up and took all the cash she'd collected. When she got back, the men she was working for beat her for losing the money and told her she'd have to work for them to pay off the debt she owed them."

Nate felt a judder in his chest. "But she got away?" he said. "She must have if you met her in the shopping centre."

"Yep. She got away. But not for long," Dex said. His gloating tone made Nate feel like punching him one.

"Shut up, Dex." Lana glared at him. "They found her the day I met her. We had such a laugh that day. Nicking stuff. Minnow was good at it. Anyway, we'd just left the centre and were on our way to get some pizza when these two men came up to us. One of them took Minnow's arm, the other took mine. The one who grabbed Minnow opened his jacket and showed us a knife he had hidden underneath. They made us go with them to where they'd parked their car and when we got there, they forced us to get inside." Lana swallowed. "I was in the front seat with the driver and Minnow was in the back with the man with the knife. He said he'd cut her if I

181

tried anything. They took us to a house in a part of the city I'd never been to before and when we got there, they separated us. They took Lana upstairs, and I could hear men laughing and then I heard Lana scream." Her lip trembled.

Nate pressed her arm. "You don't need to tell me any more. I can guess what they did to her."

Lana nodded. "I never saw her after that. They moved me on to a different house. You know what the worst thing was? I was glad they'd taken her upstairs instead of me. Does that make me a terrible person?"

Nate shook his head. "No. It's what anyone would think." He couldn't bear to see her upset. He'd never felt that way about a girl before. Suddenly all he wanted to do was hug her to him and tell her everything was going to be all right. Instead, he muttered that he was sorry about Minnow.

A sudden anger stirred somewhere deep within him. He wanted to kill the men who'd hurt Lana and Minnow. Instead, he made a fist with his right hand and slammed it into the palm of his left. "Bastards."

He glared at Dex again, willing him to make some stupid comment so that he would have an excuse to punch him. But Dex seemed subdued now.

Punching his own hand was a bad idea. It was one of the only parts of his body that didn't ache from his beating at the hands of Wolf and Shark. Now it stung, reminding him of his other injuries. He leaned back on his mattress with a sigh of exhaustion and defeat. Before long, he was sleep.

He woke up much later to the enticing smell of vinegar on hot chips. Lana handed him a greasy bagful along with a can of coke and a couple of sachets of tomato sauce. The first meal they'd been given since arriving at the new trap house hours ago.

Even after eating the lot, Nate still felt hungry. No one seemed to feel like talking. In the absence of painkillers, sleep was the buffer from his pain. So, he closed his eyes.

He woke, hours later, to find the room in darkness and Lana lying next to him on the mattress, one arm across his chest. Strong emotions coursed through him again, a mixture of tenderness and protectiveness, and, this time, something else too, a feeling — both physical and emotional — that made his breathing quicken and his cheeks burn so fiercely that he feared the heat would wake Lana. It didn't and, eventually, despite his resolve to stay awake all night just to be close to her, he fell asleep.

The following morning, when he awoke, Lana was back on her own mattress, and Nate wondered if he'd dreamed that she'd lain beside him in the middle of the night. He looked at her and they exchanged shy smiles, and he knew it had been real.

In the following weeks, he and Lana grew closer. Lana never joined Nate on his mattress after that first night, and they never talked about it, but something had changed between them. For Nate, it was like being hyper aware of her, or being connected by an invisible string that tugged whenever she moved. Whenever his back was to her, he could sense when she was looking at him. Every so often their eyes would meet, and they'd smile at each other. In spite of their miserable circumstances and precarious situation, when this happened, Nate was as close to happiness as he'd been in his entire life.

Inevitably, Dex noticed. At first, he went quiet, which wasn't that noticeable because he wasn't much of a talker anyway, but after a couple of days, he began to make snide comments in front of Wes. Nothing too obvious, but enough for Nate to feel that while something beautiful had been flourishing between him and Lana, something ugly was stirring between the two of them and Dex.

One afternoon, when he and Wes were in the room where they weighed and bagged the goods, the front door banged — Lana returning from making a delivery. Dex looked at Nate and said, "Your girlfriend's home." Then he turned to Wes and made a crude gesture, slipping the middle finger of his right hand in and out of a circle he'd formed using the thumb and index finger of his left.

Wes laughed, but Nate noticed that he watched Lana carefully when she came into the room. Fortunately, she didn't look at Nate first, but Nate knew that now Wes had found out that he and Lana had feelings for each other, he would find some way to use it to his advantage.

Lana had told Nate she'd been warned that her gran would be harmed if she ever stepped out of line. For Dex, it was his little brother, and for Nate, his mother. So much leverage, and that didn't even include the threat to their own lives.

Since the day Lana had told Nate about Minnow, there had been no more mention of trying to escape. Nate wondered if Lana had gone off the idea and he wasn't sure how best to broach the subject again, or if he should even mention it at all.

In the end, it was Lana who touched upon the subject of escape one evening after the three of them had been locked in their room for more than twenty-four hours straight, with nothing but a bottle of coke and a loaf of bread to share among them. After the first couple of days at the new place, they'd been allowed out to work and to use the bathroom, but in the early evening they were imprisoned in this foul-smelling bedroom where there was nothing to do. This time, it seemed they'd been forgotten.

Nate was lying on his mattress, staring at the ceiling, when Lana came over and sat down beside him. Dex sat up and made a stupid remark. "Mind if I watch?" Nate felt his anger rise.

Lana told him to ignore Dex, saying they all needed to talk. "We need to get out of this place. I don't know about you two, but I can't take much more of this. And I'm scared of what'll happen next time Wolf and Shark come back."

Nate knew she was thinking about what had happened to Minnow. Wolf had been back to the house to collect the money on more than one occasion, and he'd spent a lot of time looking at Lana in a way that had made her feel uncomfortable. So far, he'd always been in a rush. Next time, he might have more time on his hands.

Dex rolled his eyes. "Count me out. I'm not going to risk my arse, but I'm happy for you two to have a go." He leered. "I meant at escaping, but don't mind me if you want to have a go at the other thing too."

Lana's eyes narrowed. "You disgust me. You won't help in an escape attempt, but you don't mind us taking a risk that'll help you if we're successful."

"Just looking after number one. If you don't succeed, shit's all on you. If you do, I benefit when you tell the police about this place. Win, win."

Lana turned her back on him and looked at Nate. "I've got an idea."

Nate wanted to tell her to keep it to herself until they could discuss it without Dex listening in. But when would that be? Even if they whispered in the middle of the night, he might be awake listening to them. He nodded at Lana.

"I mostly visit the same clients every time I go out. What if I contact Wes and say I've got a problem with one of them — they're refusing to pay or something."

"Wes wouldn't go round there to sort it out," Nate said. "He wouldn't leave us here alone, if you're thinking I could break out while he's away. He'd call on Wolf or Shark."

Lana frowned. "There has to be a way." After a few moments' silence, she said, "I could just not come back here with the cash. I could go to the police instead and hope they get here before Wes finds out."

"Wolf and Shark would hunt you down and kill you. Then they'd kill your family." This time, Dex's voice wasn't sarcastic or gloating. He was merely stating a fact. "Didn't take them long to find your friend Minnow, did it?"

"The police could protect us. I saw a film once where this woman agreed to go to court to help get some criminals put in jail. After the trial, the police gave her a new name and house and everything so no one could find her."

"It's called witness protection," Nate said, remembering watching a film like that with his mum. "They give you a whole new identity. It's like starting your life all over again somewhere else as a different person."

Dex wasn't convinced. "They'd still find you."

"It'd be a risk," Lana said, "but I can't just stay here and wait for things to get worse."

She looked at Nate, her eyes shining with excitement. He couldn't disappoint her. "When you're late back from the drop, maybe me and Dex can do something to distract Wes to give you time to get to the police."

"Like what?" Dex's tone was laced with doubt. "I already told you I'm not doing anything risky."

Nate sighed. He felt Lana's soft touch on his arm, making his heart beat faster, emboldening him.

Dex gave them a scornful look. "You're both crazy."

"It's crazier to stay here for ever, hoping to be rescued," Lana said. "Ignore him, Nate. Let's make a plan."

CHAPTER TWENTY-SEVEN

Steph
21–22 May 2019

News came in of a serious incident on Burton Road. DC Joey Fairbairn gave Steph the details. "It's a serious assault, ma'am. Man jumped off the back of a motorcycle and stabbed a teenage girl."

Steph knew there was no one else available. "We'll take it," she said, signalling for Elias to join her.

Almost a month had passed since Cole Burke's murder and they were right in the thick of that investigation. The last thing Steph needed was a distraction in the form of another serious crime.

They arrived at a scene of chaos. A crowd of bystanders, all possible witnesses, a row of cars parked up with two wheels on the pavement, grim-faced paramedics and, in the midst of it all, a clutch of uniformed officers trying to keep everyone calm.

Steph recognised one of them. "What have we got, PC Sterne?"

Tim Sterne filled her in. "The driver of the bike swerved on to the pavement and his passenger jumped off and went straight for the victim, like he was targeting her, apparently. He pulled her close to him — some people thought he was hugging her — then he pushed her away and made off with her bag. According to witnesses, it was all done so fast nobody even realised she'd been stabbed until the bikers were already tearing off. A couple of people even thought at first that the bloke who stabbed her was her boyfriend. Others believed it must have been some sort of robbery."

One word in Tim's account leaped out at Steph. "Targeted? Was that word used by one of the witnesses?" She scanned the faces of the bystanders as if it were possible to pick out the right one.

"Yes, ma'am. One of our own, actually. An off-duty special constable, Jane Bell. I've worked many a shift with her since she started, so I can vouch that she knows what she's talking about."

Steph almost groaned aloud. Of all the people who might have witnessed the incident! Instinctively, her gaze shifted to the vegan café on the other side of the road, run by some friends of Bell. Was Bell in there now, watching her? She was certainly not among the dwindling crowd of pedestrians.

Tim must have followed the direction of her gaze. "She's in the café you're looking at now. I took a brief account from her and sent her on her way. She was pretty shaken. SC Bell got to the girl first, you know, held her until the ambulance arrived."

Steph raised an eyebrow. "Did the girl speak to her?"

Before Tim had a chance to reply, she cut him off. "Never mind. I might as well hear it directly from the horse's mouth." She turned to Elias. "Would you believe, SC Jane Bell was a witness! She's in the café over the road. I'm going across to interview her. You carry on here." Under her breath, she swore, "Bloody hell! I thought I'd seen the last of that annoying woman."

"Ma'am." It was PC Sterne's colleague. She could tell from his face it was bad news. "Call's just come through. The girl didn't make it."

Steph nodded, then turned to Elias. "No more than we expected. This is now a murder scene. Make sure it's treated as such."

As she walked towards Veganbites, Steph felt increasingly paranoid. Bell was almost certainly watching her. The sheer bad luck of Bell witnessing the incident irritated her beyond measure. Bell could have just gone home, but instead she'd gone to the café from where she could keep a watchful eye on how things unfolded. That was so bloody typical of the woman.

Steph didn't waste time when she entered the café. She marched straight up to the table where Bell was sitting. "Special Constable Bell. I believe you were a witness to the incident out there." She sat down opposite Bell and had just asked for an account of her version of events when Frieda Arya approached their table, smiling broadly.

Steph lived off Burton Road and Veganbites was her local café, but she'd stopped coming after discovering that Frieda and her husband Karun were friends of Jane Bell. She smiled at Frieda, whom she actually quite liked, and ordered her coffee brusquely, hoping Frieda would pick up that she wasn't here to chat.

The coffee arrived lightning fast. Of course Bell asked how the girl had fared. She didn't know the victim was dead. Steph supposed she'd have to tell her. She made a bit of a hash of it, rushing out her words to get it over with. "The girl's heart gave out in the ambulance, and they weren't able to revive her. I'm sorry. I'd forgotten you wouldn't have known that."

Bell mumbled something that Steph didn't quite catch. Steph was keen to get on with the interview. It was going to be a long enough day, and it wasn't as if Bell had known the girl, but Steph supposed she'd better allow her a moment to process the news. It was a relief when she pulled herself together after a couple of sips of tea.

Bell described how she'd noticed the motorbike approaching. She'd been as shocked as everyone else when it swerved suddenly, mounting the pavement.

"The rider on the back jumped off and grabbed the girl. From then on, my focus was on her," Bell said.

When she related how the girl had struggled to speak, Bell's voice trembled. She had a right to be shaken, Steph conceded. It couldn't have been a pleasant experience, and to top it all, the girl was dead.

Steph cleared her throat. "I believe you took charge of the situation. Asked people to stay back, preserved the integrity of the scene." It was the closest she could bring herself to telling Bell she'd done a good job in challenging circumstances. She was eager to press on, but she waited while Bell regained her composure.

Bell wiped away a tear. "She was struggling to say something to me. It seemed really important to her. It was a name — Nate."

Too fast, Steph repeated, "Nate?"

Bell was sharp, Steph observed. She asked, "Does the name mean something to you?"

Again too fast, Steph denied that it did. She switched, abruptly, to asking Bell about the licence plate of the motorbike, and when Bell admitted she'd been too focussed on the victim to check, Steph berated her, saying it was just as well that one of the other witnesses had had the sense to take a photo using their phone. It had already been confirmed as fake.

Steph made no comment when Bell suggested that the incident was probably drugs-related. Above all, she wished to prevent Bell asking pertinent questions and trying to insinuate her way into the investigation. Steph made a clumsy reference to Bell's and Elias's little pact, then she as good as reminded Bell not to stick her nose where it didn't belong.

"Ma'am," Bell said, not meeting her eye.

Steph was in a hurry to leave. It was the first time she'd been in Bell's company since she'd attempted to bribe her, and she was feeling agitated. Every moment she lingered reminded her that she owed her continued role as a DI to Bell's — and Elias's — discretion.

* * *

A day passed before they were able to identify the victim as Lana Kerr, a missing teenager from Nottingham.

"So, we have another Nottingham connection." Five minutes ago, Steph had concluded the latest team briefing on the investigation into Cole Burke's murder. She'd provided updates, then outlined the reasons why she believed the murder of Lana Kerr might possibly be linked to the case they were already investigating. Then, she'd delegated tasks to the various members assembled. Now, she and Elias were engaged in a video-link conversation with John Sulley and Terry Munks, along with the superintendent of EMSOU's Regional Organised Crime Unit, Ian Pryor.

Pryor was well versed in Lana's case. "The alarm was raised by children's services when Lana failed to return to school after the summer break. Mrs Kerr was completely clueless about her daughter's whereabouts. She didn't even know when she'd last seen Lana. A neighbour stated that she hadn't seen her around much during the school holidays. Her mother was very hazy about her daughter's comings and goings, what she was getting up to or who she was with. Out of sight, out of mind. I quote, 'Up to Lana what she does, not my effing responsibility anymore, is she? She's sixteen.' When we pointed out that her daughter was only twelve, she just shrugged and asked how she was supposed to remember something like that.

"Unsurprisingly, she didn't even know how long Lana had been missing. She'd stopped coming home regularly and, I suspect you've worked this out already, Mrs Kerr spends most of her time high on something or other and hardly knew what day it was. Her parting words to my detective were, 'If you find the slut, make sure you tell her she's not welcome here anymore.'"

"Poor kid," Elias said.

Pryor agreed. "One of far too many. As you'll be aware, the trouble in a case like this is that you're really at a disadvantage from the start, not knowing with any near certainty when the child went missing. We eventually narrowed down the time frame for her disappearance to sometime in mid-August. A member of the public responded to a missing person's alert. She reported that she thought Lana might have been one of two girls who'd been caught on camera nicking a couple of bottles of coke from her shop.

"We identified Lana from the footage. We also managed to identify her partner-in-crime. She was thirteen-year-old Daisy May, also known as Minnow because she was small for her age. Daisy was already known to us. She'd run away from her home in Birmingham two months previously. It was thought she might have gone to London. Her mother claimed her behaviour had become challenging after her partner moved into the family home. It transpired that Daisy had accused the partner of trying to abuse her, but the mother had dismissed Daisy's claim as attention-seeking nonsense."

Steph sighed. For everyone listening, Daisy's story too was depressingly familiar. "British Transport Police at Birmingham provided CCTV footage of Daisy boarding a train to Nottingham with an unknown white female," Pryor continued. "She was seen again on footage obtained from Nottingham station. EMSOU-ROCU was involved in the search, but after alighting from the train, Daisy just seemed to disappear until she appeared on that footage with Lana Kerr. We got hold of CCTV material from various locations in the city after that. The girls were spotted in several different places right up until the end of August last year. Daisy had substantially changed her appearance. She'd cropped her hair and dyed it black, leading to speculation that she was attempting to disguise herself, either from us or someone else. There were no more sightings of either girl after that."

There was a silence as they all considered the possible implications of this.

"The fact that Lana was transported to Lincoln and possibly held in a cuckooed house seems to confirm that both girls were picked up by county lines practitioners," Terry said.

Steph thought of what Kaz had said about seeing a boy and girl arrive at her house with the man she called Shark.

Kaz had said in her statement after her initial interview that she thought the girl had long hair and the boy had a red birthmark on his face. But how reliable a witness was Kaz? Could the girl have been Lana? Had Daisy even made it to Lincoln? If so, was she being held in another trap house somewhere in the city? There was no way of knowing for certain.

The meeting concluded with an update on the surveillance operation on Michael and Tommy Dodd. "We'd stop-and-search them but that would give the brothers Dodd a heads-up that we're watching them. No one's been seen travelling to Lincoln so far, but I don't need to remind you that the resources at our disposal don't always stretch to running full surveillance on everyone we suspect of being involved in organised crime."

"Can we link the Honda used when Lana Kerr was murdered to the Dodd brothers?" Steph asked.

"Sorry. As you know the plates were fake, and we've drawn a blank so far. My guess is they know it's hot and they're keeping it — and themselves — off the streets."

CHAPTER TWENTY-EIGHT

Jane
30–31 May 2019

After speaking with Shelby and Drew, Jane had been tempted
to drive straight to Faye's house, but it was book group that
evening and she'd barely have time to get home and have
something to eat before meeting Allie to walk to Veganbites,
where the group met. In the end, she decided that she needed
time to think before making her next move. Also, she'd been
looking forward to a pleasant evening in the company of
friends, and there was no reason to put that off.

On her drive home from Somersby, she considered what
she had discovered. She knew that Nate had been important to Lana. From Caleb, she'd learned that his friend Drew
knew some lads who were possibly linked to a county lines
gang operating in Lincoln. Her former colleague, Geoff, had
seen Drew in the company of an older lad, Wes, who'd been
expelled from school for drug-related offences.

From speaking with Drew and his sister Shelby, she'd discovered that Wes had been grooming Drew. Crucially, Drew
had met Nate through knowing Wes — they lived in the same
geographical area, though they'd attended different schools,

probably because Nate had been enrolled late for a school in Lincoln and missed the opportunity to attend the one closest to his home. Both Drew and Nate had fallen prey to Wes, who had introduced them to Cole Burke, a local dealer. Burke had a connection with an organised crime gang based in Nottingham.

The last piece of information had come from an unknown source — Faye's ex-partner, Shane Watt. Jane had no idea how reliable his information was. Had his worry been less about what could happen to Drew and more about not wanting Faye and his daughter anywhere near the lad?

Jane had checked, and DI Warwick was the SIO on the investigation into the murder of Cole Burke back in April. Warwick had recognised Nate's name, Jane was sure of it.

Had Warwick been searching for Nate since Cole Burke's death? What if she had no clues as to his whereabouts? What if Nate's or someone else's life depended on her finding out?

Jane's front tyre grazed the kerb as she parked her car. "Damn. I'm going to have to get in touch with her." She slammed the door shut. She toyed with the idea of calling Warwick immediately, then thought better of it, reasoning that Warwick must already know about Nate's connection to Burke and about Burke's connection with organised crime. She wouldn't appreciate being sent on a wild goose chase after Shane Watt. First thing in the morning, she would find out if there was anything relevant that Faye could tell her about Shane Watt and, if so, she'd contact DI Warwick.

"So, have you managed to find out much about that poor girl who was murdered last week? Or about the boy she mentioned, Nate?" Allie asked the minute they met.

"Not about Lana, no. I've made a few discoveries, but none of them have got me very far." Without revealing too much detail, Jane told Allie about Caleb approaching her after her talk at the school, and how she'd tracked down his friend Drew.

"I also discovered that Drew had met Nate. Anyway, I got a sort of lead this evening that I'm hoping might help me find out what's happened to Nate."

Allie gave her a concerned look. "I hope you're not putting yourself in danger with all this, Janie."

Jane sighed. "No. I've decided to get in touch with DI Warwick and tell her what I know. I think Nate's name meant something to her. She probably knows everything I've discovered already, and a whole lot more besides, but I don't want to take the risk that I might be withholding information that could help her with her investigation into Burke's — and Lana's — murder. She's the one best placed to deal with all of that and, I suppose she is good at her job, even if her manner does get my back up."

"Well, it's good that you can admit that," Allie said. "Honestly, the pair of you are pride and prejudice incarnate."

Jane smiled. "Which of us is which?"

"I'll let you be the judge of that," Allie said diplomatically.

"She's arrogant and dismissive of me. She thinks she's better than me just because—"

Allie cut her off. "Because she's a trained detective with years of experience?"

Jane gave her a sour look. She'd been about to say, "just because I'm only a special". Allie's words compelled her, reluctantly, to consider matters from Warwick's perspective.

"I seem to remember someone complaining about teacher trainees thinking they knew it all after a couple of hours in the classroom. Seems to me that the pair of you have more in common than either of you thinks."

"Rubbish."

They arrived at Veganbites. Jane felt her ill-humour evaporate as soon as she stepped over the threshold into the warm and welcoming atmosphere. Her friends were all there. Even Ed, she noticed, was there already, a sure sign that she and Allie were late. He'd saved a seat for her next to him. They had begun a tentative romance some months before, much to the delight of Allie, who'd been trying to get them together since Ed had joined the group.

Ed was an artisan blacksmith whose work had earned him a gold medal from the Worshipful Company of

Blacksmiths, no less. He wasn't from Lincoln. He'd moved there from 'down south', but not to the city. His home was in a village a few miles north of Lincoln, which was one of the reasons he was often late.

Their relationship was evolving slowly and steadily. They were both used to living independent lives — in Jane's case after the death of her husband, Sam — in Ed's, after a messy divorce. It seemed to be working well for them, living separately but together. Jane wouldn't be the first to suggest a change to their present arrangement.

Ed greeted her with a kiss. "Hi. Everything okay? You looked a bit frazzled when you walked in."

"Busy day, that's all."

Ed usually spent the night at Jane's after book group. There was a bottle of Merlot and two glasses laid out on her coffee table for them to drink later. She was looking forward to cuddling up on the sofa with him to watch a movie, then going to bed with him.

"Where's Peter?" Karun asked.

"He sent his apologies," Allie said. Allie had once announced that her husband Peter had expressed an interest in joining the group, but so far he hadn't attended a single meeting. Allie no longer bothered to explain why he couldn't make it, but everyone suspected he'd only agreed to come to get Allie off his back and had no intention of actually attending.

Jane waved at Thea, who was carrying a tray of drinks across to the comfy seating area. "I've got coffee for you two," Thea said, meaning the late arrivals.

Karun followed behind Thea, bearing cake. This evening it was a malty chocolate cake. Jane saw Allie eye it with slight suspicion. She would never be convinced that egg- and dairy-free cakes could look — and taste — as good as the 'real' thing. Once she'd even asked Karun if he secretly used real butter and eggs.

As always, they began with a catch-up session, moved on to a discussion of the monthly book, and ended with friendly conversation. The catch-up session lasted a little longer than usual this evening because two members of the group, Jan and Yvonne, had just returned from an extended trip to Poland to see Jan's relatives.

"So, Jane," Jan said. "A little bird told me you had a nasty experience last week."

Jane felt all eyes on her. "Yes. Have you heard the details?"

Jan nodded. "Frieda told us. It must have been a terrible shock."

"It was. She was so young. All her life in front of her. Such a terrible waste." Jane looked around, noted the gazes of sympathy. "All the clichés are true."

"All because of drugs," Jan said, shaking his head. "County lines, yes? An inadequate term to describe such evil. I say give poorly-off kids real opportunities to do well in life and have a share of the rewards and maybe no need for them to look elsewhere to make easy money."

Jan's words prompted a lengthy discussion about county lines, after which they moved on to discussing the pros and cons of decriminalising Class A drugs. At one point, Jane looked at Thea and thought she seemed a little subdued. She waited until Thea caught her gaze and mouthed, "Everything okay?" Thea smiled and nodded. Perhaps she was upset about all the talk of violence and vulnerable people being imprisoned in cuckooed houses. A few months ago, Thea's best friend had narrowly escaped being harmed at the hands of a deranged killer who had kidnapped her and held her captive.

Jane grabbed her after the discussion ended. "Are you sure you don't want to stay at my place tonight?"

Thea glanced over at Ed. "What? And spoil your romantic evening with the lovely Ed? Not a chance." She gave Jane a hug, looked over her shoulder. "Besides, my taxi is already here."

The following morning, Ed left early. Jane had a free day until a tutoring session in the afternoon.

She arrived at Faye's house just as she was leaving to take her daughter to her nursery. Faye Crowther was immediately suspicious when Jane asked her if she could speak with her about her ex-partner Shane Watt. "Why do you want to know about Shane? We're not together anymore."

"You didn't tell me last time we spoke that it was Shane who warned Drew and Shelby they were in danger. You just said she'd asked a friend for advice. Shelby said you might know where to find Shane. There's something urgent I need to ask him about."

Faye looked dismayed. "Shelby promised she wouldn't tell—"

"Look," Jane assured her gently, "Shelby wouldn't have betrayed your trust if I hadn't convinced her that it was very important. A matter of life and death, even." Jane told her about the murder of Cole Burke, and about Lana and Nate. She suspected that Faye knew at least some of the facts already, as she didn't seem all that shocked to learn that the gang Drew had been working for might have been responsible for killing Lana and abducting Nate.

When Jane had finished, Faye said, "I don't understand how you think Shane can help you. Shane might be an addict, but he would never hurt anyone, and he's not a dealer."

"I'd just like to talk to him because I think he might be able to help me find Nate. You must have some idea where he is. Please, Faye. These people killed Lana. They might kill Nate too, if we don't find him first."

Faye appraised Jane for a few moments. "I still love Shane, you know. I'd have him back in a heartbeat if he could get on top of his addiction." She sighed. "I . . . I didn't want to ask him to leave, but I had to think of Jessie — the kind of people Shane might have brought to our door — I didn't want to make him homeless, but I had no choice."

"I understand," Jane said, seeing tears well up in Faye's eyes. "You acted to protect your child. It was the right thing to do."

Faye hadn't, in reality, made Shane homeless. "I rang Shane's brother in Norfolk and he came to collect him, but Shane left him a note after a couple of days, saying he didn't want to burden him. He said he was going to try to straighten himself out." She wiped her eyes and gave a sniff. "When Shelby told me about Drew being in big trouble with drug dealers from Nottingham, I said I'd get in touch with Shane to see what he advised. He said the only thing they could do to avoid being hurt was to get away. You can be sure that Shane wouldn't have scared them unless he really did think they were in danger."

Jane's impatience got the better of her. Instead of comforting Faye, as would normally be her first instinct, she pressed on. "Do you know where Shane is?"

Faye breathed in and exhaled slowly, as if used to using the self-calming technique. "Shane's here. In Lincoln. He doesn't come to the house, and I don't know where he lives, but sometimes I see him standing at a distance, watching over us. I'll be pushing Jess on the swings at the park, and I'll look up and he'll give me a nod and a smile, then just walk on. I think — hope — he's getting himself sorted out. That he's keeping away until he's better. Maybe seeing us every now and again, even at a distance, helps him by reminding him of what he's missing."

It was obvious that Faye wanted desperately for this to be true. Jane found herself rooting for them all. She waited, hoping Faye would have some more information for her.

"Okay," Faye said at last. "I swear I don't know where Shane is. I haven't made any effort to find out, but he has friends. I could give you their contact details, and maybe you could speak with them. Maybe one of them will be able to help you. I need to go now. I'll be late for work if I don't get Jess dropped off at nursery in time."

Jane squeezed Faye's arm. "Thank you."

She left Faye's house with a list of names. For a few minutes, she sat in her car, resisting the urge to drive straight to the first address, but she knew how taking matters into her own hands would appear to Warwick. Better to let Warwick decide what to do with the information. She tried calling her and when the call went straight to voicemail, she left a text. As soon as Warwick got in touch, she would show her Faye's list and tell her everything else she'd found out.

CHAPTER TWENTY-NINE

Steph
31 May 2019

Alec Healey's handler, Greg Boyce, contacted Steph and arranged a second meeting.

Alec had been busy. "Your man Cole Burke and two other dealers had a wee bit of an arrangement goin' on before the boys from the city moved in. They each kept to their own patch, their own list of clients. High demand for their goods, so plenty of room for everyone. No problem as long as nobody got greedy an' tried to poach someone else's customers. It seems that a county lines operation, probably based in Nottingham, moved here back in February or March. The local dealers were advised they could either work for them or fuck off. Clients were given new contact details to place their orders. Accordin' to the rumour mill, Cole Burke had a second phone that he used only for certain clients and continued dealing to them on the quiet. It seems that your man didn't know how to take a warning. Either that or he was a wee bit thick."

There was a short silence, meant, no doubt, for everyone to appreciate the extent of Burke's stupidity.

"Well, no' surprising, the city outfit was on to him pretty fast an', well, they had to make an example of him, didn't they?"

Steph thanked him for the information. "Have you got anything else for us, Alec?"

"Aye, I've got something else for you, lass." Another silence during which Steph could all but hear the drum rolls. "I've got a lead on Shane Watt. So, I'm guessin' you had no idea that Shane has a kid? A wee lassie. She lives with his partner, or ex-partner. And, before you ask, I don't have the partner's address. I only know she lives on the Cathedral Estate and her name's Faye. No idea what the kid's called."

"How old is the child?" Steph asked.

"Around two or three."

"If the little girl is in pre-school, she might be registered with a nursery," Elias said. "And the council might be able to help with a home address."

Steph gave out some rare praise. "Good work, Alec. Do we know if Shane's likely to be living with his partner and child?"

Alec shrugged. "I did say 'ex-partner'. She kicked him out when he cleared out their bank account to fund his habit. But she might be able to give you some pointers as to where to find him."

"Let's hope so. Any luck on tracking down where Nate Price might be being held?"

"Still putting out feelers on that one. I'll get back to you."

"Keep in touch," Steph said.

After Alec had gone, Steph said to Elias, "We need to make a start on finding Shane's ex. Can you take this back to the team and get them to check out local nurseries and play-groups, and any clubs that cater for carers and toddlers? The child probably won't have Shane's surname, but no harm in checking. And I need someone to contact the housing department at the council, see if we can find out this Faye's address that way. Can I leave you to sort that out, Sergeant?"

"Yes, boss."

An hour later, Elias greeted Steph with a triumphant grin. "Got it."

"Got what?" Steph asked. "A part in Corrie Street?"

"The name and address of the nursery attended by Shane Watt's daughter. I've contacted them and they've confirmed that Faye's daughter, name of Jessica, is there today. Faye will be collecting her at two."

Steph was underwhelmed. All it had required was a ring round. Bound to produce a result sooner or later. Still, she said, "Nice work, Sergeant. Let's go now."

Steph plugged in her safety belt. "Put your foot down, Elias. I want to get there before it closes."

"No problem, boss."

They made it with five minutes to spare.

The nursery manager, who introduced herself as Carrie Hadfield, showed them into her office to wait for Faye Crowther. They stood discreetly by the window. Before long, Carrie pointed to a woman in a Waitrose uniform. "That's Faye. The one with the little pink scooter. She often brings it along for Jessica. I'll just pop outside and ask her if she'd mind stepping inside for a bit. No need to mention that the police are here in front of the other mums. It'll only encourage all sorts of rumours."

Steph was surprised Carrie hadn't asked whether Faye was in some sort of trouble. Either she wasn't a nosey person or she was used to the police turning up at her nursery.

She and Elias watched from the window as Carrie drew Faye aside and whispered a few words in her ear. Heads immediately swivelled in their direction, eyes following them as they made their way into the building. Steph could almost hear the other parents and carers speculating. *Has Jess been naughty today? Is she unwell? Hope it's not contagious. Maybe she's . . .*

Faye seemed on edge when she arrived in Carrie's office holding her daughter's hand. Carrie had obviously explained the situation on the way in.

Faye's eyes fixed on Steph. "Carrie said you're detectives, and that you want to talk to me. What's happened?"

Steph raised an eyebrow. "What do you think has happened?"

At this, Faye clutched Jessica closer to her, causing the child to look up at her with wide, startled eyes.

"Would you like me to read to Jessica while you talk?" Carrie offered. Faye nodded. They waited while Carrie led the child from the room.

"Relax, Ms Crowther. Nothing's happened to anyone as far as we know. We'd just like to ask you some questions about Shane."

Faye looked confused. "Shane?"

Steph gave a sigh. "Jess's father?"

"But I've already told Officer Bell everything I know about Shane," Faye said. "Don't you people talk to each other?" She looked from Steph to Elias and back again.

Steph stared at her. "Special Constable Bell? She's been to see you?"

"Just this morning. She'd spoken with Shelby and Drew. She went to see them because she thought Drew might be able to help her find Nate."

If Faye had told her Jane Bell was the head of MI6, Steph would have been less shocked. She swallowed.

"I'm sorry to have to bother you with the same thing all over again, but SC Bell is not an experienced police officer. She's only a . . . a volunteer. You mentioned Shelby and — Drew, was it? Let's start with them."

CHAPTER THIRTY

Jane
31 May 2019

Jane's tutoring session ended a few minutes early. As she shut the lid of her laptop, a loud knocking at her front door made her jump. *All right, all right. I'm coming.*

Jane stared at the woman on her doorstep. "Oh. Hello, ma'am. Sarge. Did you get my text?"

"What text?" DI Warwick's tone, cool at the best of times, dripped liquid nitrogen.

"I sent you a text this morning, ma'am. I have some information that I thought might be of interest to you." Jane looked past Warwick to where DS Elias Harper stood at her back, gesticulating, mouthing something that she couldn't interpret but which she thought might be, 'watch out'.

"All right if we come in," Warwick said. It wasn't a question. Jane stood aside to let the irate DI stomp past. Elias followed, avoiding Jane's eye.

Warwick had been in Jane's house before. She made for the sitting room but didn't sit down. There was no preamble. "I want to know what you know about Shane Watt and Nate

Price, and why you've been snooping around asking questions about them."

Jane picked up her phone and checked that her text had sent. It hadn't. There was one of those annoying red triangles next to it and a message saying, 'failed to send'. *Dammit.* She held her phone out to show Warwick.

"Why wouldn't you have checked that it had sent? Oh, never mind. Just answer my previous question, if you can remember it."

"I haven't been snooping. I didn't even know Shane Watt existed until yesterday. As you know, I held Lana Kerr as she was dying. I felt a sort of responsibility towards her—"

Warwick interrupted with one of her customary grunting sounds. "When will you learn that your naive sense of attachment to victims is misplaced? You aren't responsible for them, and you sure as hell are not responsible for investigating their murders. You are not a trained detective, and your amateur meddling does more harm than good. There are correct procedures to follow. Failure to adhere to them can result in hours of work being compromised. At worst it can mean a guilty person walking free because of shoddy police work."

Warwick was red in the face. Jane bristled at the word 'meddling', but, mindful of what Allie had said about Warwick being a trained detective with years of experience, she bit her tongue and tried looking at things from Warwick's point of view.

Maybe the source of Warwick's antipathy wasn't arrogance, she reasoned. Maybe it arose out of passion for her job. *She cares about doing things the right way because she wants to ensure justice for the victims. She's worried I'll cock up the investigation by not adhering to proper procedure. It's not personal.* A less generous thought intruded. *Why should I make all the effort? Takes two to tango.* She sent it floating off on a puffy cloud of broad-mindedness. This hostility between her and Warwick was unprofessional and unproductive. Jane's friends were always telling her that she was by nature a kind and tolerant person. Well, DI Warwick had certainly got under her skin and shown her another side of herself. A side that she didn't much care for. *Damn woman brings out the worst in me.*

Jane was weighing up what to say when Warwick got her second wind.

"You're a special constable. You do not go off conducting your own investigation. Do. You. Understand?"

She doesn't make it easy. Jane made an effort. "Sorry. You're right, of course. Ma'am."

Warwick looked slightly taken aback but recovered quickly. "Of course I'm bloody right."

Jane winced. *You just can't give an inch, can you, DI Up-Yourself?*

Warwick cleared her throat, "So, my question."

Jane told her everything. How she'd been approached by Caleb at her school talk on county lines, and how he had expressed concerns about his friend, Drew. "When I spoke to Caleb's form teacher, who happened to be an old colleague of mine from my teaching days, he mentioned that Drew had been associating with an older boy called Wes who'd been expelled from school some few years previously after he was found to be involved in drug dealing.

"I taught Drew's sister, Shelby, a few years ago, and when I heard that Shelby was looking after Drew, I was concerned and paid her a call to see if there was anything I could do. That was when I met her neighbour, Faye, who helped me find where Shelby and Drew were hiding out."

Jane recounted the conversation she'd had with Faye that morning.

When she finished, Warwick said, "DS Harper and I have been investigating Cole Burke's murder. We've also been searching for Nate Price. We believe he's been abducted and coerced into working for a county lines operation in Lincoln. The fact that Lana Kerr mentioned Nate's name to you was deeply concerning."

"So, the same people who killed Lana might still have Nate," Jane said.

"Yes. And it was this Drew who told you about Shane Watt?" Warwick asked.

"Yes. Apparently, Shane was one of Cole's clients and he warned Drew off working for him. Initially, Cole never let on to Drew about the gang takeover. Shane knew that Drew lived next door to his ex-partner, Faye, and their daughter, Jessica. I think he might have been worried about county lines people calling on Drew because of the danger it might represent for Faye and Jessica. This was before Cole Burke was even murdered—"

"Watt would have felt vindicated when that happened," Warwick interjected. "Wes knew where Drew lived, and that he was being cared for by his sister, a young woman on her own. The county lines people could have moved in right next door to his family. This might also explain why Watt disappeared. Not only was he afraid because of his association with Cole, he was also afraid of leading gang members to Faye and Jessica." Warwick looked at Jane. "We know that when you spoke with Faye Crowther, she gave you contact details for some of Watt's friends. Do have them still?"

"Er, yes." Jane suspected she knew what was coming next. She was right.

"On no account do you follow them up. Understood?"

"Yes, ma'am. Do you think Shane knows where to find Nate?"

When Warwick ignored her question, Jane said, "So, why are you looking for Shane, then — er, ma'am?" She expected an abrupt reminder to mind her own business.

"We're hoping that Shane might know some of Cole's ex clients. If we can find out who they are, we can set up a surveillance operation, learn who's supplying them now, in the hope it might help us locate the cuckooed house, which in turn might lead us to Nate."

"But not the people at the top," Jane commented.

"It's not always possible to get to the top, but any disruption in the supply chain, hopefully one that leads to a sizeable seizure of drugs and keeps them off the streets, is a win of sorts. We know the drugs are coming from Nottingham, and we've got a team from EMSOU-ROCU on board."

Jane was emboldened by Warwick's sudden willingness to share. "Shane recognised Drew because he lived next door to Faye and his daughter. When I spoke with Faye, she said she thought Shane was watching over her and Jessica from a distance, presumably in case the gang moves in on Faye, threatens her, or worse. It might be worth having someone keep an eye on Faye. It could lead to Shane, if he's watching his family at a distance."

"Yes, that had occurred to us," Warwick said, for once without any hint of sarcasm. "But it was good thinking."

Jane's eyes widened. Had Warwick just complimented her? Not only that, she was sure Warwick's lips had twitched into something like a smile. Blink and you'd miss it.

"Thank you, ma'am."

"Do you have any other information for us, SC Bell?"

"No. There's nothing else I can think of. I found out the name of Nate's school, but I expect you know that already, and I suppose you've found out where he lives too."

Warwick raised a disdainful eyebrow. "Of course."

"Will you check Nate's house again? If he manages to get away from the cuckooed house, which I know is unlikely, he might go home."

"Thank you, SC Bell. Please try not to tell us how to do our job."

"No, ma'am." *Wouldn't dream of it.*

CHAPTER THIRTY-ONE

Nate
20–21 May 2019

Nate and Lana immediately began planning their escape. Neither of them said it, but Nate suspected that, like him, Lana believed any delay would only make them think twice, maybe even change their minds.

"Can we run through it one last time?" It was the night before the Great Escape as they'd taken to calling it. Nate knew the plan by heart, but he needed to hear it again. He had to be sure there was nothing they'd missed. He lay beside Lana on her lumpy mattress, and she nestled against him. From across the room came the sound of Dex's steady breathing. So what if he was only pretending to be asleep? He knew about the plan, and he'd made it known that he considered it reckless and stupid.

Lana whispered in the darkness. "In the morning, I'm going to an address I've been to a lot of times before to do a drop. When I leave there, I'm going to walk off in the same direction as usual, in case the client is watching me, then at the next street corner, I'll go the opposite way from normal and walk for about five minutes before I stop and ask someone how I get to the nearest police station."

"A shop assistant or someone like that," Nate reminded her urgently. "Not just someone at random off the street. They could be anyone."

"I know, I know. That's what I meant."

"Sorry."

"When I get to the police station — or if I manage to wave at a police car and attract their attention — I tell them my name and say I was kidnapped in Nottingham by drug dealers who're making me work for them." Lana searched for Nate's hand and held it. "What if they don't believe me? What if they take too long to believe me? Wolf and Shark will come here and hurt you and Dex. Then they'll kill your mum." She gripped Nate's hand so tightly his fingers felt like they were being crushed.

"Shh. That's not going to happen. Remember the motto."

"Failure's not an option." Lana said quietly, relaxing her grip.

Nate had said it before, but he said it again. "The police will have heard of you. When kids go missing, they put their names on some kind of database. If you give them your name, they'll check it and know that you're missing. I saw someone on the news talking about drug dealers abducting kids even younger than us. It's a big thing now, and the police know about it. They're bound to believe you."

Lana had told Nate something of the circumstances that she'd left behind at home. He knew she dreaded being sent back there, but she feared staying at this house even more.

They lay quietly for a while, until Dex groaned, and turned in his sleep. Nate sighed. He was reluctant to leave Lana's side. "I'd better go back to my own mattress in case Dex wakes up and sees us." He began to rise.

Lana tugged on his sleeve. She whispered shyly, "Will you kiss me first?"

Nate caught his breath. He wouldn't have dared to ask her, even though he'd been wondering for some time what it would be like to feel his lips on hers. Swallowing, he whispered back. "Yes."

He felt for her face and found her nose, then traced a line from there to her lips. Emboldened, he moved his hand down to cup her chin like he had seen people do in movies. Lana tilted her head upwards and he lowered his lips to hers.

His dry lips brushed against her dry, flaking lips, and he felt the split in the middle of her lower lip that bled sometimes, making him wish he could fix it. He'd never kissed a girl before. He didn't know what it was meant to feel like, but now he knew that it felt like nothing he'd ever felt before, and in a very good way.

"Goodnight," he whispered, drawing away with reluctance. Then the words tumbled out before he could stop them. "I love you."

Silence. Nate tensed in embarrassment, wishing he hadn't spoken. Why couldn't he have left it at the kiss?

Then, "I love you too." Lana's voice, tremulous and soft, making him release the breath he had been unaware he was holding, which was just as well, for his chest immediately swelled with joy until he felt like his heart would burst.

In the morning, Wes watched over Nate as he counted out Lana's packages. She was expected to return for more later. That way, if she was stopped by the police, the loss would be minimised. Unfortunately, it also meant that Wes would be expecting her back in just over an hour and a half.

Nate avoided looking at Lana as much as possible, but he could sense that she was on edge. Her hand shook as she concealed the packages amid a collection of other items in her backpack. He felt sick with concern for her.

Wes didn't seem to notice. Deliveries were not usually made during school hours, but a customer had requested a morning drop. He reminded Lana, "Remember, anyone asks why you're not at school, you say you live in Nottingham and your school's closed for a teacher training day. You've come to Lincoln with your mum because she works in an office here, and her boss said it was okay for you to come to work with her for the day. You've just popped out to get some sandwiches for her and you."

"I know, I know. Same as always," Lana said.

Nate smiled, remembering what Lana actually did when this situation arose. *I just give them the finger and tell them to mind their own business.*

Nate watched her make her way to the door. She looked back over her shoulder at him and smiled, a sad, shy sort of smile, which made him want to rush over and hug her to him for ever. Instead, he mouthed, "I love you."

Then, Lana was gone.

A few minutes passed. Then, Wes crossed the room to Nate and slapped him hard on the face. "That's the last you'll see of your girlfriend, you traitorous little shit."

Dex was looking down at the floor.

"Dex?" Nate said in a thick voice. His face was numb. "What have you done?"

Dex wouldn't look at him. Wes patted Dex on the shoulder. "Done good, haven't you, Dex? At least there's one loyal soldier I can count on in this house."

CHAPTER THIRTY-TWO

Steph
31 May 2019

"At least she hasn't compromised our investigation." Steph glanced at Elias, but he was looking the other way. She had been ranting on a bit.

Apparently, he'd been listening. "She's found out practically as much as us in a week. She's even given us a lead on Shane Watt's whereabouts. If she hadn't spoken with Faye Crowther first, Crowther would never have given us information on Shane Watt. All credit to her for tracking Watt down."

His words rekindled Steph's resentment. "Come on, DS Harper. She's been giving talks about county lines at half the schools in Lincoln. Sooner or later, she was bound to come across someone with a connection to Nate. This other boy, Wes, used to go to Caleb's school. He probably stalked vulnerable-looking kids around the perimeter. It was sheer luck that that kid came up to Bell after her talk at his school, otherwise she'd still be completely in the dark about everything. He set off a chain of connections that would have been hard to miss, even for an inexperienced special."

Even as she said it, she knew she was being unfair. Sure, Bell had been lucky, but she'd also asked the right questions of the right people and followed a logical thread that had led her to Shane Watt.

"You told her she'd done well," Elias pointed out, quietly. "You wouldn't have said it if you didn't mean it. I appreciate it must have been hard. You would never have said something like that to her a few months back."

"Only because she was practically panting for praise." Steph fell silent, aware that she sounded rancorous, troubled by the thought that she had not always been this ungenerous. Was it really possible to find a middle way between the 'little ray of sunshine' Kaz remembered and her present self?

Surely, she still had the capacity to be kind? She'd been sincere when she told Frieda Arya that she was grateful to Bell for saving her life. She'd meant for Frieda to tell Bell what she'd said, but why had she baulked at telling Bell herself?

Had it been fear of opening up a channel to better relations — perhaps even friendship — with Bell that had restrained her? She'd pulled back and hardened her attitude, seen Bell as a threat. Was she letting Cal win every time she behaved this way?

There was something else too. Usually when Elias spoke to her like this, it fanned her resentment of him. She hated that her sergeant had this hold over her. It was a form of blackmail.

She'd been hostile to Elias even before he'd struck the deal with her about seeking help for her issues in return for his silence. As she was hostile to most people. Those PCs at the station had been right when they described her as hard and uncompromising. People were a threat until you knew otherwise. It was unwise to trust them. She'd created her hard persona to keep people at a distance. If no one could get close to her, no one could hurt her. But in keeping everyone at arm's length, she was pushing away the good along with the bad.

She'd convinced herself that Elias was ambitious, that he planned to undermine and usurp her, destroy her reputation and take her place in the police hierarchy. She'd interpreted what she thought of as his over-familiarity with her as lack of respect. Now she was less certain. From talking with Dr Bryce, she was beginning to recognise that Elias could actually be a good and loyal colleague and friend who'd have her back — if she let him. Why else would he have urged her to seek help rather than ratting her out to the powers that be, thereby saving her career?

Steph sighed. All this introspection and self-analysis was exhausting and time-consuming, and she had a job to do. She dug out her phone and consulted the list of Shane's friends that Faye had given them, stared at it for a moment, frowned. "What was the name of that psychiatric nurse who worked for the rehab team? The one who said he treated Shane Watt when he worked in A & E at Lincoln County?"

Elias thought for a moment. "Colm Doyle."

"There's a 'Colin D' on Faye's list. No surname. If she'd never seen the name Colm written down, she might have thought it was 'Colin.' It's pronounced similarly. Could it be the same person, I wonder?"

Elias looked sceptical. "Bit of a long shot, boss. He didn't say he was Watt's friend, only that he'd come across him at the hospital. If he is the same person, why wouldn't he have mentioned to us that Watt had a partner and a child? He would have known that sort of information might help us trace him."

"Unless he didn't know Shane had a family. But, if he is a friend of Shane's, wouldn't it be odd if he didn't know something like that? He might have deliberately withheld the information to stall us finding Watt. I think we'll speak with him first."

"One way to find out if he is Colm Doyle." Elias took out his phone. "Hello. Detective Sergeant Elias Harper speaking. I have a question about one of the names on your list of Shane's friends." After a pause, during which Steph surmised Faye was speaking, Elias asked, "Colin. Do you happen to know his surname? It's Doyle. Thank you, Ms

Crowther. You have a good day." To Steph, he said, "Looks like you might be right, boss."

Steph had instructed Elias to obtain addresses for all three of the people on Faye's list. Another phone call, this time to Kaye Flyte at the Antisocial Behaviour team to establish Doyle's present whereabouts, established that he was on a week's leave. "You should be able to catch him at home. He said he was doing a bit of decorating this week."

Fifteen minutes later, Doyle opened his door in answer to their knock, dressed in paint-spattered white overalls. He looked over his shoulder, a sure tell if ever Steph had seen one. "Your mate Shane helping you decorate, is he?"

Doyle frowned. Steph didn't give him the opportunity to deny it. "Before you get going, Colm, let's cut the crap, shall we? We know Shane's in there."

They didn't, but Doyle's blush was all the confirmation they needed. "I don't know what you're talking—"

Before he could complete his sentence, a voice called from further down the hall. "It's all right, Colm. Let them in."

Steph recognised Shane's voice. "Thank you, Mr Watt," she called out, as Colm abandoned his pretence and beckoned them inside.

Shane, too, was in white overalls. On his head a red baseball cap, spotted with white paint, in his right hand, a roller.

Steph smirked. "It's been a while, Shane, but we're pleased to renew our acquaintance with you. We met your ex-partner and your daughter yesterday. They're both fine. Then again, you know that. You've been keeping a watchful eye on them, haven't you?"

"Leave Faye and Jess out of this," Shane growled.

"Faye and Jessica are fine, but a twelve-year-old girl is dead, and at least one young lad that we know of may be in grave danger. Isn't it time you told us what you know?"

Colm squeezed Shane's shoulder. "Maybe it's time, man." Shane gave him a nod. He put down his roller, stepped out of his overalls and handed them to Colm. Colm showed everyone into his small kitchen. He smiled at Shane. "I'll be right back."

In his absence, Shane prowled the kitchen, making Steph nervous, given his tendency for flight. No one spoke until Colm returned, minus his overalls and equipment.

They all sat down.

Steph addressed Watt. "Last time we spoke, Shane, you were in a hurry to get away. As I remember, you were upset at hearing that Cole Burke had been tortured and murdered, but you were unwilling to give us any information that might have helped us find his killer."

Shane clasped his hands behind his neck and leaned forward, pressing his elbows together.

"Look, I went to stay at my brother's place in Norfolk for a bit after Faye asked me to leave, but I wasn't there long. When I got back to Lincoln, I badly needed a fix. I called Burke to sort it and arranged to meet one of the kids he had running deliveries for him. The kid turned out to be Faye's next-door-neighbour's brother, Drew. Imagine what a shock that was for me. I didn't want trouble finding its way to Faye's door. I'd heard the rumours that Cole was working for a county lines operation. I'd planned on speaking to Shelby, but as it happened, Faye contacted me first — and, well, you know what my advice to Shelby was. I felt bad about scaring her and her kid brother, but I did it to protect Faye and Jessie. Like I said, I didn't want trouble finding her through me, or anyone else. But I did it for the kid too. He could have got himself into serious trouble."

"Why didn't you tell us any of this when we spoke to you in the café that day just after Cole's murder?" Steph asked.

Watt didn't answer for a moment.

"The truth? I was scared. Scared the gang that killed Cole would get to me through my association with him. Scared of what might happen to Faye and Jessie. When you said he'd been murdered, I panicked and decided the best thing would be to disappear for a bit. The last thing I wanted was for a gang member to see me talking to the police." He looked at Steph. "And yeah, I was also scared you'd think I killed him. You told me I was a suspect."

"You didn't disappear entirely. We know you've been watching over Faye and Jessica."

"I've been cautious."

Steph nodded. "We think the people who killed Burke also killed Lana Kerr. You know about Lana?" Shane nodded. "We also believe that another boy — Nate Price — who acted as a runner for Cole has been abducted by the gang and is being held in a cuckooed house. So, as you'll no doubt appreciate, we're eager to find Nate before anything happens to him. If it hasn't already."

Steph decided to confide some information in Shane. "Nate's name was the last word Lana ever spoke." She let that sink in. "So any information you can give us on Cole Burke might help us find and save him. What did Colm mean just now when he said he thought it was time you told us?"

Shane looked to Colm, who gave a nod. To Steph's surprise, Shane got up and left the room. Startled, she made to rise, but Elias beat her to it and followed him. They both returned moments later, Shane carrying a fraying canvas backpack. There were zipped pockets on either side, and from one of these he extracted a mobile phone with a cracked screen. He handed it to Steph. She stared at it in disbelief. "Is this what I think it is?"

Shane nodded. "It belonged to Cole. That's why I bolted that day you saw me outside his place. I wasn't really trying to scramble over the wall into the dyke, I was getting rid of the phone. I dropped it over into the grass on the bank. I went back and retrieved it a couple of days later."

"What were you doing with Burke's phone? How did you get hold of it?"

Shane met her gaze. "I got a light-fingered acquaintance of mine to swipe it from him when he was in the pub. This was just before he was killed. He had me in his list of

219

contacts and I didn't want a criminal gang getting hold of it and seeing my name."

Colm produced a charger and connected the phone to a socket. The phone asked for a password.

"It's shit," Shane said. Steph stared. "The password." He spelled it out. "S H I T."

"I know how to spell it. It's just a stupid password," Steph snapped. "How did you work it out?"

Shane shrugged. "I always start with four-letter words. Got it in three."

Steph checked Burke's contacts — his list of clients. Her eyes widened. She looked at Elias and saw her own excitement reflected in his eyes.

"And you've been withholding this evidence since then? You must have known it might have helped us with our investigation into Burke's death."

Shane stared at his hands. "I know what you're thinking. A junkie doesn't care about anything but his next fix. I'm not proud of myself."

"Maybe not, but that doesn't alter the fact that if you'd spoken up sooner, we might have saved a life," Steph said.

Colm said, "You cared about your family, Shane, and it wasn't your intention to do any harm." To the others, he said, "Shane came to me after Cole Burke's death. He knew that if Cole had spilled any information on him to his killers, if he'd told them Shane might have his phone, his life could be in danger."

Steph was as angry and disgusted with Colm as she was with Shane. "And he's been staying with you ever since. You lied to us before when we asked if you knew of his whereabouts. You failed to mention that he had a family. I could arrest the pair of you right now for withholding evidence and obstructing the course of justice."

"Shane hasn't used at all since he's been staying with me. With my help he's going to get clean." Colm spoke as though that exonerated the pair of them.

"Well good for you both!" Steph snapped. "While you've been cleaning up, we've been investigating two murders, at least one of which might have been avoided if you'd had the goddamn guts to speak with us sooner." She glared at Colm Doyle just to reinforce that she regarded him as equally at fault.

Shane scratched at the AMC motto on his arm, making it bleed.

"Easy," Colm said, reaching out to press his shoulder.

Infuriated, Steph turned away. All this time wasted. She signalled to Elias that it was time to leave.

CHAPTER THIRTY-THREE

Nate
21–30 May 2019

Nate shrank back in horror at Wes's words. Then he launched himself at Dex, hammering him with his fists and screaming every swear word he knew.

Wes wasn't exactly in a rush to come to his loyal soldier's aid. A few moments passed before he pulled Nate off Dex and shoved him roughly down on a chair. Nate couldn't bear to look at Dex, but he had the satisfaction of hearing him howl like a baby.

"So much for your little plan," Wes informed him. "Lana's a dead girl walking."

"What do you mean?" Nate knew exactly what Wes meant.

Wes leaned over him. "See, if there's one thing Shark and Wolf hate more than anything else, it's disloyalty. Lana will get what's coming to her."

No! What had he done? Fear for Lana, and guilt at his own part in her likely fate were all that restrained Nate from attacking Wes. He sat there, enraged but paralysed.

Throughout the rest of the day he waited for news, hollowed out by anxiety. Wes had locked him in the bedroom. Gazing over at the mattress where Lana had slept, he hoped that she'd be sleeping there again that night, because the alternative was that she'd never sleep anywhere again.

Night came and no one joined him in the bedroom. Had Dex been rewarded for his loyalty? His treachery? Was he sharing a room with Wes now, as one of his trusted soldiers? Nate didn't care. He never wanted to see Dex again.

In the middle of the night, he heard the sound of a car engine outside the house. Fear wrenched his gut. He had not yet been punished for his part in Lana's escape bid, and he dreaded the moment when Wolf or Shark turned up to give him what he deserved — just like Lana.

It wasn't Wolf or Shark, just the neighbours returning after a late night. How would they react if they knew what horrors were playing out next door? By the time they did, he would be dead or holed up in some other cuckooed house. At that moment, neither fate seemed more or less attractive to him.

Two days of solitary confinement followed, during which he was given only a bottle of water. Finally, he was allowed out to work. A delivery must have arrived, for there was weighing and bagging to be done. He sat at the table opposite Dex, neither of them speaking. Around noon, a pizza delivery arrived. Wes threw one of the boxes at Nate.

"They're not coming for you." Nate started at the sound of Dex's voice. Wes had left the room, but he'd be back within minutes. "Wolf and Shark. I told Wes it was all Lana's idea. That you knew about it, but didn't want to go along with it, tried to talk her out of it. That's the only reason you're not dead."

"Is Lana . . ?" The word stuck in Nate's throat.

Dex shrugged. "Dead? I don't know for sure. Wes isn't saying anything, but why wouldn't she be?" Then, angrily, "It's all your fault. Lana had accepted how things were until you came along and got her all wound up again." His voice shook. Nate realised that he was upset. It occurred to him that Dex had known Lana for longer than him. Maybe he'd had feelings for her too.

One day, about a week or two after Lana's escape bid, a new courier arrived at the house, a boy of fifteen or so called Spencer. He arrived alone — Wolf and Shark hadn't been around since the day of Lana's escape, which suggested they were lying low. All the more reason for Nate to fear that Lana was dead.

Spencer seemed nervous. He probably hadn't been doing this for long. Nate wondered how he'd been recruited, what he'd been threatened with to remain. He had a look about him that Nate recognised. It was the same look Lana had had, the one Dex still had, the one he'd probably see in his own eyes if he could look in a mirror. It was a look shared by the legions of children lost to the evils of county lines.

CHAPTER THIRTY-FOUR

Steph
3–7 June 2019

A wealth of intelligence could be extracted from a dealer's phone. Shane Watt's gift of Cole Burke's phone was one that Steph hoped would keep on giving.

The phone had been passed to the Digital Forensics Unit at EMSOU, where it would be picked apart to reveal Burke's call history, his text and voicemail messages, his photos, videos, contacts and internet use.

Data would also be sought from the phone service provider, from which the unit's intelligence analyst would gain additional call information and be able to map where the phone had been used. With luck, they would be able to identify calls made between Burke and his clients, particularly if his clients had registered their phones. Buyers were generally less solicitous about security.

So it was with some eagerness that Steph welcomed John Sulley's request for a meeting to discuss the intelligence that their analyst had obtained from Burke's phone. This time, Terry and John arrived in person and Steph and Elias sat down with them in a meeting room on the second floor at

Newport House to hear what they had to say. Steph was amused to see that her sergeant had his fingers crossed.

"Okay." Terry looked younger in the flesh. Steph reassessed her age as late thirties, not the forty-something she'd looked on the video link. She had spiked up her hair and wore dangly silver earrings. There was a comradely warmth in her eyes as she looked at them over the rim of her black-framed specs. She smiled at Elias. "Don't look so worried, Elias." Then it was down to business.

"We got the names of around a dozen of Burke's regular clients who'd registered their details when purchasing their phones, meaning that it was a walk in the park — or more precisely, around the databases — to confirm their last known addresses. Now, as you're aware, we simply don't have the resources to put all the names we've got under surveillance, so we're concentrating on two of Burke's regulars, a web developer by the name of Chris Bolan and a local businesswoman, Jackie Prothero. Both were in the habit of ordering their coke once a month, on approximately the same day — creatures of habit fortunately for us. Assuming they haven't given up their habit, they must be buying from another source, possibly our county lines dealer.

"Superintendent Aidan Caldicott has authorised directed surveillance. He'll be liaising with your boss this afternoon, so hopefully, we can get going with immediate effect — which is important as Burke and Prothero's key dates are imminent." Terry looked to John for confirmation of the dates, and he nodded.

"If we're lucky," Steph dared to hope, "we might get a courier who'll lead us to the cuckooed house where Nate Price is being held. Luckier still, and he'll lead us right back to his contact in Nottingham."

After imparting the information, Terry and John left promptly.

Elias turned to Steph. "What now?"

"Now we wait."

For the first three nights after surveillance was set up on Chris Bolan's house in Yarborough Crescent, all was quiet. No one was observed approaching his property, other than the postman and a woman with flyers for a pizza delivery service. Jackie Prothero's home overlooking the West Common on Long Leys Road was similarly quiet. Then, on the fourth day, Bolan was observed returning home in the middle of the afternoon instead of his usual time of six thirty in the evening.

Steph was on tenterhooks as she awaited updates from the surveillance team.

Half an hour later, a teenage boy with a canvas bag was spotted approaching Bolan's house, then turning up the path to his front door.

One of the surveillance team described the boy as white with a purply-red birthmark covering one side of his face. He looked to be around thirteen or fourteen. A moment later, an image of his face appeared on Steph's phone, and she instructed Elias to run it through the Compact Missing Persons system and the intelligence database in the hope of hitting a match.

"Dexter Curtis," Elias informed Steph promptly. "From Boston, Lincolnshire. Parents are both dead. He was living with his aunt and uncle in Spalding when he went missing. A neighbour of his aunt and uncle claimed to have spotted him hanging out in town with some older kids, but the sighting didn't lead anywhere. His eight-year-old brother still lives with his aunt and uncle."

Elias was interrupted by the voice of another member of the surveillance team. "Bolan's just come to the door and accepted a package from the kid. He handed over something in return, and the kid put it in his bag. An exchange has taken place."

"Right," Steph said. She didn't need to give any instructions. The officers had been well briefed. Bolan wasn't who they were after today. Instead, their brief was to follow the delivery boy.

Dexter was observed delivering packages to several more properties within walking distance of Bolan's place. One of them was Jackie Prothero's address.

A member of the surveillance team had followed him on foot, while relaying his location to his colleague, who in turn kept Steph up to date by mobile. After around one-and-a-half hours, Dexter was seen entering an end-of-terrace house on North Parade, a residential street ending in a cul-de-sac with steep steps leading up to Yarborough Road. Steph was informed that he'd gone inside. "Let me know when there's some action," she told the surveillance team.

"This could be the house where Nate's being held," Elias said.

"Again, we wait." Steph appreciated that the frustration she felt was shared by everyone involved. She drummed her fingers on her desk.

Beside her, Elias sighed and said, "*Though patience be a tired mare, yet she will plod.*"

"Oh, for fuck's sake, Elias. What have I told you about spouting the bloody Bard while on duty?"

Elias moved on from Shakespeare to the voice of doom. "Poor Nate's probably already dead. They killed Lana, why would they spare him? And what about Dexter Curtis, and anyone else who's in there against their will?"

Steph said nothing. The knowledge that they could be putting lives at risk while they gathered evidence was a constant, nagging worry.

A few moments later, Elias reported back on the owner of the property on North Parade. He was Glynn Stewart, a man in his fifties with a history of poor mental health. He had lived in the house with his mother — who had also been his carer — until her death, just over a year ago.

His nearest neighbour said that Glynn's mum had been "a bit peculiar", having "kept to herself", and that, referring to Glynn, "The apple didn't fall far from the tree."

Steph knew that vulnerable adults went largely unnoticed. She'd seen it again and again in her line of work

— adults with autism, personality disorders or other mental health issues being arrested for behaviours associated with their condition, a lot of the time because the support they needed just wasn't there. Such individuals were often socially isolated, with few friends or family, which was what made them such easy targets for criminals.

There were no new updates until the following morning. Steph was sitting alone in her office when a call came through from Terry Munks.

"Just to give you an update. Late last night a car parked outside the house on North Parade and a man got out accompanied by a lad. The man, we think, was Michael Dodd. Very early this morning, the lad — a white male of around fifteen years — was seen leaving the house. He boarded a train for Nottingham and was picked up again by our people at the station here. Something that might be of interest — on his way to Lincoln Station, he stopped to 'chat' with an older white male, early twenties possibly. I'll send you some images in a sec. A member of the surveillance team followed him from the station in Nottingham to a property in Forest Fields, which is now under surveillance. There'll be someone on his tail the minute he leaves the house. But don't expect too much. His transactions with the gang are probably limited to receiving instructions on his burner."

"Have you looked into the tenant or owner of the property?" Steph asked.

"I was just getting to that. George and Karen Green. Two kids, one a lad of fifteen, name of Spencer. I'm guessing our courier lives with mum and dad. They're all clean."

"Okay," Steph said. "You mentioned some images."

"Sending them now. First one is Spencer Green. Second is the unidentified white male he spoke with on his way to Lincoln Station."

Steph checked the first photo, of a lad poised at that awkward stage between boyhood and manhood — gangly and pimply, a bit of fuzz on his chin and upper lip. She scrolled to the second photo. And gave a start.

"You still there?" asked Terry.

"What? Yes. Sorry. It's just that I recognise the man in the second picture. His name's Noah Shore. He works in a barber's shop underneath the flat where Cole Burke lived and was murdered. Or at least, he worked there back in April. I don't know if he's still employed there. I do remember him being a bit jittery when we spoke with him directly after Burke's murder. We thought he might have been buying drugs from Cole and was worried we'd find out. We ran a background check on him at the time. He was clean. Plus, his name wasn't listed as a contact on Burke's phone."

"Still, it's a bit of a coincidence, him speaking with a kid who has a possible county lines connection," Terry said. "A kid who doesn't live in Lincoln."

Steph agreed. "Especially when that kid appears to be linked with the county lines operation that's taken over Cole's customers." She thought for a moment. "He was probably ordering his fix. We can't risk bringing him in for questioning."

"Want us to place him under surveillance too?"

"Yes, please, Terry. I'll forward his details to you. And thanks for the intel."

"No problem," Terry said. "Speak again soon."

More waiting. But the threads were beginning to pull together, and Steph felt more optimistic than she had in weeks.

CHAPTER THIRTY-FIVE

Nate
13 June 2019

Around three weeks — as far as Nate could calculate — after Lana's escape attempt, Dex told him that he'd overheard Wes speaking with Wolf or Shark, and that it sounded like they were soon to be on the move again.

"I'm not surprised. We've already been here a while," Dex said. "After a bit, the neighbours start to get wind that something's not right."

Nate wasn't surprised either. Part of him couldn't wait to get out of this place with its memories of Lana and the brief happiness they'd shared as they drew closer together, all tangled up with the terrible fate that he feared had befallen her. Another part of him believed that he'd be leaving something behind that he'd never be able to recapture.

Wes gave nothing away. He rarely spoke or interacted with Nate or Dex these days. It was weeks since he'd had a break from this place. Nate wondered why he did it. Was he being paid so much drug money that it made it worth the monotony, the isolation and sheer boredom of existing here week after week? It seemed to Nate that Wes was as much a prisoner as they were, for who would choose a life like this? Only a person for whom life offered no better prospects.

It seemed incredible to Nate now that he had been so easily — and cheaply — bought. A bag of fish and chips was all it had taken for him to latch on to Wes. Of course, it had been about more than just the gifts — he'd really believed that Wes was his friend. Looking at him now, Nate could scarcely believe he'd been so gullible.

Wes clocked that he was watching him. "What are you looking at?"

"What happened to Lana?" It was the first time he had asked.

"Can't you guess?"

"Is she dead?"

Wes yawned. He actually yawned. "Who gives a shit?"

Something snapped. Weeks of suppressed rage and resentment and a whole lot more besides welled up and erupted. Nate shot out of his chair and headbutted Wes in the chest, sending him careening backwards on to the stone hearth. He sat astride him, slamming punches into his face over and over until he realised that Wes wasn't retaliating. He drew back. Wes was out cold.

Nate saw his chance. He sprinted for the door, but before he reached it, he heard Wes, apparently back in the land of the living, roaring to Dex, "Stop him!"

Now in the hall, Nate looked around, frantically, for something to use as a weapon. There was an old-fashioned barometer, like the one that his gran used to have, hanging to the side of the door. He lifted it off the wall and held it, raised, like a cricket bat, ready to take a swing at Wes as soon as he came barging through the door.

Dex barged through instead. Nate's nostrils flared as he raised his weapon, but before he could take a swing at him, Dex lunged forward and snatched the barometer. To Nate's astonishment he began hitting himself over the head with it, all the while exclaiming loudly, "Ouch! Aaah!" Blood dripped from a cut self-inflicted on his forehead.

Nate finally got it. Dex was helping him escape. "Come with me," he hissed, but Dex shook his head. Nate didn't stick around to persuade him to change his mind. He unlocked the door and bolted.

Outside he was assaulted by sensations he hadn't experienced in weeks — fresh air, the tickle of a light breeze, sunlight on his face. It took a moment to process. Then, he ran.

Adrenalin carried him a long way before a stitch in his side forced him to stop. Bending low over his knees, he sucked in great gulps of air, but not for long. Wes must be after him by now.

His long captivity and lack of wholesome food had weakened him. His lungs burned, his muscles cramped, and every time he stopped, it took longer to recover.

"Are you all right?" a woman with a toddler said. "You look terrible."

Nate's tears turned to hysterical laughter, causing her to draw her child closer and scurry away. Nate bit down on his fist to stop the laughter, only stopping when blood began to trickle over his knuckles. Then, he ran. Again.

When he could run no more, he walked, stumbled, walked a little more, eventually ending up in a part of town that seemed familiar. He had passed this way with his mum the day they arrived in Lincoln from Gainsborough. If Nate could have foreseen then what lay ahead of him, he'd have turned around and got straight back on the train.

As he turned a corner on to a cobbled street, he realised why the area seemed familiar. He was on Castle Square, with the cathedral on one side of him and the castle on the other, and between the two, standing outside the tourist information centre, was a man with a white ponytail playing a violin.

A woman stepped towards the violinist's open case and tossed a coin inside, drawing Nate's eye. When the small crowd had dispersed, and the man began turning over the leaves of the book on his music stand, searching for something else to play, Nate ran forward and pushed him, knocking him off balance. He took advantage of the man's surprise to help himself to a handful of coins from the case. Glancing back over his shoulder, he hoped he hadn't hurt him.

The stolen money paid for a bag of chips and a bottle of coke from a fish and chip shop, after which Nate felt some of his strength return. Enough for him to walk home. He needed to warn his mother that she might be in danger. Wolf and Shark would be out looking for him, and Angie could be a target too.

He was looking up at his mother's bedroom window when he heard the familiar voice of the old man who lived downstairs. "She ain't there, duck. Still in the hospital, far as I know."

Nate stared at him. "Hospital? W-what happened?"

Mr Thom shrugged. "Don't know, lad. Police came round and then an ambulance. It were all go for a bit."

"No!"

"She'll be all right, duck. They'll fix her up at the hospital, no worries."

"Wolf and Shark . . ." Nate's voice trailed away. How had they got to Angie so fast?

"I have to go." Sick with fear, Nate stumbled away.

They'd got to her. That was the only explanation. Mr Thom had said "she's still in the hospital", suggesting she'd been there a while. That didn't make sense. How had Wolf and Shark got to Angie first? Nate was tired and confused. His head hurt and he couldn't think straight. If Angie was in the hospital, she was safe for now, unlike him. They would still be looking for him.

He ran until he got the shakes, like Charlie Sullivan's mum when she went on her running machine. She'd hold out her trembling hands, saying, "Used up all my energy. I need some calories," which Nate and Charlie knew was code for coffee and cake.

It was a while since he'd thought of his Gainsborough friends, Charlie and Alfie. Thinking of Mrs Sullivan gave him a choky feeling in his throat. He wished he could bury his face in her bosom. Was that pervy? He didn't mean it in a sexual way — he just wanted to feel safe, cared for. If he'd had his phone, he could have called Charlie now, and his mum or dad would jump in their car and come for him.

Then he thought about Lana. At his most despairing, he feared that she was dead — Wolf would have made sure of that. Even so, he clung to a happy image of her in hospital being looked after in a comfy bed next to his mum, who'd given up drinking for ever. Now he really was slipping into the realms of fantasy. It was time to focus on satisfying his hunger instead of feeding off his daydreams.

There was some money left from the old man's takings, but, counting it now, he realised there wasn't enough for another takeaway. He'd have to look for a shop — one of those that sold all sorts and stayed open late. He'd walk until he found one.

Who knew a bag of crisps cost so much? They wouldn't even fill him up. In one of the fridges in a Spar shop there were some sandwiches that had been marked down because the use-by date was less than three hours away. Egg mayo, chicken mayo, ham, and cheese and pickle. He was spoilt for choice. All at 20p each. Nate grabbed one of each.

"You feeling hungry, duck?" the woman at the till asked. She was picking at her nails and didn't sound interested in knowing the answer.

"They're not all for me. My mum sent me out to get some for us all. Her and me and my big brother." Even half-starved, he didn't want her to think he was greedy.

If she didn't hurry up and serve him, Nate would rip the packaging off the chicken mayo sandwiches and stuff them in his mouth.

"Bit of a cheek charging for these really. They'd only be going in the bin in the morning. But I don't make the rules. You want something to drink? Them big bottles of cola are on special offer. Two litres for 89p."

It would leave him with only ten pence, but drinking was as important as eating, and with two litres of coke and four lots of sandwiches, he wouldn't have to worry about food the following day. "Yeah, okay. Can I have a bag, please?"

"I'll have to charge you ten pence for that."

"Whatever." Nate handed over everything he had.

The cola wasn't going to last as long as he'd thought. He'd only taken one long drink from the bottle and already it was a quarter empty. Half the sandwiches were gone. After eating the chicken ones, he still felt hungry, so he opened the egg mayo ones, telling himself to save one triangle for the morning. Then he remembered his mum once saying that eggs can make you sick if they're too old, so just to be on the safe side, he ate the second one too. Shame he hadn't been able to stretch to a bag of crisps. A sandwich wasn't the same without crisps, though being honest, he'd been too hungry to notice until he was on the second lot.

Darkness was closing in around the city, and it was no longer warm. Nate thought nostalgically of the puffer jacket he'd bought with the money he'd earned from Cole. *Cool* and *toasty*. That's how he'd felt wearing it for the first time.

The river he'd been following took him by surprise, widening unexpectedly into a small lake upon which narrowboats and cruisers bobbed silently in the glow of the lights from nearby buildings. The area was teeming with activity, even this late in the evening. There were people everywhere — gathered outside a cinema, queueing for a table in one of the many restaurants, or just strolling along the lakeside, dressed for an early summer's evening, as though they couldn't feel the chill in the air that was sending feverish shivers through Nate's limbs.

He thought he'd mingle with the throng. This wasn't the sort of place where Wolf and Shark would hang out. It was too bright, too . . . shiny. People like them belonged in the shadows with others of their kind, living off the misery and pain of kids like him and Lana, and Dex. The kids no one cared about.

He walked on, unseen, a shadow among the evening revellers, feeling like the ghost of a boy from another century where the notion of childhood had yet to be invented.

His footsteps led him, eventually, to the High Street, with its long, steep climb back to the looming cathedral, now bathed in soft floodlighting that made the sky around it glow like golden mist.

He was exhausted now, the grimness and anxiety of the day's events weighing on him — a solid, crushing force, sapping his strength and stifling his spirit.

There was a word for this, he knew. Despair. It meant without hope that things will get better. People on the news said it a lot — people who'd lost loved ones or their homes and possessions in wars, or in floods or fires or natural disasters. *That's what I am.* Nate reached the top of the hill and stood, utterly spent, near the place where the old man had played his violin earlier in the day. *A natural disaster.*

He walked through the biggest of three stone arches leading to the cathedral and stopped, remembering from a lesson in primary school that the cathedral had suffered its share of natural disasters. It had been burned by fire, almost completely destroyed by an earthquake, and at least one of its towers had collapsed in a storm, yet here it was. Maybe there was hope for him yet. The thought cheered him a little.

He walked alongside the cathedral until he came to some steps that led to a long, sweeping hill. He followed the curve of the hill downwards, coming eventually to a park where he found a brick shelter, somewhere to spend the night.

CHAPTER THIRTY-SIX

Jane
13 June 2019

Jane was doing routine paperwork when she received a call from Frieda. She was worried about Mr Kendrick. A customer had just mentioned that he had been mugged on Castle Square. Frieda was tied up at the café. Would Jane mind checking if he was all right? Jane set off immediately, hoping to find Merlin still there. He was in his favourite spot outside the Judge's Lodgings, playing an uplifting duet with a young woman, probably a student.

An audience of shoppers and tourists had stopped to listen. Jane listened too, feeling the music lift her spirits. She looked up suddenly and caught sight of the towering west front of the cathedral piercing a brilliant blue sky. For a few moments she experienced a sense of pure joy.

A voice to her left said, "Isn't it beautiful? They sound like angels. I can see you're very moved, my dear." It was an older woman. She patted Jane's arm before moving away. Jane looked after her, irritated. The sound of the woman's voice had broken the spell and brought her back down to earth. It would have been nice to have experienced that sense of bliss for just a few moments longer.

As soon as the violinists' bows stilled, there was a short round of applause before the little throng of people moved on. Quite a few threw coins into Merlin's open violin case or complimented the players. One or two consulted the time with irritable looks, as though resenting the musicians for delaying them, stealing precious minutes from their busy day.

Jane approached Merlin and the young woman. She dropped a two-pound coin on to the faded blue-velvet lining of Merlin's case, saying, "Thank you. That was beautiful, though I'm afraid I have no idea what the two of you were playing."

Merlin smiled at her. "Just some little thing by Haydn."

"Catch you later, Merl," the girl said, blowing him a kiss.

"Have you got a minute to talk, Merlin?" Jane asked.

"Of course."

They sat on one of the benches in the square, near the triple-arched Exchequer Gate leading to the west front of the cathedral.

"A little bird told me that you were mugged this morning."

"*Tsk tsk* . . . Frieda's been telling tales."

"She also told me that you were reluctant to report the incident."

"I didn't feel the need. Only my pride was injured. He took a few bits of loose change, that's all. If he'd had any sense, he would have snatched my violin. It would have sold for a pretty sum." He caressed the body of his violin lovingly. "To be honest, he was such an unkempt, scrawny little tyke that I didn't begrudge him a share of my meagre takings. I hope he spent it on a good feed."

"Hmm. I'd advise you to pop along to the station so they can take details for a crime report, Merlin. Might help us find him."

"I see you're wearing your special constable's hat this morning, Jane, even though you're not in uniform."

"You should take this more seriously, Merlin. Frieda said he pushed you over. You could easily have been hurt."

"It was more a matter of losing my balance than being pushed over. Don't go birching the little urchin on my account, Jane."

Jane gave a deep sigh. "Can you describe him for me, at least? I promise I'll do nothing more than clip him around the ear if I spot him."

To her surprise, Merlin tapped his two front teeth. "I looked up and saw him listening to me play for a bit before he . . . unbalanced me. He seemed a bit out of breath, and he was breathing in through his mouth. I noticed there was a bit of a gap between his two front teeth. Other than that, he looked skinny and uncared for, poor little fellow."

Jane stared at him. Merlin frowned. "Now remember your promise and don't go throwing him in prison."

"Prison is the last thing he needs," Jane said quietly. "He's had enough of being locked up." She gave him the bare bones of the story, without revealing too much.

Merlin listened attentively, only interrupting her once to ask her to explain the term, 'cuckooed house'. He shook his head sadly when she'd finished. "Why do we as a society allow our children to live in such misery?" He sighed. "Perhaps he'll come back again when he runs out of money. I'll look out for him. If I see him again, I'll alert you immediately."

"Thanks, Merlin."

Jane left him to resume his busking. Feeling that she had to do *something*, she texted or emailed Nate's picture to every-one she could trust to look out for him, adding a few words of caution. "If you do spot him, contact me immediately. Do not put yourself at the slightest risk. The people Nate's mixed up with are highly dangerous."

She also texted DI Warwick to update her. Warwick was looking for Nate too. As were the predators, Wolf and Shark.

With all that looking, surely someone must find him soon. Jane made a silent wish. *Let it be the right someone.*

At 6.30 p.m. Jane began getting ready for her shift but her mind was on her visit from DI Warwick and DS Harper two weeks earlier. She assumed that by now they must have tracked down Shane Watt and interviewed him. If only she could be a party to what they'd learned. Warwick must have uncovered a lot by now. As the SIO on the investigation into the murder of Cole Burke, she must have quickly gleaned that there was a connection between his death and Lana Kerr's, which must only have been confirmed when she learned that Lana's last word was Nate's name.

In Burke's case, the motive for his killing could have been a territorial dispute, but why would they kill a twelve-year-old girl? For disobeying them? Betraying them in some way? Lana had been carrying cash in the bag that the biker snatched after fatally stabbing her. Had she been planning to escape with the money and been found out?

There was no need to imagine the conditions Lana must have been kept in at the cuckooed house, the abuses to which she had probably been subjected. Jane had listened to harrowing accounts from officers who'd been involved in freeing victims of cuckooed houses. She sighed. *Better get a move on or I'll be late.*

Tim Sterne greeted her with a grin when she arrived at the station. "Ready for another thrilling ten-hour shift then, Jane? I'm hoping for a quiet night. Left hip's giving me gyp. Smothered it in some anti-inflammatory stuff Meg got but it's bloody useless."

It wasn't the first time Jane had heard about Tim's hip. "You should see someone about that."

"I'll see the barman down the Crown soon as I'm off duty." It wasn't the first time she'd heard this joke either, and they both knew the pubs would be long closed by the time they got off, but she smiled indulgently.

It seemed that Tim's wish for a quiet shift was not going to be granted, for within twenty minutes they were alerted to

241

a disturbance on a residential street on the Cathedral Estate, where there had been complaints of noise, bad language and brawling outside an end-of-terrace house. When they drove up, they discovered that a family birthday party had got out of hand after the guests had been drinking all afternoon and early evening.

The revellers had spilled out of the house on to the street. Some were singing and dancing, others staggering about drunkenly chattering, but several individuals were talking in raised, angry voices, and the situation looked volatile.

"Reckon that lot are going to start kicking off soon," Tim said. "Let's get some back-up."

By the time another two response vehicles turned up, Jane and Tim were in the thick of it, receiving abuse from all sides as they struggled to prevent the heated arguments erupting into violence.

They'd hoped to avoid making arrests — some of the partygoers were on their side, trying, with Jane and Tim, to encourage the more argumentative and unstable among them to call it a night and go home. Others berated them for harassing their friends and family, all adding to the disturbance and making Jane's and Tim's job harder.

Unfortunately, a man and a woman had to be arrested when they turned on two of the newly arrived officers. This had a sobering effect on the others, and people began to disperse, restoring calm and order to the street at last.

Back in the car, Tim remarked, "What did I say about wanting a quiet shift? There's no such thing. Still, the adrenalin's done wonders for my hip."

Jane laughed. "No need to go to the Crown for medicinal purposes now then."

Tim put her straight. "You're wrong there. I need it all the more now to calm my nerves."

"I might just join you if we can find a landlord willing to serve us at four in the morning. Tim, while we're on the Cathedral, do you mind if we just swing by a house on Lancaster Way? It's only a minute from here."

Tim turned around at the next junction. "Anywhere in particular?"

Jane had done her research on Google Street View, so she recognised the block of flats where Nate lived immediately. "Do you think we could just park outside that block for a couple of minutes while I take a walk around?"

Tim raised an eyebrow, but he didn't object.

"You can wait here if you like," Jane said.

Tim yawned. "Might as well stretch my legs."

Nate and his mum lived in the maisonette above the flat on the corner of the block. As they approached the ground-floor flat, a man appeared from the shadows at the door, leaning on a walking frame.

"What's going on? Seems to be a lot of interest in this block lately. Police have been by more times than I can count. I've been sat by my window all day and I seen them at least three or four times." He must have seen Jane look up at Nate's house, for he added, "You won't find nobody at home up there, duck. She was taken away in an ambulance weeks ago and I've not seen nothing of her since."

"What about her son, Nate? Have you seen him?" Jane asked.

"Funny you asking that. Hadn't seen hide nor hair of him for ages, until today. Turned up when I was taking some rubbish out to the bin."

Jane tried to contain her excitement. "You're sure it was him? Nate Price? Did you speak to him?"

The man looked as though he'd received an insult. "I just said, didn't I? It were him all right. I saw him with my own two eyes."

Jane apologised. "Go on."

The man told the story in his own way and in his own time. "When I saw him, I thought to myself, that looks like the young lad as lives upstairs. He were right scrawny, like. Blow over in a gust o' wind. Anyway, he seemed right upset when I told him his mum was in the hospital, like he didn't know anything about it. Said something right strange too."

"Oh?" Jane said. "What was that?"

"It were something about wolves and sharks. Like he thought his mum had been attacked by a monster. Thought I'd heard wrong. Either that or the lad wasn't all there. He took off like one of them sprinters in the Olympics."

"Right. Thank you, Mr, er?"

"Eric Thom's the name."

Jane contacted Warwick by text immediately. She wasn't entirely surprised to receive a phone call almost at once.

"What do you want, Bell?" DI Warwick's tone wasn't exactly hostile but neither was it friendly.

"I've just been out on patrol, ma'am. We were on the Cathedral Estate near the block where Nate Price and his mum live. I thought I'd just take a quick look, make sure the premises were secure."

Warwick didn't comment. Jane suspected she was thinking something along the lines of *Does she really expect me to believe that she just happened to be passing by that particular block of flats?*

Jane felt herself flush.

"And?" Warwick prompted. "Was everything in order?"

"Yes, but that's not why I called. While I was there, the downstairs neighbour came out." Jane told her what Eric Thom had said.

"That's useful information. Thank you for letting me know, SC Bell."

Is that all you have to say? "Right," Jane said. "That's two sightings in one day. At least we know Nate's alive and that he might not be being held in the cuckooed house anymore. Unless he was making a delivery. But it's wonderful to know he's alive, isn't it, ma'am?"

There was a moment's silence. Then, in a voice that sounded sincere, Warwick agreed. "Yes. It's very good news." She cleared her throat. "Thank you, SC Bell. Was that all?"

"Yes, ma'am. I hope you find him soon. Ever since poor Lana uttered his name, I've been worried on his behalf."

"I'll make sure you are informed of the outcome of the investigation."

Jane recognised a dismissal when she heard one. Still, she said, "I . . . If there's any way I can contribute, in my role as a special constable, I mean . . . I know it's unlikely, but if the occasion should arise, perhaps . . ." She faltered, imagining Warwick's face, sour at the very thought.

Warwick didn't hesitate. "*If* such an opportunity should arise, I'll be sure to let you know."

"Thank you, ma'am." Then, out of devilment, Jane added. "I hope to hear from you soon, ma'am."

Jane hoped she'd earned some Brownie points from DI Warwick. By their standards, the exchange between them had been reasonably civil. At least, on this occasion Warwick couldn't accuse her of meddling — Jane had been on duty when she'd come across the information. It didn't matter that neither of them had been fooling the other on the coincidence of her route that evening taking her to Nate Price's doorstep. Each had been aware that a level of mutual deception was taking place — and accepted it. Jane saw that as progress.

She'd stalled after giving the information, partly to irritate DI Warwick, but partly in the hope that some reciprocation would take place. Warwick's tone had made it quite clear where she stood on that.

CHAPTER THIRTY-SEVEN

Steph
13 June 2019

Steph filled Elias in on what Bell had told her about a boy answering to Nate's description stealing money from Mr Kendrick.

"If he's escaped, and he's on the streets, they'll be looking for him." Her brief euphoria at hearing that Nate was alive quickly turned to anxiety that he wouldn't stay that way for long.

"He could have been making a delivery, then returning to the house." Elias said.

Steph shook her head. "I don't think so. If he's stealing money, he's more likely to be on the run." Elias nodded, grim-faced.

Terry Munks and John Sulley contacted Steph by video link with news about Spencer Green.

"Spencer left his home first thing this morning," Terry said.

"Let me guess. He wasn't going to school."

"Nope. He went for a haircut."

Steph leaned forward in her seat. "In Lincoln?"

Terry looked puzzled. "No, in Nottingham. Why?"

Steph frowned. "Because the young man he spoke with before getting on the train to Nottingham — Noah Shore — works — or worked — in a barber's shop in Lincoln, remember?" There was a silence, during which Steph could tell from Terry's face the way her mind was heading, but it was John who got there first.

"Think there might be a spot of money laundering going on?"

Steph nodded. "It's a possibility, but we shouldn't jump to that conclusion just because a hairdressing business is one that often deals with cash. Then again, we do need to consider how the drug money is being cleaned."

"To be fair, the kid did come out with a level two fade," John commented dryly. "We'll get this place checked out. In the meantime, we've got something else for you. Terry, want to take over?"

"Sure," Terry said. "Michael Dodd, aka Shark. He's in Lincoln, at the house on North Parade, also as of this morning."

If Nate truly had managed to escape, had Shark arrived in Lincoln already to track him down? An image of the two bikers swooping down on Lana at the traffic lights on Burton Road in broad daylight flashed into Steph's mind, ramping up her fear for the boy's safety. And where, she wondered, was the other brother, aka Wolf?

Terry continued. "Our tech guys managed to install a covert CCTV camera on an empty house across the street from the suspected cuckooed house, just in case our surveillance team missed anything. We now have camera footage as evidence to back up their pictures. The Dodd brothers have a background in trafficking drugs. They're known to be violent. The tenant of that house, maybe even the kids who're the victims of child trafficking and or criminal exploitation, will hopefully testify against them. How do you want to move forward with this, boss?"

Steph leaned back in her seat again, thinking. She knew what Terry was asking. They had a choice. Move now on the cuckooed house or carry on with the surveillance in the hope that, in time, it would lead to arrests and convictions further up the chain?

"Let's keep going with the surveillance, while we can. Step up the surveillance on Spencer Green and Noah Shore. This is going to be a decision at a higher level than either of us, Terry."

Elias butted in. "But we could move on Michael Dodd while he's at North Parade. There's bound to be evidence of dealing in there — merchandise, cash, scales, deal bags. Not to mention whatever we get off their phones. We could hopefully gather enough evidence to persuade the CPS to authorise a charge under the Modern Slavery Act 2015, or conspiracy to supply Class A drugs."

Steph let her sergeant rant. If he were in charge, they would be raiding the house at dawn. To tell the truth, it was what she wanted too. Let her at the door of that house right now and she'd batter it to splinters with the big red key herself.

She relayed the information to her boss, who in turn would liaise with his counterpart at EMSOU. Ultimately, the decision to act or wait was in their hands. She hoped it would be a no-brainer for them, too.

Later in the afternoon there was more news. Terry Munks contacted Steph to say that Noah Shore had been tailed to the Park Estate in Nottingham.

Steph wasn't well acquainted with Nottingham, but she was aware that the Park Estate was a premier residential enclave located on what had once been Nottingham Castle's deer park. Right in the heart of the city, yet strangely apart from it, the estate boasted gated entrances and was lit at night by gas lamps, for heaven's sake!

"You need money to live in that area," Elias commented.

"Subject approached a large modern residence on Newcastle Drive and mounted some stairs to the side of the property." Terry gave the number of the house.

"We need information on the owner of that property, right now!" Steph barked. Elias stepped up, finding out in minutes. "The owner is a Mr Kenneth Shore."

"Bloody hell. Don't tell me we're on a wild goose chase here, and Noah Shore is just visiting a relative?" Steph said.

"It's not his father. His name is Syd," Elias said. "An uncle, or cousin, maybe?"

John Sulley interrupted. He'd been googling. "Kenneth Shore is the owner of a number of hairdressing salons in Nottinghamshire. He's fifty-six years old, a widower with two grown-up daughters, both of whom live on the Park Estate. Both work in one of their father's salons. Gives a bit more credence to the money laundering angle, doesn't it?"

Steph nodded. "Agreed. We confirmed what Luca Esposito told us about his shop having been in his family's hands for generations, and a first look at the finances suggests he's not involved. Which begs the question, what was Noah Shore doing working for Luca when he could have been working at one of his Uncle Kenneth's salons?" My guess is he was there to keep an eye on Cole Burke. The Shores suspected Cole of cheating on them somehow and sent Noah to the salon to befriend him."

"Think they're using one or more of Shore's salons to store drugs?" Elias said.

Terry Monks rubbed her hands together. "Let's get the go-ahead to put the daughters' houses and some of the salons under surveillance ASAP."

Steph's nerves buzzed with excitement. They were closing in, she was sure of it.

Hours later, still waiting for news of when — or if — they would get the go-ahead for an early raid, Steph's phone vibrated. Bell again. What the hell did she want this time? Steph put the call on speaker so that Elias could listen in. Bell had been to Nate's house and spoken with a neighbour who had seen the boy earlier in the day. Steph thanked her for the information and tried to wind the call up quickly, but Bell blabbered on and on, prompting her to say to Elias when she finally got rid of her, "That woman still doesn't know when she's being dismissed. I mean, does she really believe that there's anything more that she, as a special, can contribute to a complex investigation such as this?"

CHAPTER THIRTY-EIGHT

Jane
14 June 2019

"Jane, I've seen him!" Thea's voice was shrill, worse than any alarm clock. "I texted you, but you didn't answer. Don't tell me you're still in bed."

"I was on duty half the night, remember?" She glanced at her clock. It was barely six. She'd been in bed for less than two hours. "What the heck are you doing out at this ungodly hour?" Jane was still drowsy with sleep, otherwise she wouldn't have said, "Who have you seen, anyway — Lord Lucan?"

Thea groaned. "Ha ha. How many times have I told you only old people like you get that reference? Nate, of course. I've found Nate Price."

Jane was wide awake now, feet planted firmly on the floor, phone clamped to her ear. "Where? Where have you seen him? Is he okay? Is he still there? Are you with him?"

Thea's answers came fast and staccato. "I'm in Temple Gardens. Yes, he seems okay but he's asleep in that little pavilion thingy at the bottom of the gardens so I haven't asked him. Any more questions, Jane? I thought you'd be in

251

a rush to get your butt down here before he wakes up and does a runner."

"On my way. And don't say 'butt'. It's an Americanism."

"Arse then. Get your arse over here."

"Much better." Jane smiled as she groped for her jeans, tripping, Mr Bean-like, in her haste to put them on.

Temple Gardens was an area of public open space sloping down, in a series of grassed terraces, from the city's north escarpment to the busy eastern by-pass of Lindum Hill. More significantly from Jane's point of view, the gardens were less than a five-minute sprint from her house.

As she rounded the side of the Usher Art Gallery, she caught sight of Thea in her bright jogging gear hailing her from the pavilion near the bottom of the gardens. As the distance closed between them, Thea jogged the rest of the way towards, her, removing her ear buds.

She seemed less certain of her discovery now. "I was sure he looked like the boy in picture you showed me, but I could only see the side of his face. Now that he's turned to face the wall, I'm beginning to doubt myself. I hope I haven't dragged you out of bed for nothing."

Together, they crept over to where the boy was lying, curled up in the pavilion, clutching a carrier bag to his chest, like a teddy bear, for comfort.

The pavilion and its attached terrace wall was Grade II listed, but sadly affected by vandalism. It was a popular hang-out for rough sleepers and addicts, providing a modicum of shelter from the elements, and Jane was surprised to see that the boy had no other company.

"Should we wake him up?" Thea asked.

Jane hesitated. "If it is him, I'm worried we'll startle him and he'll bolt." Perhaps if you do it and I stand back out of the way. He's more likely to relate to someone his own age."

Thea seemed thrilled at the suggestion. She was so young, Jane thought. This was all an adventure to her. She didn't understand the depths of human misery he represented to Jane.

With reluctance, Jane moved to stand out of sight at the side of the shelter. Fortunately, at this time of the morning there was little traffic noise from Lindum Hill.

Scanning the area, she felt a sense of unease. This was an easily accessible public space. They were alone now, but who knew for how long? Someone could approach from almost any direction. If this boy was Nate, they'd need to act quickly.

"Hi." The sound of Thea's voice focussed her attention. "You okay? I was just out for a run, and I saw you there. You look a bit young to be sleeping rough."

Silence. Jane could imagine the boy's wary eyes, looking at Thea, the stirrings of an adrenalin rush honing his senses for fight or flight. Which would it be?

Thea gave a little chuckle. "It's all right. I'm not after your sandwiches. I'm having porridge and a banana for breakfast when I get home. After my shower, of course. I'm Thea, by the way. What's your name?"

Jane held her breath, hardly believing he'd answer, but after a few moments, a croaky voice said, "Nate."

"Cool," Thea said more casually than Jane could have managed. "Hey, your voice must be breaking, unless you're just thirsty? Can I sit down? I need a rest after all that running. I went all the way over to the South Common."

You did, did you? This was interesting news for Jane. She'd warned Thea that the South Common had a slightly shady reputation. She didn't like the idea of Thea running there alone at all hours of the day or night.

There was a shuffling sound, presumably Nate rearranging himself on the seat to make room for Thea.

"I don't mind if you eat your sandwiches. You look as if you need them. What have you got? Ham. I wouldn't eat those. I've given up meat for the sake of the planet. Well, except for the odd bit of chicken. You have to wean yourself off slowly in case you get withdrawal symptoms. Bit like coming off alcohol or drugs. Not that I'd know."

Jane cringed. Nate was unlikely to find Thea's remark amusing, given his mother's addiction to booze and his experience with an organised drug gang.

It also occurred to her that the remark might have put Nate on his guard. This was how kids like him were recruited into crime — they were groomed by other kids just a little older than themselves. He had to be wondering if he should trust Thea.

The silence lengthened. Then Jane heard a kind of glugging sound. She'd noticed a bottle of cola on the ground under Nate's seat. He must be drinking, or he'd offered some to Thea.

Jane stepped out from her hiding place. The boy on the bench beside Thea choked on his drink.

"It's all right, Nate," she said, seeing Nate's eyes grow wide. The bottle of cola dropped from his hand. He was poised to run.

"My name's Jane Bell. I'm a police officer. I want to help."

Maybe he believed her, or maybe Thea's presence reassured him, or maybe he was just too weary to run anymore. He looked at Jane with haunted eyes and whispered one word, "Lana?"

Jane couldn't bring herself to speak, but her face told him what he most feared.

She and Thea caught him as he fell.

CHAPTER THIRTY-NINE

Nate
14 June 2019

He really wanted to trust the girl but he didn't know if he should. When the woman stepped out from behind the shelter, he was going to run — except he really didn't think he had the energy — or the will.

The woman said she was called Jane Bell and was from the police. But she didn't show him any ID.

Is Lana dead? He could only bring himself to whisper her name. The woman's face crumpled.

Nate didn't hear any more. He felt like he was falling.

When he came to, they were both looking at him with concern — at least that's how it seemed. Should he trust them?

He'd trusted Wes and Cole and look where that had got him. Part of him had always known, of course, that there was something off about the relationship he'd had with those two. He'd known what was in the packages he delivered for Cole, known that what he was doing was against the law. Maybe he'd even known all along that they were using him, but it had seemed a fair exchange in return for the friendship they'd seemed to offer, the sense of belonging. How quickly Wes had shown his other side when Cole was out of the picture.

He looked at the woman who claimed to be a police officer but who wasn't in a uniform. "Are you going to arrest me? I've done bad things. I delivered drugs for a man called Cole."

"No. I'm not going to arrest you," the woman said. "People have been looking for you, Nate — the police. We knew you were being held somewhere against your will, that you were probably being mistreated. I want you to know that you're not in any trouble. You're a victim. I know that this man, Cole, would have given you things like clothes and trainers, maybe even cash, to run errands for him. That's called grooming. When an adult does this to someone who's still a child, and persuades or coerces the child into committing crimes, it's called child criminal exploitation, and it's the adult who's in the wrong, not the child. Do you understand, Nate?"

Nate wasn't convinced. He was still worried he'd be seen as a criminal. "But I knew what I was doing—"

"It might take a while for you to understand fully, Nate. For now, I want you to trust me, okay?"

Still hesitant, he decided to take a risk. He was so, so weary of dealing with this alone. "Okay. What will happen to me now? My neighbour told me my mum's in hospital but I don't know what happened to her. Did she get beaten up?"

"No. She had an accident. She's fine, and she's being well looked after. As for what will happen to you, I'll be honest, I don't know. It won't be my decision, but I can promise that whatever does happen, you'll be safe."

The woman and the girl were looking at him the way Charlie's mum used to. "I . . . I trust you," he said, his voice a bit wobbly.

The woman smiled. "Come on, then. My house is about five minutes' walk from here. You'll be safe there. You look like you need a shower and something to eat. And don't worry. Everything's all right now."

Nate hadn't felt safe for a very long time. He moved to stand up from the bench. As he did so, he looked past the woman and the girl.

And saw Wolf charging across the grass towards them.

CHAPTER FORTY

Jane
14 June 2019

"What is it, Nate?" Jane swung around to see what had caused the rapid change in Nate's expression. A heavy-set man in leathers was barrelling down the slope towards them.

Nate wailed, "It's Wolf. He'll kill me."

Wolf was upon them already. "Found you at last, you little fucker."

Bloodshot eyes darted from Nate to Jane to Thea. "Step aside, ladies, if you don't want to get hurt. Not that I care if you do. Collateral damage and all that."

"I'm a police officer," Jane said.

"Is that right?"

Jane really didn't see it coming. She heard some words that sounded like *Think I give a fuck?* followed by a scream that sounded like Thea.

Then everything went dark.

CHAPTER FORTY-ONE

Steph
14 June 2019

This is it, Steph thought. The culmination of months of painstaking investigative work beginning with the murder of Cole Burke. *It ends at dawn.* It couldn't come soon enough.

She and Elias had been up all night. The raid on the house on North Parade had been authorised very late the previous evening, and a line of police vehicles had been ready to move since the early hours of the morning. Steph and Elias were accompanying them, along with their EMSOU-ROCU colleagues Terry Munks and John Sulley.

The moment before action was always a tense one after weeks or months spent patiently gathering intelligence and waiting as the surveillance began to garner evidence and results.

In just fifteen minutes or thereabouts all hell would break loose, but for now the atmosphere was charged, edgy and expectant.

Then the order was given, and the convoy set off, gliding seamlessly along near-empty streets while the city still slept.

Steph glanced at Elias, sitting stiffly in his protective vest. "Okay?"

"Yes, boss. Just a bit hyped. Can't wait to get to the property and see this through."

"You and I both," Steph said.

They turned into North Parade and their car slid past the rows of cars parked in residential parking bays, coming to a halt behind the fleet of other police vehicles blocking the middle of the road.

As it was a murder investigation and weapons could be involved, the house would initially be entered by armed officers. Steph watched as they piled out of their vehicle and began to group around the cuckooed house.

Dressed all in black, they were wearing protective helmets and goggles, with the lower parts of their faces covered. They carried rifles and some had ballistic shields. The assault on the house had been carefully orchestrated and everyone involved knew their respective roles inside out.

"This is it." Steph watched as, in response to a signal, two unarmed officers moved forward and sliced the door from top to bottom using a chainsaw. They were quickly relieved by two others who took it in turns to ram the door of the house with the enforcer. Their grunts and heaves resulted in a hail of splintered wood and shattered glass until — at last — they were through.

At another signal, armed officers surged forwards, yelling repeatedly, "Armed police! Stay where you are!" A terrifying wake-up call for the occupants, and half the neighbourhood besides.

"Come on!" Steph had got out of the car when the team had moved on the house. Now, she and Elias approached the entrance, with Terry and John close behind. They stood back from the door, awaiting the signal that would tell them they were cleared to go inside.

"Armed police! Stay where you are!" The yelling reached a crescendo, then began to subside. Inside, the team would be checking every room in the house, rounding up and securing the occupants.

A man was already being marched down the hallway towards them, hands cuffed behind his back. Behind him, another man, younger and ginger-haired, also cuffed and howling in protest. The first man was Michael Dodd, aka Shark. The other, the boy they knew as Wes Savage.

"Where's Tommy Dodd?" John Sulley demanded, sullen looks from Dodd and Savage his only answer.

Steph and the others advanced to the open door of the living room. There, they found a scared-looking lad with a vivid birthmark on his face — Dexter Curtis — and a man who looked drugged and bewildered — Glynn Stewart, the owner of the property.

Officers in uniform were tearing the room apart in the search for evidence. Steph asked them to leave for a few moments.

She addressed the terrified boy with the birthmark. "Dexter Curtis?"

He nodded, scared. "Where's Nate? Is he okay?" His face brightened, momentarily. "He must be okay if you're here. I never thought he'd make it."

Steph ignored his comment. "When did you last see Nate?"

"Yesterday morning. I helped him get away." He shivered. "It was the least I could do. I'm glad he made it. I'd have felt bad otherwise. I wish I'd never told now."

Steph frowned. "What do you mean, Dexter?"

The lad shrank away from them. "Didn't Nate tell you?"

"We haven't spoken with him yet. Nate's missing. If there's anything you can tell us that might help us find him—"

Dex's eyes flashed with fear. "What about Lana? Did you find her? Did they kill her?"

"Yes. I'm sorry, Dexter." Steph's tone was brisk. She couldn't afford the time to worry about the boy's feelings. With Tommy Dodd still on the loose, Nate could be in grave danger. "What did you mean just now when you asked if Nate had told us something?"

Dexter paled. His voice shook. "It's my fault. I told Wes about their plan to escape, and Wes told Wolf and Shark. That's how they got to Lana. Nate went for Wes when Wes suggested that Wolf and Shark killed Lana. He managed to escape. Wes hurt himself when Nate pushed him, and he couldn't get up without feeling dizzy . . . I was supposed to stop Nate, but I let him get away. No one told me anything after that."

Before Steph could respond, Terry jumped in, concerned, no doubt, that Dexter was becoming more and more distressed. "What happened to Lana wasn't your fault, Dexter. I'm sure she wouldn't like to think of you blaming yourself."

Steph was impatient to get on. "We arrested two men just now. The other man, Tommy Dodds, or Wolf as you called him. Where is he?"

"I dunno. They don't tell me anything. My guess is he's out looking for Nate. Wolf and Shark have eyes everywhere. Wherever Nate is, Wolf'll find him."

Steph's nerves were taut. It wasn't that she'd expected to find Nate at the house. Until Bell had informed her of the recent sightings of the lad, she'd feared him dead already. Now that she'd learned that, as of yesterday evening, he was still alive, it was imperative that they find him before Wolf got to him first and ripped him apart with tooth and claw.

Her phone buzzed. Jane Bell. What the hell did she want at a time like this?

Steph hesitated to answer. Whatever Bell wanted couldn't require her attention as urgently as the present situation. Irritated, she spoke into her phone. "What is it, SC Bell? I'm busy. Can't it wait?"

Bell's voice sounded thick and incomprehensible. Steph couldn't make out a word. "I can't understand you . . ."

A pause, then, another, different voice was in her ear. "DI Warwick. It's Thea Martin. I'm with Jane. She can't speak properly because that man hit her in the face. He's got Nate."

Thea wasn't much easier to understand because she was talking at the speed of light quadrupled.

"What man? Slow down, Thea."

"Nate called him Wolf. He's got Nate. You've got to do something. Hurry! Please!"

CHAPTER FORTY-TWO

Nate
14 June 2019

Wolf's fist slammed into the woman's face, knocking her out instantly. The girl called Thea screamed and dropped to her knees beside her. Nate felt his arm grabbed and he struggled to remain standing. A warm trickle of urine ran down his leg.

This is it. I'm going to die. He sank to the ground, and Wolf dragged him back to his feet and half-pushed, half-pulled him across the grass.

"Why don't you just shank me here?" Nate screamed at him. "Like you did Lana."

Wolf grabbed him by the throat. "Maybe I should, the amount of trouble you've caused, you pissing little bastard. But it's for exactly that reason that I want to take my time with you."

Nate tasted vomit in his mouth and swallowed it, remembering what Wolf had done to Cole, how he'd made him suffer.

He wouldn't make it easy for Wolf. He didn't want to die a slow, agonising death at this monster's hands. If he made him angry enough, Wolf might lose it and kill him here — now — fast. So, Nate let his body go limp, hoping it would become a dead weight that Wolf would have no choice but to drag or carry, slowing him down.

Even as a dead weight, his body must have weighed less than a sack of feathers, for Wolf lifted him with ease and heaved him up and over his shoulder. Nate screamed, pummelled his fists against Wolf's back, used his teeth and nails on the skin of his neck. Wolf growled but did not stop.

"Put him down!"

It was the girl, Thea, sprinting towards them from behind. In seconds she had overtaken them, disappearing from Nate's sight. Then, suddenly, Wolf went down, taking Nate with him. They both landed awkwardly — Wolf on his right shoulder, pinning Nate underneath him.

"Get! Off! Him!" After tripping Wolf up, Thea had reappeared and begun kicking Wolf in the ribs to encourage him to roll aside, so that Nate could get out from under him. Wolf lashed out at her with one arm.

Everything seemed to happen at once after that. Police sirens wailed in the distance. There was the sound of a dog barking frantically somewhere nearby. Then, suddenly, it was upon Wolf, growling and tearing at his trouser leg as he struggled to rise using his one good arm. The dog must have sensed Wolf's weakness, for it went for his uninjured arm, giving Wolf no choice but to lie still.

"Allie!" Thea cried.

The woman she called Allie looked at her pet in horror. "Dudgeon! Get off him!"

"No!" Thea cried. "That man was trying to kidnap Nate."

The older woman froze. Nate could tell from the way she stared at him that his name meant something to her. Her face took on an angry set. Turning back to the dog, she commanded, "Good boy, Dudge! Guard!" Then, she looked at Nate. "You're the missing boy that Jane's been looking for." She cast about her. "Where is Jane?"

Thea, winded, pointed to the other side of the park, where Jane was slowly rising to her feet. The woman called

Allie squinted. "Oh, my goodness! Is that her? Is she all right?"

Thea nodded at Wolf. "No thanks to that brute. He punched her in the face."

Nate was struggling to hear them now because the police sirens were so loud. From the direction of the sound, he saw at least six officers spilling out of their cars and running across the grass towards them.

Nate looked at Thea. "I'm not going to die."

Thea hugged him to her. "No, you aren't. Not on Jane's watch."

CHAPTER FORTY-THREE

Steph
14 June 2019

The sight of Jane Bell's friends, Thea and Allie, and Allie's Staffordshire bull terrier growling and snapping viciously at the injured man on the ground, almost stopped Steph in her tracks. Panting from her dash from the car, she exclaimed, "What the—!"

"The man on the ground is Tommy Dodd," Elias said. "And the boy is Nate Price, like Thea said."

"I know that!" Steph snapped. "Where's Bell?"

"Over there!" Elias pointed across the park and, following his line of sight, Steph saw Bell walking unsteadily towards her friends.

Steph surveyed the unlikely bunch of people — Thea Martin in her multicoloured leggings and cropped running top, Allie Swift in polka-dot trousers that looked suspiciously like pyjama bottoms and an oversized pink hoodie. The boy, grimy and malnourished, high-fiving Thea with a gap-toothed grin — and the snarling, leather-clad man on the ground, looking like some archetypal pantomime villain, being restrained by four PCs, while another made a fuss of the Staffie with the unlikely name of Dudgeon.

Elias cautioned Dodd. His face contorted in agony as a uniformed PC cuffed him and dragged him to his feet. "Watch my bloody shoulder!" At the sound of his raised voice, Dudgeon growled and bared his teeth. Dodd drew back. "Keep that vicious beast away from me!"

Steph stepped forward. Her face inches from Dodd's, she said, "You call yourself Wolf. *You're* the beast. Compared to you, that dog is a helpless little kitten."

Allie piped up, "His bark's worse than his bite, really. Dudge wouldn't hurt a fly."

Steph suppressed a smile. She addressed the PCs. "Best take Dodd off to hospital, I suppose, and get that shoulder popped back into place." She wished she could do the job herself, minus the anaesthetic.

Thea and Allie moved to support Bell, who was looking a bit wobbly. Her nose was bloody and she had a burgeoning black eye.

"Thank goodness you got here in time," she panted, looking at Steph.

Steph nodded, cleared her throat. "Looks to me like you and your motley crew had the situation more or less under control, SC Bell."

CHAPTER FORTY-FOUR

Steph
18 June 2019

Steph and Elias interviewed Wes Savage under caution. His legal representative was present, a softly spoken woman with deep laughter lines around her eyes and mouth. Her job wasn't exactly a barrel of laughs, so she must have found her fun elsewhere. Wes had decided to cooperate in return for a more lenient sentence.

"Tell us about your relationship with Cole Burke," Steph began.

"I met Cole in Luca's barber's shop. He was in the seat next to me wearing a Man United T-shirt and we got talking about footie, like you do. We went for a pint afterwards and then he asked me up to his flat and offered me some weed. I told him I was looking for a job but I wasn't having a lot of luck and he asked me if I wanted to make a bit of money working for him."

Steph interrupted. "Did you understand that the work he was offering you was illegal?"

Savage answered without hesitation. "Yes. I started off doing deliveries. Then, a few months later, Cole gave me a bit more responsibility. I'd go to London a few times a month and bring back the merchandise."

"And, for the record," Steph said, with a look at the recording device, "by 'merchandise', you mean what, specifically?"

Wes gave a shrug. "Heroin, crack cocaine, meth, anything and everything. Then Cole came up with the idea of recruiting a couple of kids to do the local deliveries. He'd heard that's how the organised gangs operated, using kids because they were less likely to be stopped by the police."

Steph nodded. "You recruited Drew Wilson and Nate Price?"

"Yeah. Drew didn't last long. He went off somewhere with his sister and never came back, but by then Cole and me had a bigger problem. I went round Cole's place one night and there were two men there."

"These men were the brothers Michael and Tommy Dodd?"

"Yeah, but they prefer Shark and Wolf. Scares the kids."

Steph ignored his slow smirk. "Go on."

"They told us their people were taking over and offered us the opportunity to join them."

"And you agreed?"

"It was better than the alternative."

"Which was?"

"Get out of the game altogether, find a proper job earning next to nothing."

"So, you went to work with — who — the Dodd brothers?"

Wes snorted. "Not them. That pair are as thick as shit. No, they were just the muscle. We never got to know who we were working for. That's how they operate."

Steph nodded again. She knew only too well how organised criminals operated.

"I was put in charge of looking after the kids in the cuckooed house. Wolf and Shark came and went, attending to business. Sometimes one of them would be there for a few days at a time. They'd often drive kids over from Nottingham, plugged up with gear. Other times the kids travelled alone, by train."

Steph felt a surge of anger. "You bullied and threatened these children. Put them in fear of their lives and for the lives of their loved ones."

"Yep. Discipline was part of my job." He looked at them, no hint of shame in his neutral expression, no emotion at all as far as Steph could see. "I chatted to them and made friends with them, found out what made them vulnerable."

All part of the job. Wes had admitted he'd believed he had prospects within the gang. Steph sat back in her chair for a few moments, arms crossed, letting a thin silence permeate the room. People were uncomfortable with silences. It made them eager to talk, not that Wes was holding back.

Was she like him? When she'd waited before calling for help while Cal bled out before her eyes, she'd known exactly what she was doing. No amount of therapy would ever entirely convince her that she'd hesitated because she was in shock.

Dr Bryce's words came back to her. "He would have died anyway. The injury he'd inflicted on himself was catastrophic. It's unlikely emergency services could have saved him, even if you'd contacted them immediately." And her own reply, *I could have done something. I could have tried to stop the bleeding* . . . And on, and on. Except for the one thing she'd left unsaid because she'd been too ashamed to admit it — *I watched him die and I felt nothing.*

Elias gave a meaningful cough. He was giving her one of his concerned looks. Wes's legal rep was staring at her, waiting. No one is comfortable with a protracted silence. It makes them think something is wrong.

Steph came back to herself. She looked at Wes, "Why was Cole Burke murdered?" They already knew the answer to that, but she needed to hear it from him.

"Cole was stupid. He thought he could carry on more or less as before. He had a select group of clients on a separate

271

phone that he continued to supply, thinking he wouldn't be found out."

Jackie Prothero and Chris Bolan among them. Two of the names extracted from Cole's phone that the EMSOU had placed under surveillance, and who had led them to the house on North Parade. It hadn't taken either of them long to find a new supplier after Cole's murder.

Wes shifted in his chair, sat up straighter as if to big himself up. "I was the one who brought it to Wolf and Shark's attention. One of the clients Cole had been dealing to on the quiet got in touch with me. He'd been told he could get a better deal elsewhere and was shopping around.

"I told Wolf and Shark what I thought Cole was up to, and they took it back to their bosses."

Ah, yes. Their bosses. In another interview room, in another city, Steph knew that Terry Munks and John Sulley would be sitting down opposite Kenneth Shore and other members of his family — his wife, his brother, his two daughters and their husbands, and his nephew, Noah, all of whom had been arrested and charged with an assortment of offences including conspiracy to murder and conspiracy to supply Class A drugs for starters.

The CPS had been consulted regarding charging and remanding them in custody while further enquiries were conducted and additional evidence gathered. Further charges of false imprisonment and child abuse were likely to be added once CPS had sight of the full evidential file. Not to mention the financial evidence that was already accumulating to prove that they'd been laundering drug money through their hairdressing business.

The process of gathering evidence for additional charges could take weeks or even months, but as the CPS had agreed that there was sufficient evidence on the initial charges, at least there was no prospect of anyone involved being released on bail before they appeared in court.

Steph pressed on. "And that was when Noah Shore became involved?"

"Yeah. They put Noah in the barber's shop below Cole's flat. He approached Cole and said he'd heard he could get hold of some coke for him. That's how they got proof that what I said was true, that Cole was betraying them. Noah was given a number to place his orders with Cole. The number wasn't one we recognised, proving Cole was using another phone for his own clients. Like I said, Cole was stupid. They sent Wolf and Shark round to take care of him."

"Like they later took care of Lana Kerr," Steph said.

"She was stupid too. It was that kid Nate's fault. Lana knew how it was until he turned up. She wouldn't have tried to escape if he hadn't gone and fucked her all up emotionally."

Steph stared at him. "What do you mean?"

"She fell for him, didn't she? Made her think they could get away and be together, live happily ever after and all that Romeo and Juliet bullshit." Wes shook his head. "Bloody feelings. Better off without. Just get on with what needs doing, that's my motto. That and look out for number one, 'cause no one else will."

Steph caught her breath. The back of her neck prickled, and her skin felt moist. Wes must have had feelings once — Wolf and Shark too, presumably. What had happened to them to turn them into the callous, unfeeling creatures they were now?

She thought of her sessions with Dr Bryce — how much she was learning about herself, how far she'd progressed. Looking at Wes Savage was like looking at a future that, but for the intervention of Elias and Jane Bell, could easily have been hers.

Steph announced that she was stopping the tape. She'd had as much as she could stomach for now. She spoke the time aloud and switched it off.

She and Elias stood up. Elias looked at Wes and said in a quiet voice, "Best not to reference things you know nothing about."

Wes looked at him, blank-faced.

"Romeo and Juliet didn't live happily ever after, you moron. The play was a fucking tragedy."

"Feel better?" Steph asked him outside the interview room.

"Not really. He needs a name."

"What?"

"Wolf. Shark. They're predators. He should have a name too."

"He has one already," Steph pointed out.

Elias frowned, then understood. "Savage by name, savage by nature."

CHAPTER FORTY-FIVE

Steph
24 June 2019

Midsummer's evening. Steph walked across the cobbled square towards the imposing gated entrance to Lincoln Castle, glad there was no sign of rain. The play was being performed outdoors, and she didn't want a sudden downpour interrupting her enjoyment of watching Elias make an ass of himself.

Elias hadn't been kidding when he warned her to bring a cushion. The seating was indeed uncomfortable, but it did have the advantage of being set out within the stone curtain walls of a well-preserved Norman castle, under a clear blue midsummer sky.

It was a balmy evening. A lot of people were fanning themselves with their programmes. Steph was glad she'd gone with the linen shift dress. There was a thin cotton cardigan in her bag in case it turned chilly later.

She'd come alone. Elias had invited her for drinks with the cast after the performance, which she'd agreed to attend with the caveat that she'd stay for just one drink. She was sipping a deliciously chilled Sauvignon blanc at that moment, which was already making her feel relaxed.

A voice behind her commented on the wonderful setting. It occurred to Steph that her experience of the castle grounds probably differed from most other people's. For her, a visit to the castle usually meant attendance at the Crown Court, which was located in its grounds.

She closed her eyes, enjoying the warmth of the early evening sun on her face.

"DI Warwick! Hey!" Steph opened her eyes, cringing inwardly at the sound of Thea Martin's voice. She gave a weak smile. Worse was to come.

The seats on either side of her began filling up with familiar faces. There was Allie Swift and her husband, Frieda Arya from the Veganbites café, Jan Mazurek and his partner Yvonne, and a lean, good-looking man who appeared to have his arm around SC Bell. Two older men also appeared to be part of the group. Steph recognised one of them. He was a busker who often played his violin in Castle Square or on High Bridge in the centre of town. She'd also seen him in Veganbites, and she'd heard Bell's account of the part Merlin Kendrick had played in helping her track down Shane Watt. The other man must be Giles Brimble, who'd also played his part.

Steph hadn't seen Bell since she'd interviewed her following the arrest of Tommy Dodd in Temple Gardens. As far as Steph was concerned, serendipity had once again played a part in leading Bell to a positive result. Still, she had to admit that Bell's tactic of telling everyone she knew to look out for Nate had very likely saved the boy's life.

Was it also serendipity that had led to Jane Bell's seat being right next to Steph's, with Frieda on her other side? Steph thought that was more likely to be Elias's doing, since he'd reserved her a seat in the front row. Had he and Bell been conspiring behind her back again?

"Good evening, DI Warwick." It was SC Bell. Bell gazed up at the cloudless sky. "I hope the weather's kind to us."

Steph nodded. "I checked the forecast. No rain until tomorrow afternoon, then only a light shower." *Good God, we're talking about the bloody weather.*

Bell introduced her companion, Ed, who also made some comment about it looking like the weather was going to hold.

There had been a subtle shift in Steph's relationship with Jane Bell since the incident at Temple Gardens. When she'd spoken with Bell the day after the event, Steph had thanked her for the part she'd played in rescuing Nate Price and facilitating the arrest of Tommy Dodd. Bell had deflected the praise on to Dudge, but she'd been pleased, Steph thought, or perhaps just relieved not to have been given a tongue-lashing for sticking her nose in where it didn't belong.

Now Steph was way out of her comfort zone. For a moment, she considered finding an excuse to move seats, but how could she do that without appearing rude? She sighed. Her famous thick skin was in danger of becoming transparent if appearing rude was something that was going to bother her in future. Next thing she knew, she'd be letting her guard down all over the place. The thought made her shudder.

Bell noticed. "Are you cold? I've got a spare cardi in my bag if you need it. I've got my jacket."

Steph declined the offer. "I'm fine. If anything, I'm a bit warm." *And not just from the heat.*

Steph remembered that she had some news to share with Bell. She cleared her throat. "They found the girl. Lana's friend, Daisy May."

When Bell didn't react immediately, Steph realised it was because she was possibly afraid to learn the girl's fate. She reassured her. "Alive. In bad shape, obviously. I won't go into the details. I think you can probably guess how she'd been treated."

Bell nodded, eyes full of compassion, prompting Steph to say, "I'm sorry. I hope I haven't spoiled your evening."

Bell gave a sad sort of smile. "Life goes on. I heard the other day that Nate Price is being fostered by a family in Gainsborough where he used to live."

"Yes," Steph said. "They have a son, Charlie, who was one of Nate's best friends before his move to Lincoln. It's

277

unlikely that Angie Price will ever be able to look after him properly. It's a good outcome for Nate."

She was about to say that things were looking positive for Shane Watt and his family too, but at that moment, the stage lit up and a hush settled over the audience.

As always with Shakespeare, Steph struggled with the language, but managed to get the gist of the plot. Elias was hilarious as Bottom, partly because of his accomplished performance, and partly, well, just because he was Elias and she knew him.

At the end of the play, responding to Puck's invitation to '*Give me your hands, if we be friends*', Steph joined in with the enthusiastic applause.

Jane Bell looked her way and smiled. "Elias was excellent. He's a man of many talents, it seems."

"Yes. I'm lucky he decided to exchange a life on the stage to become my sergeant." A pause. "And my friend."

"I'm glad you appreciate him, DI Warwick," Bell said.

Steph nodded. Then, "We're not at work, now. Call me Steph."

Bell reciprocated immediately. "Call me Jane."

"Right . . . er . . . Jane. But don't go thinking this is the beginning of a beautiful friendship or anything."

Jane smiled at her. "Not at all, ma'am."

THE END

Made in the USA
Monee, IL
11 December 2021